Wrong

LP LOVELL   STEVIE J. COLE

Jeanette,
You're a wrong'n.

Editing: Ashley Mac Editing Services and Ellen Widom

Photographs and model: Uncovered Models, Drew Truckle
and Hannah Nichol Photography

Cover Design: SM Piper

Chapter 1
Jude

This won't be the first time I've killed someone, and it won't be the last, so why is my heart pounding so damn hard right now?

Most people might say that what I'm about to do makes me one sick fucker, but when someone slaughters your family, you, in turn, kill theirs. I'm doing this for revenge, pure and simple. Merciless vengeance, it's just how it goes in my world: you use violence and power to enforce your rules. When you make a living illegally, you learn how easy it is to prosper from others' fear, although not all bookies are as brutal as I am. Having a conscience is where other bookies fail. Brutality is the difference between making a few dollars and making a million. You cannot be weak and survive in this profession, and the moment someone no longer fears you, you're fucked.

I'm not fucking weak! I'm trying to psyche myself up, slightly pissed that I'm finding this harder to swallow than I thought I would. I know the only reason I'm still standing here with my pulse banging in my ears is because this particular situation involves a woman. You'd think it would be no problem to follow through with, seeing as how I don't really have morals—right and wrong, I don't play by those rules, I wasn't raised to. Hell, I grew up in a house where arsenals were kept in every room "just in case." I witnessed my first murder when I was only twelve. So I can't understand why I'm conflicted right now. A soft moan and the thud of the headboard hitting the wall carries down the hall, and I shake those thoughts from my head.

Marney and I press our backs to the wall. My heart is still thrashing around like a caged gorilla. I try to regulate my breathing, but it's nearly impossible with all the adrenaline that's flooding my system. I stare at the door. I want to utterly destroy Joe Campbell, I want him to be so miserable death is the only thing he has left to look forward to, and if this is the way I have to do it, so be it!

There's only one light on at the end of the hallway, and it's just enough that I catch Marney make eye contact with me, then nod toward the door. I push away from the wall and kick the door in, startling the man and woman fucking on the bed. She shrieks and scrambles to her feet, covering herself with the sheets.

The man jumps up. Taking a boxing stance, he throws a punch at me. I duck and pull the gun from my belt, cocking it as I aim directly at his head. He freezes and tosses his hands in the air. I narrow my gaze and realize this is not a middle-aged man. This is not Joe, which fucks everything up.

"Shit! Where's Joe?" I shout at the woman now cowering in the corner.

"He's not here," she sobs. Her eyes fix on me, taking in each detail of my face.

I glare at the man still frozen in front of me.

"Don't hurt us, please," he grovels.

"The safe is in the basement. There's over a million dollars in there," the woman frantically offers. "Take it! Take whatever Joe owes you," she pleads, her voice trembling.

"Shut up," Marney shouts.

I clench my jaw. "Oh, you're gonna pay, sweetheart, but this debt can't be paid in anything but blood." I tilt my head to the side as her eyes focus on mine. She's shaking and crying. "Your husband took something from me, and I'm going to take something from him."

I swing my gaze to the naked man and stalk toward him. "Too bad for you, you chose the wrong woman to fuck around with. Wrong place, wrong time." I stop about three feet in front of him, point the gun at his face, and pull the trigger. His body jerks backwards and collapses to the floor with a thud.

A shrill, drawn-out scream pierces the air, falling silent when the woman pulls in a large breath only to scream some more. I turn, the gun still raised, and she runs across the room toward the door. I go to pull back on the trigger, and I can't. I really didn't think it would be this hard to kill a woman.

Marney catches her and slams her onto the ground, pressing her down by her throat. "It's not personal. This is all for your husband."

"Please don't kill me. I'm a mother...my boys...please!" she weeps.

"I'll make it quick. I promise." His tone is vacant of any emotion, completely monotone and matter-of-fact.

Headlights stream through the window, bouncing around the dark room, and she lets out another tortured cry. She fights, yanking and jerking. She bites Marney's arm and I watch an animal-like scowl shoot over his face as he pulls his gun, shoves it against her temple, and BAM. She lies completely still. Marney wipes the blood splatter from his face with his sleeve. "Now what? Not as effective since we couldn't tie the bastard up and make him watch, huh?"

I shrug, leaning over and pulling up the man's body. "Put them in the fucking bed."

Marney grunts as he pulls the woman from the floor and tosses her onto the mattress. I step back and look at the two bodies piled on the bed. I grab the woman's blood soaked hair, lifting her face and dropping it by the man's limp dick. "Open her mouth," I tell Marney, laughing.

"You're fucking kidding, right?"

"See what he thinks about walking in on this shit." I can't help but smile. This right here is beyond fucked up.

Marney shrugs, parts the woman's lips, and I push the flaccid cock into her mouth.

We make our way down the stairs and let ourselves out the back door, walking through the woods for a good two miles in silence. When we come to the edge of the tree line, Marney grips my shoulder. "You did your pops right just then. He would be proud."

A run-down cab sputters up, the brakes squeaking as it comes to an abrupt stop. Richard hangs his hand out the window to signal that he's alone. We climb in and Richard glances back at us in the rearview mirror. "Damn. You two look like you bathed in blood. What the fuck did you do?"

"What had to be done," I mumble, and slump down in the seat.

I'm fucking wrong, and I know it.

Chapter 2
Victoria

It's one in the morning, and I've been on shift for twelve hours. I'm reaching my physical and emotional limit. I've had a night full of heart attacks, drunken injuries, and drug overdoses.

I'm just about to call it a night when the doors to the ER crash open. The medics rush in a stretcher, and all I can see is blood, a lot of it.

Dr. Phillips, one of the ER doctors, is running behind the team, shouting at various staff. "Multiple gunshot wounds!"

"Devaux!" he yells at me. "Let's go, keep his heart going until we can get to the operating room! Let's move!" he barks frantically. I hop onto the gurney and place a knee on either side of his body. The gurney is rushed through the hospital corridors, doors flying open in our wake as a team of doctors and nurses work frantically to keep the man alive.

I pump his chest rhythmically, trying to keep his heart from stopping, from giving up.

We burst into the OR I hop off the gurney and check his pulse. Nothing.

"He's got no pulse!" I shout while the nurses hook him up to the monitors.

People move like clockwork, everyone knowing their place and operating like a well-oiled machine. Clothing is cut from the man's lifeless, bloodied body as a defibrillator is wheeled next to him.

"Clear!" Dr. Phillips shouts, and holds the paddles on the patient's chest. His back bows off the bed, his body contorting in shock.

I stare at the flat green line on the monitor, marking his lifeless state.

"Clear!"

Again they shock him, and still nothing.

Come on, live. Just fight a little harder, I think to myself.

The doctor shocks him three more times to no avail.

"Time," Dr. Phillips says.

I glance at the clock on the wall. "One twenty-two," I call out.

He's pronounced dead, and everything stops. The fight is over, and we lost. It never gets any easier. I've been a resident in the ER here for nine months now. I've seen death on a daily basis—it's part of the job—and still, the fragility of human life always surprises me. One minute someone can be absolutely fine, living their life, working their job, having a

9

family, and the next...it can all be over. Life itself can be so fleeting. You're promised nothing. And that's hard to swallow at times.

I became a doctor to save lives. And for every one that dies, there are ten more that are saved. It's what makes this job so rewarding. It's all I've ever wanted to do in life. I decided to drop everything and leave my home in England to come here and study—to make a life for myself in America.

I am living my dream, but that doesn't mean this is easy. I feel like every life lost takes a part of my soul with it. I worry that there will come a day when it no longer affects me, when it no longer hurts. I am terrified of not feeling this pain, of feeling nothing, because the day I can watch someone die and not feel a thing means I no longer have a soul. I'm terrified of becoming a monster.

I turn my back on the dead man. The frantic desperation that filled the room moments ago is now replaced by a resigned calm. Doctors and nurses remove equipment as a sheet is pulled over the man's face. Pushing through the doors of the operating theatre, I head for the locker room. As my adrenalin drops, my legs start to feel like lead. I'm exhausted. When I reach the locker room, I take a minute to collect myself. That was a rough night.

I yank my bloodied scrubs off and throw them in the laundry bin before I pull on my jeans and a hoodie. I grab my handbag and check my phone, which has three missed calls from my sister. I swear she doesn't understand the concept of twelve-hour shifts. I send her a quick text saying that I'll call her in the morning. I'm almost out the hospital doors. I can practically hear little angels singing as I catch a glimpse of the outside world. I'm so close.

"Ria!"

At the sound of my name, I freeze. *Damn it.* I turn around and meet the smiling face of my boyfriend, Euan. He has that perfect smile coupled with wavy blond hair and bright blue eyes.

Euan is a surgery resident. His father is the Chief of Surgery here at the University hospital. Let's just say, he's guaranteed a good job when he completes his residency. He is the typical American ideal of perfection. He's everything a girl is told she should want in a man: driven, intelligent, attractive and kind to me. I've worked for years to get where I am, and, I guess, I want a certain life. Euan fulfills that vision.

That may not sound romantic, but I don't believe in fairy tales. Euan may not set me on fire, but there are more important things in life than passion. Life is about goals, and I didn't travel halfway around the world to find passion. I did it to be the best, to achieve my dreams, and create the life I've always wanted.

I smile wearily. He looks so perfectly put together- even after a twelve-hour shift he looks immaculate, and, well...I don't. My hair is greasy and falling out of a messy bun. I have suitcases under my eyes right now, never mind bags, and I probably have various bodily fluids all over me. Nice.

Regardless of how disgusting I must look, he leans in and places a chaste kiss on my lips. "How was your shift?" he asks.

"Busy," I reply in a clipped tone.

I really don't want to talk right now. My bed is calling my name.

Luckily, he seems to get the message.

"Well, I'll let you go, but we're still on for tomorrow night, right?"

"Yeah, of course." I smile and nod. "I'll text you when I wake up."

He quickly kisses my cheek again and winks before walking away.

At two in the morning, I finally get home. I jump in the shower and wash all the blood and death from my skin.

My job is hard, but the longer I do it the more I learn that I have to let go of each day before moving on to the next. This is my routine: to cleanse myself of the day's events.

The scalding hot water soothes my aching muscles and clears my mind.

I'm starving, but the prospect of making any real food is just not appealing. I quickly eat a cereal bar in preparation for the twelve-hour hibernation I plan to now have. I'm on shift again tonight, and if Friday nights are bad, then Saturday nights are hell.

I'm unconscious as soon as my head hits the pillow.

Chapter 3
Jude

"He's not gonna pay, Jude," Richard argues.

I twist in my chair, drumming my fingers over the wooden desk. "Oh, no. He'll pay. No one doesn't pay me." I laugh, glancing Richard over.

He's thick, nothing but a muscle head, and he's dumb as shit, but I don't need brains in my lackeys; I need brute strength and looks that will make people piss their pants. Richard is just that—a complete mongoloid. It's a family business I run. It has to be. Money, murder, and lies are all part of this business, and my family has been at it for going on three generations.

I suck in a quick breath. "You'll make sure he pays, right?"

His mouth flips into a devious, anticipatory grin. "Yeah, of course."

"He's a dumb college kid, he most likely thinks he knows statistics and thought he'd outsmarted me. Dumbass," I mumble. "He won't have the money. Just take something for collateral. Rough him up, and don't give him more than three days to get me my money." I frown. "But make sure you're smart about it."

"I'm not a fucking idiot. Which car do you want me to take?"

"Go down to David's, he'll have a car for you. There'll be instructions inside the console about where to trade out cars in Tennessee, okay?"

The phone rings and he nods, then leaves. I raise the receiver to my ear. "Go ahead, partner."

"This is Rammer Jammer. First half bet on the underdog. Two dimes. Bottom five."

"First half bet on the underdog worth two dimes on the bottom five?" I repeat back.

"Yep."

I hang up and grab the smoldering cigarette from the ashtray, inhaling a large cloud of smoke as I quickly scribble the bet in red ink over my legal pad. This game is sure to pay out a shitload of cash, and I can't help but smile as I glance over the bets I've taken today. Politicians, preachers, cops: they're all my clients, and as long as they pay, there's not a problem. I'm a *businessman* and I take my job very seriously.

You fuck with me, I'll kill you, because no one takes anything as serious as death.

Chapter 4
Victoria

Euan smiles wide when he opens the door and sees me. "Hey."

I flash him a smile. "Hey."

He leans in and places a lingering kiss on my cheek before opening the door wider to usher me in.

"Let me take your coat." He moves behind me and eases my coat from my shoulders, ever the gentleman.

"Something smells good," I remark.

He flashes me that blinding smile of his. "I'd love to say I cooked, but you know me...I ordered takeout."

I shrug. "Takeout is good."

I just need to eat before my next shift...which will actually end up being a twenty-hour shift, and it starts in two hours.

Another wide grin. "I ordered Thai, your favourite."

We sit down to eat and Euan seems oddly quiet. Usually he has a lot to say, whether it's talking about work, or my horrible living conditions—which he thinks are abhorrent. He usually brings up my flat because that conversation always leads to him trying to get me to move in with him, which leads to me explaining why I *don't* want to move in with him.

Tonight though, he's quiet, distant almost.

"Are you alright?" I ask.

He smiles slightly and nods as he chews a mouthful of food. "Of course."

I chalk his lack of conversation up to the fact that he's just got off shift. God knows I'm a miserable bitch when I've just done a long shift. I guess he's allowed to feel it once in a while as well.

Taking a quick sip of my water, I ask, "What did you do today?"

As predicted, he launches into a detailed account of a triple bypass he scrubbed in on earlier. I don't know whether it's kind of sad or that our main topic of conversation is work.

I'm helping clear up when the doorbell chimes. He frowns and leaves to go answer it. I carry on, loading the plates into the dishwasher. When I'm done, I take a bottle of water from the fridge. Euan's still not back. Curiosity gets the better of me, and I poke my head around the kitchen door, into the hallway.

Standing in the hall is the biggest man I've ever seen. He's quite smartly dressed in a buttoned shirt and suit trousers, but despite his smart dress, there's something about him that makes me instantly wary of him. His entire demeanor is dominating and aggressive. His arms are folded across his massive chest, and he smirks condescendingly at Euan, who is talking in a hushed voice. I can't hear what he's saying, but he looks frantic.

Something is wrong.

I slip back into the kitchen and find my bag on the worktop. I dig around until my fingers close around a small metal can of pepper spray. When I first came to America, my sister made me carry it. She said that in a country where everyone has a gun, I at least needed something. I've never even thought about using it, I've never felt threatened, but suddenly, I do. Holding the spray behind my back, I peer into the hallway again. The big guy has stepped closer to Euan now, their faces are only inches apart. The guy's voice is a low growl, which Euan visibly cringes away from. I slip the can into my back pocket and make my way towards them.

"I don't have it!" Euan pleads. His six-foot frame looks positively dwarfed by the monster in front of him.

"I'm sure I can find something around here you can sell," the guy sneers, his eyes flicking up, then down the hallway. Straight at me.

I stop breathing the instant those flat eyes meet mine. A menacing smile pulls at his lips. "Well, well. What do we have here?" he lilts.

"Ria, go back in the kitchen." Euan's voice is shaky.

"Who is he?" I ask.

"No one," he snaps a little too quickly. The big guy smiles wider.

17

I can't help myself. "He doesn't look like 'no one.' He certainly doesn't look like a friend." I grind my teeth. Nothing pisses me off more than being treated like an idiot.

The stranger narrows his eyes as a muscle in his jaw starts to tick. I reach for my back pocket, my fingers brushing the pepper spray.

He turns away from me abruptly. "What's it going to be, Jones? The money, or your legs?" he growls.

"What is he talking about, Euan?"

His eyes flash to mine, a small frown line appearing between his eyebrows before he turns back to Mr. Happy.

"Look." He hesitates and glances over at me, then back to the ogre. "Can you give me a minute?" Euan nervously rubs the back of his neck.

The behemoth man seems annoyed, and huffs. "You have one minute, and then shit starts to get ugly."

"Original," I mumble.

Euan strides toward me, taking my arm and leading me back into the kitchen.

"You need to go, Ria." He's uneasy, almost guilty sounding.

"Just like that?" I cock one eyebrow at him. "You expect me to just walk out of here without a care for the bloody unit of a man that is clearly threatening you?" I snap.

"Look, just leave, Ria. I'll call you later." There's an edge to his voice that I've never heard before. Euan has always been unfailingly sweet and polite. Now, though, he's agitated and twitchy and bordering on rude.

I cross my arms over my chest. "No. You tell me what's going on right now."

"Your boyfriend owes me money, princess." The man slinks in the doorway.

"And you are?"

"Rich."

"How *much* money?" I ask slowly.

"Ria, please just—" Euan starts.

"Twenty grand," Rich cuts him off.

I almost fall over. "Twenty grand?!" I shriek.

He nods. "What the hell? No wonder you have the Hulk after you," I moan.

Rich smirks.

"Look, it's just a misunderstanding," Euan says defensively.

Rich looks almost bored now. "Nope, no misunderstanding. You pay twenty grand today, or I'm going to break your legs." He inspects his nails and continues, "Followed by every bone in your body, and ending with a bullet in your skull," he says with cold nonchalance.

My stomach tightens and the hairs on the back of my neck stand on end. I really want to say he must be joking, but his entire demeanor tells me he's absolutely serious.

"What does he owe the money for?" I ask. Rich turns those menacing eyes on me again. His gaze flicks lazily down my body before trailing back up.

He shrugs. "Gambling."

The air rushes from my lungs. "Gambling," I whisper. Gambling in a state where gambling is illegal, which means Euan now owes money to some pretty unsavoury people. "Brilliant," I say acerbically.

My boyfriend is a lowlife with a gambling problem. You think you know someone. I mean, Euan is so put together. He has everything going for him...

"Look, I can get the money. Just give me three days," Euan begs, ignoring me now.

Rich shakes his head, his lips twitching. "Now or nothing, frat boy. Your choice."

"I promise, I can get it to you in three days." His tone sounds like a whiny child.

"Enough," Rich snaps.

"Take her!" Euan grabs me by the shoulders and shoves me toward the scary man. "Take Ria as security. I'll bring you the money."

"What?!" I shout. "Are you fucking insane?!"

Rich smiles, but it's like a shark smiling at me. There's nothing comforting about the gesture.

"Dirty mouth for a little rich girl," he says. "I like it."

I stumble backwards. "I'm not going anywhere with you. His debts are his problems."

What the hell has Euan gotten me into? I should have left him here to his fate. Stupid me for giving a damn about him when he clearly doesn't give a shit about me. He's willing to hand me over to this brute, all over a gambling debt. I look Rich over again: the broad shoulders, those cold eyes, the close-shaved hair, the light scar on his cheek. All of this coupled with the new information that he's not exactly an upstanding, law-abiding citizen makes me want to run as far away from him as possible.

"This is his debt. Hell, at this point, break his legs. I don't care," I growl as my temper kicks in, but all Rich does is laugh.

Euan wraps his fingers around my wrist, but I yank away sharply. "Don't fucking touch me."

"I can get the money, baby. He'll kill me if you don't go!"

I laugh humorlessly. "Go fuck yourself, Euan."

Rich snickers like an amused child who's just found a new toy. "I'll take her, and that BMW you have parked outside."

Euan opens his mouth to argue, but quickly snaps it shut again, handing over the keys to his much-loved car. Apparently he's more attached to that than he is to me.

Rich grabs me by the shoulders, taking both my arms and crossing them snuggly behind my back with a strength I didn't know someone could even possess.

"Three days" are Rich's parting words before he hauls me toward the door.

By some miracle I manage to wiggle one arm free from his hold and grab the pepper spray from my back pocket. I hold the trigger down, and I aim straight for his eyes. He's a foot taller than me and I don't get a good shot, but it's better than nothing. He shouts out and his grip on my arm loosens, but not enough. I'm just about to swing my leg back and go for gold between his legs when I feel cold metal against the side of my neck.

I freeze.

Rich pushes the barrel of a gun into my neck, the cold metal biting against my skin. My pulse thumps wildly in my chest as a cold sweat breaks out over my skin. Guns terrify me. Maybe it's because of the number of gunshot victims I've dealt with, the amount of people I've watched die with just the pull of a trigger. Whatever the reason, it's a rational and very real fear.

"Walk," he snarls whilst rubbing at his eyes.

He moves behind me, now pressing the barrel of the gun into my back.

I open the door and step out into the cold evening air. He rams the gun into me again, making me stagger forward a few steps.

Pointing towards Euan's black BMW, he orders, "Get in and drive."

I nod and wait for him to move away before making a break for it. My heart pounds like a train as I cover the short distance back to the apartment building. If I can just...

A hand slams down on my shoulder, and I fall to my knees.

"Help!" I scream. Someone will hear me, surely.

I'm hauled to my feet, and then he brings the back of his hand down across my face. I sway from the force of the blow, and blood fills my mouth. Tears prickle my eyes as pain explodes across my jaw.

"Get in the fucking car!" he shouts.

I move silently and slide into the driver's seat, while Rich moves around the front of the car. His eyes drill into me the entire time.

Once he's seated next to me, he resumes pointing the gun in my direction. "Get on I-65."

"Where are we going?" I ask.

"Just do as you're fucking told, bitch," he snaps. "Go the speed limit. Use your fucking blinker, and if we get pulled over you better keep your mouth shut. I'm not above killing a cop."

We drive for several hours, and at the Georgia state line he orders me to pull over into an abandoned car park. I do as he says. He's stopped pointing the gun in my face now, but he still has it. I'm not all that keen on provoking him.

"Pull up behind the SUV," he says.

I pull up behind the only car in the car park and cut the engine. There's a tense silence as I wait with baited breath for him to make his next move. He takes the gun out again and orders, "Get out."

I open the door and slide out until my feet touch the tarmac.

"Come here," he says, wiggling his finger as he opens the boot of the SUV.

I approach cautiously. One glance in the back of this car has me paralyzed with fear. There's rope, a couple of shovels, and some tarpaulin. *He's going to kill me. He's going to kill me.* The thought runs through my mind over and over. He pulls a length of rope from the back and moves toward me. I don't think, I just react. I swing my leg back until my knee meets his groin. He manages to dodge at the last minute, and although I make contact, it doesn't quite have the impact I would have liked. I turn to run, but he grasps a fistful of my hair. I scream, as my scalp feels like it's on fire.

Something hits me in the side of the head, and then everything goes black.

When I come to, I'm lying on my side and my head is pounding like a jackhammer. The hum beneath me tells me I'm in a car. I try to sit up, but my hands are bound behind my back. There's also a gag in my mouth, but, on the bright side, I'm not dead. Yet. I lose track of time, but eventually the car rolls to a stop and the engine cuts off.

The boot opens and Rich grabs my arm, pulling me out. He pushes me forward and shoves my bound wrists. My shoulders scream in protest, but I say nothing.

He walks me to the front door of what looks like a normal house. It's not too big, not too small, but I notice that

24

there are no other houses near it. He marches me up the steps to the front door and knocks three times, and then the door opens. The guy standing on the other side is almost as wide as he is tall. His eyes trace over me, landing on my face and focusing on the gag. His brow furrows, and his eyes dart from me back up to Rich. "The fuck?"

"Kid wouldn't pay. Threw her to me as collateral," Rich chuckles.

I watch a slow, sick smirk crawl over the man's face, but he continues to block the doorway. "Collateral, huh? See how the boss feels about that. He does love women, so..." He moves away from the door.

There's something about the way he's smiling that makes me think I'm missing out on some private joke.

Rich drags me into the house. There's a haze of cigarette smoke that seems to linger in the air. The house is dark, with dim lighting everywhere. I hear the murmur of several men talking, then the rumble of their laughter coming from somewhere inside the house. He pushes me down a narrow hallway. All I can hear is my pulse hammering in my ears and my quickening breath. There's a dark wooden door at the end of this long hallway. That's where he's taking me. I panic. What if this boss guy is worse than Rich here? What if he plans to kill me? Or rape me? This is not happening! I will not be a victim, a statistic. In a last-ditch attempt to escape, I throw my weight back against Rich, knocking him off balance and into the wall behind us.

"Goddamn it!" he growls as I make a break for it.

I stumble down the hallway toward the door. I know I'm going the wrong way, but it's away from Rich.

He storms after me. I hesitate at the end of the hall, unsure of which way to go. I run toward the only open area there is, but I'm not fast enough because he grabs my wrist, twisting it as he spins me around. Screaming in pain, I stomp on his foot and kick him in the shin.

"If you try to kick me one more time I'll yank that pretty hair right outta your skull, sweet cheeks. Got it?" he shouts, his cigarette breath blowing over my face. He drags me back to the door and opens it, shoving me down the steps.

When we get to the bottom, I try to yank my arm from his grasp, and he rams me up against the wall, winding my arms behind my back.

"Stop fighting me!"

I groan and he twists harder, straining both of my bound wrists and my already aching shoulders.

Rich drags me in front of him, shoving me through the door at the end of the corridor with such force that I fall forward, my knees crashing into the wooden floor boards. Pain shoots through my joints.

"Ah, fuck," Rich mumbles behind me.

I grit my teeth as my entire body aches.

"What the fuck?" a deep voice rumbles over a high-pitched moan.

I lift my head slightly and peer through my tangled hair at the source of the sound. There's a large desk in front of me, and bent over it is a naked, red-haired woman, her chest pressed against the wood. Standing behind her is the biggest bloody guy I've ever seen, and he's pointing a gun at my head. I squeeze my eyes shut as panic threatens to overtake me. At least it will be quick. I wait, and nothing happens. When I open them again, he's lowering the gun. My eyes fix onto his broad chest, which is bare, the defined muscles straining as he yanks up the fly of his jeans and shoves his gun into the waistband.

I feel a blush creep over my cheeks. I'm not a prude, but equally, I do not want to see two total strangers naked. This is so not what I pictured when Rich was dragging me down that hallway.

"Get out," the big guy snaps at the girl as he gathers her clothes. She huffs and takes the clothes from him. He smacks her arse. "I'll finish with you later." I want to scream at her to fucking help me. I'm bound and gagged and yet she's glaring at me like I just interrupted her fun. News flash, sweetheart, I'd rather not be here.

"You know, your job really is a pain in the ass," she remarks.

Am I the only person in this room who finds this hideously uncomfortable?

"Go to work, Crystal, I'd hate to fire my favorite girl for being late anyway." She shrugs and walks out of the room, completely naked, swaying her hips as she goes. I feel like I just walked into a madhouse.

"The kid couldn't pay. She's a deposit," Rich says casually.

"You took a person"—he points at me—"as collateral?" His voice is a low rumble. The room suddenly feels too small. I can feel his anger like a living thing. My skin breaks out in goose bumps, and I tremble as a very real fear kicks in. "Get out! I'll deal with you later." His voice is calm, but not in a good way. More like the calm before a storm.

Wordlessly, he leaves, and the door clicks shut with a heavy finality.

I'm alone with this guy, the boss. This can't possibly bode well for me. I slowly lift my eyes to find him looking at me. Our eyes lock, and I feel like I'm staring into utter emptiness.

He's undeniably beautiful, his eyes the oddest shade of green, his face something you would see in the pages of a magazine. His body is bulky and cut, honed for a purpose. His skin is a map of ink work, winding down both arms and across his chest. He's the kind of guy you would stop in the street just to stare at, but would not want to meet in a dark alley. His beauty is overshadowed by a coldness that seeps from him, an air of danger that seems to cling to him. Everything about him screams dangerous. And I'm now bound and gagged, and locked in a room with him.

Chapter 5
Jude

I pour the whiskey into a short glass, savoring the way the ice cracks under its heat. She's damn near panting from what I just did to her. Using the back of my hand, I wipe the mess she left on my face, licking over my lips to enjoy the taste of her. This girl is one of my favorites. She gives me everything I crave: power, control, and fucking killer sex with no strings attached. "Don't move a muscle. You stay just like I had you."

Plucking a cube from the drink, I dim the lights and make my way back to her. My dick twitches as I stare at that curved ass bent over my desk. I set the chilled glass on her lower back, and it bows. "Ah, ah, ah. I didn't tell you to fucking move."

She giggles and slings her head back; her red hair flies over her bare shoulders and hits my face. "I didn't ask." She glances over at me and bites down on her lip.

"That mouth of yours is gonna get you in trouble." I arch a brow, rubbing the ice over her ass and up the indention of her spine as I say, "Move again and I'll choke you."

Her nails tap over the desk, scratching across its surface while she fights the urge to wiggle by pushing her ass against me. "Stop torturing me," she pleads.

"Honey, this isn't torture. *Trust* me!" I massage the melted ice into her skin, then fist her hair. "Torture would be not letting you fuck me, and I promise, in about five minutes I'm going to be balls deep in that pretty little pussy of yours." I tug on her hair, yanking her head back so I can kiss my way down to her shoulder.

She pushes off the desk and spins around, rubbing her hand over my jeans and clawing at me. I slowly pull my shirt off, holding it in my hand as I dig my fingers into her sides and twist her away from me. With one swift movement, I mercilessly slam her face down over the desk.

I stare at her ass, thinking about how much I love the slapping sound it makes when I lay into a woman. "I'm fucking you from behind," I say, squeezing her firm cheeks in my palms. I loop the shirt around her throat, and tug her head back to me. Sweeping my fingers over her wet pussy, I give it a quick slap, and she jumps a little from that unexpected sensation.

"Fuck, JP. I'm about to die here," she moans, grinding her bare pussy against me. "You've still got half your clothes on."

I laugh, and, keeping a good grip on my shirt, I use my free hand to unfasten my fly.

"Oh," she sighs. "Just fuck me, you asshole." She attempts to turn around, but I hold her in place. "Would you please, for once, take the gun out of your jeans? It makes me nervous."

"Don't pretend you don't like it," I say, pulling my cock out and stroking it, teasing against her entrance.

A groan bubbles up her throat. Frustrated, she slams her palm over the desk out of frustration. "Fuck me, damn it!"

"Oh, I'm gonna fuck you up," I growl as I widen my stance behind her.

I'm not gentle at all, I hold the shirt with one hand, and slam my dick into her with the other. She moans loudly, her back arching from the sudden assault.

Her breaths morph into sex-drunken moans, and she tightens around me, the sensation damn near making my eyes roll back in my head, forcing me to grit my teeth. I'm about three seconds from losing my shit when the door is suddenly thrown wide open. I instinctively pull my gun, aiming into the hall. The safety clicks and my finger rests on the trigger. Staring down the barrel, I realize its Richard, and with him is a girl, bound and gagged, on her knees in front of my desk.

"Aw, fuck," he says, covering his face with his hands. I'm taken so off-guard by the unwelcomed intrusion that I briefly stand with my cock still buried in the woman before pulling out.

"What. The. Fuck?" I shout. I glance back down at the girl in front of Richard. "What the fuck?" I ask again as I shove my dick back inside my jeans.

Crystal's still sprawled out on the desk, ass in the air, and panting. I snatch the clothes from the floor and hand them to her. "Get out." She straightens up and takes her clothes from me, a bewildered look plastered to her face. I raise both brows, then smack her ass. "Don't worry, I'll finish with you later."

"You know, your job really is a pain in the ass."

"Go to work, Crystal, I'd hate to fire my favorite girl for being late anyway."

She huffs and stomps off, not bothering to dress. She just trots past them both, completely unfazed by any of this. My eyes dart to Richard as I pull in a breath. I wipe my hand over my sweaty chest, and my gaze drifts down to the girl. She's dressed in jeans and a Vanderbilt University hoodie. Her hair's a complete mess. She's covered in grease and dirt, and her eyes are swollen and red.

"The kid couldn't pay." He smiles nervously at me. "She's a deposit."

I roll my bottom lip underneath my teeth, and bit down, fighting to maintain my calm. "You took a person"—I point at the girl—"as collateral?"

My heart repeatedly slams against my chest, a tingly heat spreading across my body from anger. This motherfucker is stupid as hell. I really want to beat the shit out of him, ram his head against the wall a few good times, but I clear my throat instead, and point my finger at the door. "Get out! I'll deal with you later." I manage to keep my tone completely calm, which is, to anyone who knows me, worse than any shouting.

He doesn't say a word, he just turns, shutting the door behind him as he leaves.

I snatch my shirt from the floor and wipe the sweat from my body. Pinching the bridge of my nose, I inhale deeply before I turn around to look at her. Blonde mussed hair hangs over part of her face, she has a nasty black bruise on one cheek, and she's staring at the floor, visibly trembling.

I need a drink to handle this shit right here. I shake my head, scratch over my stubbled jaw, and reach for the whiskey. My eyes lock onto hers as I top off the drink. I take a sip, then set the glass on the edge of the desk. Her gaze follows my every move as I grab a cigarette, place it to my lips, and flick the lighter. I take a long drag and slowly blow the smoke in her direction, the light grey cloud blanketing her.

What the fuck am I gonna do with this girl?

She hasn't stood up. She hasn't moved a muscle. I lean against the desk, and take another drag, blowing a plume of smoke at her again. She coughs weakly. She's staring at me like I'm some fucking caged animal that's been let loose.

"Hmm," I mumble, balling up my shirt as I push off the desk and walk toward her. The closer I get to her, the bigger her eyes grow. I squat in front of her and pull in another puff. The gag is so tight the material's cutting into her skin. The least I could do is take it off. Gripping the cigarette between my lips, I reach around the back of her head and unfasten the knot. The cloth falls from her face, revealing a swollen and bloodied lip. *He fucking hit her? I'm gonna kill him for this.* I brush my finger over her wounded lip, and she jerks away.

"I demand that you let me go," she says, glaring at me.

I cock a brow at her as a slight smile pulls at my lips. Feisty and British. I won't pretend the accent doesn't do something for me. I rise and turn my back to her. "I wish I could."

"This has nothing to do with me. Your stupid guy took me against my will. Your argument is with Euan, not me." She's trying her damnedest to sound strong, but I can hear the slight tremor in her voice. Yeah, she's pissed, but it's obvious that she's scared, and judging by the state of her face, she should be.

I cross my arms over my chest and lean against the edge of the desk as I take puff after puff, stewing over how fucked up this shit is. After a brief moment of silence, I say, "But you're here, so unfortunately, doll, it now has *everything* to do with you."

She hangs her head, leaving it bowed as she lifts her gaze to mine. "Please." Her voice trembles. "This is a misunderstanding. Please, just let me go," she chokes.

A sensation I'm not all too familiar with creeps through me, but I swallow that uncomfortable feeling down. There is no room in my world for guilt.

"Now, as much as I'd like to just let you leave, you see, when Euan decided to hand you over to me, you became part of that debt. I'm sure you'll understand why I can't let you go, huh?" I shrug. "Don't take it personally or anything. It's just business."

I watch as the gravity of her situation sinks in. Her eyes slowly drop to the floor, and she pulls in a ragged breath like she's about to burst into sobs. "Please," she whispers again. She looks so small and vulnerable, it forces me to look away from her.

She may be just a girl, but she *is* in *my* house, and unfortunately for her and that dipshit, Richard, she's now seen my face. She's a security risk at the very least. "You play nice, your boyfriend pays up, and I'll let you go unharmed."

Her gaze narrows. Those eyes of hers are so bloodshot, and all that does is make the deep blue of her irises pop. "Who are you?" she asks, hushed.

"A businessman." I shrug, then take her by the arm to help her up. I place her against the wall. "You gonna stay there, right?"

"It's not like I'm going anywhere," she mumbles.

I take my shirt from the desk and pull it over my head, then dig my cell from my pocket and dial Marney's number. As usual, he picks up on the first ring.

"Yeah?"

"That deal in Vanderbilt's fucked up. I've got a damn hostage now, and what the fuck am I supposed to do with that?" I groan, my eyes locked on hers.

"A hostage?"

"Yeah, a fucking girl!" Hearing it out loud sends me into a sudden fit of rage. "Someone's gonna fucking die!" I shout. I exhale in an effort to calm myself. "Call around and find out some more about this Euan kid for me. Tap his fucking line. I want to know everything about him down to what kind of lotion he uses when he jerks off, got it?"

"Yeah, sure thing," he chuckles. "So, what you gonna do with the girl?"

"I don't fucking know!"

"Well, have fun with that. I'll let you know what I find out." He hangs up the phone, and my eyes zero in on her swollen lip again.

I will fuck Richard up so bad for doing this. I take her by the shoulders and, without saying a word, turn her around, my gaze instantly falling to her bound wrists. The skin is red and raw, the flesh worn into the rope. *Bastard.* I quickly untie the knot and notice just how deeply the burns have cut into her fair skin.

She wiggles her fingers, working to get feeling back into her hands. "Thanks," she mumbles.

I don't know what the fuck to do with her, but she's got to go somewhere besides here.

"Come on, then." I reach for her arm to escort her to another room, and the next thing I know, her knee is coming at my balls. I jump back, bite down on my lip, and hiss in a breath. *Fucking bitch!* I catch both her arms in my hands, jerking her around as I pin them to her sides and slam her into the wall. She fights me, thrashing her entire body in a feeble attempt to get away.

Leaning into her, I place my nose inches from her ear. "Really?" I growl against her neck, as I press her against the wall. "Now, do you think that was a wise decision?"

"Let go of me!" she screams.

I force her harder into the wall. I'm using so much of my own body weight I doubt she can hardly breathe, much less move. "Not a chance," I say, and push into her more, my thighs now firm against her ass. She gasps, and I keep my voice calm and low as I say, "I'm telling you, girl, it's best not to test me." She squirms and her body rubs over me in a way my cock can't ignore. I back away an inch so she can't feel that I'm slightly aroused by her.

"Please just let me go," she begs. "You don't have to do this. I won't tell anyone. I won't call the police. I promise."

"I don't trust anyone, not even pretty little blondes. And you know what usually happens to people I don't trust that try to kick me in the balls?" My hold on her tightens, and I yank down on her arms. "They end up in a fucking body bag."

She grunts and, without warning, drives an elbow into my stomach. To my surprise, she actually has some force behind it because it knocks the breath from me. That little stunt makes my hold on her let up, and she wiggles from my grasp, running for the door. I storm after her, my heart thrashing in my chest. When I catch up to her, I grab the ends of her long hair, yanking her head back so hard she stumbles and falls to the floor. I drag her back down the dark hallway, and she's pitching a fit. Screaming, yelling; she's clawing at my hands so hard that her nails are slicing through my knuckles.

"I'm gonna fucking kill Richard for this shit," I grumble. She lets out a scream so shrill I'm certain only dogs can hear it, and I cringe. "You can't just make things easy for me, can you?" I mumble as I plop down in the office chair and pull her onto my lap. "Had to go and make me act like an asshole."

She's still fighting me, slapping me, wiggling around. I manage to yank the drawer open despite her bucking like a rabid mule, and I fish out a zip tie. "Would you just fucking *be still*?"

She screams again, then I grab her by the waist, and in one swift movement, I lay her face down across my lap, wrapping one leg over her thighs to hold her there. "I don't guess you're gonna put your hands behind your back without a struggle, huh?" I ask, my tone dripping with sarcasm. She grabs onto the edge of the chair. I guess she thinks that's going make it more difficult for me to get her hands? I just laugh and take both arms, bringing them behind her back. I fasten the restraint, then pat her on the back. "You gonna behave now? Not try to kick me in my balls again, huh?"

"Fuck you!" she shouts, still struggling underneath my leg.

I trail my eyes down from her hands to her ass, and unfortunately, the way she's continuing to thrash around combined with the sight of her flipped over my lap and tied puts my dick in a compromising position. I shift my hips, adjusting the semi-hard on I can't seem to fucking get rid of, then I feel her teeth tear into the upper part of my thigh.

"You crazy...." I hiss at the throbbing pain and grab a fistful of her tangled blonde hair, jerking her head away from my leg. It shouldn't turn me on, but fucking hell, I love a feisty girl. *Fuck, I'm sicker than I thought. I probably need to get the hell away from her.*

I rise and she falls from my lap to the floor. Before she has a chance to try and stand, I pick her up, and toss her onto the couch across from my desk.

"You really don't know when to just stop. Fuck, I was being nice to you!" I say as I loom over her, wiping the sweat from my brow.

"Yes, I'll just lay down and let you kill me," she says with bitter sarcasm.

"Who the fuck said anything about killing you? Don't fuck with me, and you won't have to lay down and get killed. Damn!" I drag my hand down my face. This is such a fucking pain in the ass. "Don't fucking move. I'm done playing with you. Just sit right there." I arch my brow as I point at her, and she looks away. I'm pretty sure she's afraid to move now.

I fall back in my chair and sit, staring at her and wondering how in the fuck this is ever going to go right.

"I had no idea he was mixed up in any of this shit." Her face crumples and her head falls back into the couch. "How could I not know?"

The longer I sit here and look at her, the harder that guilty feeling tries to bubble to the surface again. The professional in me knows what I should do, but that dirty, miniscule part of me that still has some deformed part of a conscience is screaming that I shouldn't. If this were a man, I would have one of my guys kill him, but it's a fucking girl, and I'd really rather not kill her. I can lie, cheat, steal, kill; I can do a number of horrendous things without batting an eye—as long as it doesn't involve a woman. And as fucked up as that mess with Joe's wife was, I can't go there, even though I know it's probably safer for me to; I can't kill her.

"You just..." I shake my head, "stay there." I stand and pace in front of my desk, then grab the bottle of whiskey, twisting the cap and tossing it to the floor. I turn the bottle up and suck back several mouthfuls of the burning liquor while staring at her. I take one more large gulp, then sit on the floor and slump against the door.

"If you try to leave, you'll have to get through me. I've been pretty fucking patient up until now. Don't test me." I flip my shirt up to reveal my gun. "Just so you know, if I have to kill you to get my fucking money, I will."

Her chin drops to her chest, and she cries. And I drink. I drink until my eyes fucking cross because I see no solution to this situation that I like. At some point, she falls asleep, and I keep tipping back the bottle, watching her. She's just lying there, arms behind her back, hair matted to her face. I skim over her, stopping to admire her breathing. She's out cold, and each large swell of her chest forces her breasts up. That is one thing that gets to me, for some reason, watching a woman breathe—the way their breasts rise and fall, it's a turn-on, and the fact that her hands are tied behind her back is just making each draw she pulls in more pronounced and slightly labored. *Fuck me!* I have to shake off that automatic response my body has to it. I keep watching her for God only knows how long, my dick pressing against my jeans like goddamn roadkill. I can't take it any longer.

I manage to stand, but only briefly before staggering and falling into my desk. "Fuck this," I grumble and grab the knife lying on the desk. "Just fuck it!" I stumble toward her, losing my balance several more times before I kneel next to the couch. I stare at her, flipping the knife in my hand. I shouldn't do this, but I'm drunk. I take the blade and slip it between her wrists, and the zip tie snaps free. I guess even soulless motherfuckers like me have a weakness. Fuck it to hell. I rub my hand over my head, dropping the knife to the floor when I fall into the wall. I settle back against the door, and my eyes grow heavy. *Great! The damn room is spinning.* I lean my head against the door and pass out.

Chapter 6
Victoria

I wake up and my head is pounding. My shoulders ache where my arms have been tied behind my back for so long. Just as I think that, I realise that my hands are no longer bound.

I don't remember him untying me.

I sit up quickly. Looking down at my hands, I notice that my wrists are marked from the restraints. I guess I only have myself to blame for that, but I wasn't going down without a fight.

My eyes dart around the small room. It's dark, the only light coming from a small lamp on the desk. There are no windows, and the walls are bare, with the exception of one picture of a naked woman hanging over the side board covered in various bottles.

The door is opposite me, and there, slumped against it on the floor, is that man. His head is resting on his shoulder, and he does *not* look comfortable.

Good, I hope he has a stiff neck for days to come.

I study his profile, watching as his chest rises and falls on heavy breaths. He's intimidating, dominating, and scary as hell. This man is as predatory as they come. Everything about him screams deadly. I don't know what the hell Euan is into here, but this shit is serious.

My eyes drift down his chest of their own accord, tracing over the broad muscle. They skim lower, lower, and that's when I notice the dim glint from the gun in his lap. His fingers are wrapped firmly around it, one a whisper away from the trigger. *Shit, is he planning to shoot me?*

I slowly rise to my feet. My head spins, but I manage to steady myself. I tiptoe across the room, watching to make sure his breaths remain even. *Maybe I can just pry that gun from him? Shit, can I?*

Worth a try. I drop into a crouch in front of him, reaching out cautiously. He doesn't move. My fingers just brush the cool metal of the gun when his hand darts out and latches on to my wrist, squeezing hard.

"You should know I'm a *very* light sleeper," he whispers without opening his eyes. I jump, and fall back on my arse. *Shit!* "Nice try, though." Opening his eyes, he sits up. "What exactly were you gonna do, sweetheart? Kill me?" His gaze narrows accusingly on me, and I try to tame my pounding heart.

"No, just escape," I whisper.

"Mmm, I see." His eyes rake over me. "I untie you and you try to kill me. You see the problem I have with that?"

"I wouldn't try to kill you. *I'm* not a murderer," I huff.

"You'd be surprised what people will do to survive," he says quietly.

He crawls toward me, the gun clasped in his hand, which makes me nervous to say the least. His lips kick up in a smirk. He's like an animal stalking his prey, toying with it.

"You really should look at this particular situation like this, I'm your saviour. I didn't kidnap you. I'm most likely gonna fuck up my own guy for busting those pouty-ass lips of yours."

My saviour! Is he serious right now? My temper flares. I have been bartered in exchange for a bloody debt to this man, who clearly has the morals of an alley cat. I'm not a fucking object to be traded and exchanged at will!

"Oh, spare me your chivalrous bullshit," I interrupt him. "You're going to beat the shit out of your guy because he's an idiot." My hands are trembling as I attempt to scramble back away from him. I know I should be careful how I speak to him, but honestly, if he wants to kill me, he will.

He sucks in an agitated breath and continues, "...and I haven't killed you, although I probably should seeing as how you just tried to steal my gun."

He's moving slowly, stealthily. All I can think is how much his movements resemble a big cat. This damn room is so dark, which doesn't help. His cold eyes lock with mine, making me recoil even more. For every inch I move backward, he seems to move forward two. The last thing I want is him anywhere near me.

I laugh nervously. "Don't you think you're being a bit over-dramatic?" I try to keep my voice level, but it wavers under that murky green gaze. Honestly, I wouldn't even know how to shoot a gun. One look at his expression, and I know I've said the wrong thing.

His eyes narrow as he growls. I can smell the whiskey on his breath as it blows across my face. I panic. I don't know why I do, but out of instinct I lash out, slapping him across the face. His head snaps to the side slightly before his gaze swings to mine, and a sick grin twists his lips. "Wrong fucking move, sweetheart."

Oh, God. I think I'm going to throw up. The look on his face tells me that I'm in for a whole world of shit right now.

"I'm sorry!" I blurt, but it's too late. I thought he was an arse yesterday, but that's nothing compared to this. He's going to kill me. I know it. A muscle in his jaw ticks, and the next thing I know I'm flat on my back. He violently slams me to the floor, his large body pinning me to the ground. His hand wraps around my throat, pressing me mercilessly into the wooden floor boards. I gasp and panic, fighting against his hold. The more I struggle, the more his fingers threaten to tighten.

"You have no idea who you're fucking with, little girl." He inhales, the air hissing through his clenched teeth. Those icy eyes of his bore into me, and he leans in until his face is inches from my own. "If you did, you'd learn I'm not a person you want to provoke."

I feel his fingers press into my throat a little more, and the weight of his body lays over me, nearly suffocating me. I gasp desperately as my lungs start to falter.

My pulse quickens, hammering through my veins as fear consumes me. He's going to kill me, right here, right now. I'm going to die in his basement and no one will ever find me. My senses are heightened; I can hear each labored breath I manage to pull in echo through my ears, and all I can smell is him. The earthy scent of his sweat and cologne mixed with a touch of whiskey, it makes my stomach churn. All I can think is that I'd rather he shoot me than strangle me. I'd rather bleed out than have the life choked from me.

He moves until his lips are almost on my ear. "I am that guy your father warned you about." he hisses, the heat from his breath touching my neck, making me tremble underneath him as sheer terror grips me. "I am that man that you pray you never run into in a dark alleyway on the wrong night. Do *not* mistake my pity for weakness. I will put a bullet in your skull without a second fucking thought. Do you hear me?"

I buck underneath him, trying to throw him off me as my basic desire to survive kicks in. His fingers constrict around my throat, and I claw at his arms, trying to pull him away. Of course it's pointless. He must be at least three times my weight, but my survival instincts are determined to give it a bloody good shot. His eyes lock with mine, unyielding, unforgiving, and ice cold. As adrenaline floods my veins, my breathing grows shallow, my vision swims.

"Do you hear me?" he snarls in my face. I gasp and cough under the pressure of his fingers, managing a small nod. He tightens his hold again, and dark spots skitter across my eyes as a low hum rings through my ears. I'm about to lose consciousness. Suddenly, the pressure releases, and his weight is gone.

I roll onto my stomach, dragging oxygen into my lungs. I choke and cough violently. My eyes are streaming, as tears pour down my face. My throat is screaming in pain, and my chest hurts. I've never been so scared in my life. For a second there, I really thought he was going to kill me. It takes a certain type of person to choke the life out of someone. Shooting someone is one thing, but being that close, watching the panic in their eyes....I'm dealing with a monster. Lifting my head, I find him leant over his desk with his hands braced against the wood and his head hung. He looks so calm.

"Shit!" he shouts, making me jump.

I crawl away from him until my back is against the wall. I watch him warily, my chest heaving as he starts to pace in front of his desk.

He raises his head and moves toward me, stopping directly in front of me. "Come on." He gestures for me to stand, and I do, but I keep my back to the wall the entire time.

He eyes me carefully, his gaze flicking down to my throat before he stalks away from me. "Come on I said," he shouts. I do as he says, because honestly, the last thing I want to do is piss him off.

I push off the wall and gingerly follow him out of the office. All I can do is stare at him. He's so large, his frame seeming to fill the hallway. His shoulders are rigid, his steps hard as he storms through the house. When his hand reaches to his pocket, I tense, fearing he's changed his mind and is going to shoot me.

He pulls a phone to his ear. "Get down to the guest rooms, now!" he snarls. I suddenly feel very sorry for the person on the other end. Apparently his treating me like shit isn't personal.

I have to almost run to keep up with him as he navigates a set of stairs, and then along another corridor. At the end of a hallway, we reach a door. He slams it opens, stepping aside to let me in. I keep my eyes trained at the floor, unable to look at him.

Oh, God, is this going to be a torture chamber or something?

I peer inside the room and find a double bed, a chest of drawers, a TV. It's just a bedroom, or maybe a prison cell.

Hurried footsteps tromp down the hall, followed by a deep southern male voice. "Hey, what's up?"

"I have a job for you besides bringing me my fucking whiskey," Jude barks.

I keep my head hung, but peep up through my hair at him. His jaw is clenched as he narrows his eyes at me.

"You're gonna watch her." He points at me. "Don't let her escape. No phone calls. Don't fucking trust her. Got it?"

"*Her?* A girl? You want me to watch a girl? Why is a girl even here?"

"Problem with that?" His tone is clipped.

"No," the other man responds quickly.

I hear the door click shut. Knowing he's gone, I raise my head and find a young guy standing just inside the door. He looks up at me from beneath his long brown hair.

"Hey." He smiles shyly and rubs his hand over the back of his neck. He's not like Rich, or the other guy. He's just a kid. He can be no older than twenty.

"Hey." I say quietly. If I am going to be locked in a room with one of these guys, I'd much rather it be with this kid.

He stands in front of the closed door for a long time before he speaks.

"Fuck!" The sound of the psycho screaming is followed by a loud thud that shakes the wall. I jump and this kid remains completely unfazed.

"Uh, I'm Caleb," he tells me. He's staring at me like he's never seen a woman before...and maybe he hasn't.

I stare at him, study him, really.

I swallow. "Ria. I would say it's nice to meet you, but, well, you know, kidnapped and all."

He frowns, looking utterly confused. "Wait, what? Jude kidnapped you? Jude?" He shakes his head and then resumes glaring at me like he has no idea what on earth to do with me. "That's fucked up," he mumbles, and his eyes dart to the floor.

This guy may well be my only hope....

Chapter 7
Jude

I shut the door, groaning as I rub my hands down my face. I nearly make it to the end of the hallway before my anger gets the better of me. "Fuck!" I scream, pulling my fist back, and slamming it through the sheetrock. Pain splinters up my arm, and I watch the flurry of debris settle. I shake my head and suck in a lungful of dust. This is some fucked-up shit Richard's gotten me into, and I'm going to beat the everloving piss out of him for it.

On every fucking level, women are a weakness of mine. And that is something most people who know me are aware of.

I tromp up the stairs to my bedroom, fuming. I kick open the door and rip the black t-shirt over my head. I grab the edge of the dresser, lean in, and stare at my reflection. There's an angry handprint on my left cheek and several raised welts on my arms from where she clawed at me in a pitiful attempt to get me off of her. The look of absolute fear plastered to her face when I pinned her down by her throat flashes through my mind, and I have to close my eyes.

She fucking hit me and I lost my shit. What did she expect? I grip the edge of the dresser so hard my knuckles fade to bone-white.

I pull my shirt on, straighten it out, then grab my Colt 45 on the way out of the door.

I pass the room *that* girl and my brother are locked in, and stop to pound my fist over the door. "Caleb? Tie her up any time you take her to piss, got it?"

"Yeah, Jude. Got it," I hear him shout through the wall.

And then…. "You are *not* watching me piss!"

I shake my head. Caleb should have fun dealing with that one, I just worry he's too damn nice. She's unfortunately an attractive woman, and half the guys in this house are fucking Neanderthals. Caleb's the only one with enough restraint not to touch her. Hell, I barely had enough restraint last night. She has one hell of an ass, an accent that makes everything sound filthy, and a smart mouth. Everything about her is just asking to be fucked.

I pass through the living room, eyeing the guys glued to the television. "She doesn't leave, and no one fucks her, understood?" I point at Bob in particular.

They wave me off. And I leave, washing my mind of her while I tend to business.

Chapter 8
Victoria

I've been in this room with Caleb for nearly three days now. I'm starting to wonder what the hell is going on. Three days, Euan said. Three days, and he was supposed to pay the money, and I walk free. Then again, I don't exactly trust the word of a guy who would sell out his own girlfriend to a bunch of criminals as collateral. I won't pretend I'm not hurt; I am. I would never say that Euan is the love of my life or any of that crap, but I thought he cared about me, respected me. I thought he was a decent guy. How wrong I was. Panic is starting to kick in now, and it feels as though the walls are closing in on me. I have to get out of these four walls.

Shit, what if I never get out of here? What about my job? My life? What if they kill me? It's the waiting that's killing me, the not knowing.

I glance at Caleb, sprawled casually across the small double bed. He's wearing a football jersey and keeps intermittently yelling at the TV, watching some game. He's completely absorbed in it. I study him carefully. He's the typical American college kid with shaggy, dark hair and dark eyes. He's good looking, albeit he is still rather wiry for his height, but I can already see that he will bulk out.

I hate to admit it, but he seems nice. He hasn't given me one death threat. He seems genuinely concerned about my welfare, even though he clearly has no idea what to really do with me. I haven't really spoken to him since we've been locked in here. I'm not going to acknowledge a guy who is aiding my captor. He doesn't seem bothered, though. He's perpetually chirpy, constantly trying to feed me, asking if I want to watch a film. He's wearing me down without even bloody doing anything. I feel like I'm going mad. He obviously works for that maniacal psychopath, but he doesn't fit in with a gang of murderous thugs like Jude and Rich. Why is he here?

"Yes!" he shouts at the TV.

I'm sitting on the floor with my back to the wall, trying my best to block out the irritating ruckus of the TV.

"Is it really necessary for you to watch this in here? Can't you go and find another room?" I huff.

He shakes his head, his eyes never leaving the TV. "No can do, chick. I have to stay with you, but I also have five grand riding on this game. Not fucking missing it."

"You do know that gambling is a fool's game, right?"

He flashes me that wide, boyish smile of his. "Not when you're a statistical genius. It's all about calculated risk."

"You're a statistical genius, really?" I ask sarcastically. He looks like the quarterback. The attractive guy with nothing going on between the ears.

"Not me," he chuckles. "Jude. He's got to know exactly which odds are in his favor. He's good at it. Really good."

I frown, because I have no idea what the hell he's on about, but I don't want to talk about that bastard.

I steer the conversation away. "So, do you have any plans for your life, aside from working for that fuck-wad?" I'm genuinely curious. I can't help but think that he's better than this.

He glances away from the TV again and cocks an eyebrow at me. "I'm a paramedic," he says, shocking the shit out of me.

"Wow, okay. So why the hell are you working for Jude?"

"You're nosey." His attention flicks back to the game. "I don't work for him, well, not really. He's my brother. I just help out. All this mess just comes with being part of the family."

I gasp. "I'm sorry, you're related to him?" I ask incredulously.

He nods, still not looking my way.

What the hell? How on earth can he and Jude possibly share the same genetic makeup? Jude is dangerous and scary as fuck, whilst Caleb is almost sweet. I don't know, maybe that's just what they want me to think. Maybe he's every bit as bad as his brother. I look at his boyish face, and I just

56

cannot summon even a fraction of the fear I feel toward Jude. Now that he's said it though, I see the similarity in their features. The line of his jaw, the set of his nose, broad and straight.

"How unfortunate for you," I mumble, and draw my legs to my chest.

He smiles. "You know, you really shouldn't judge him. You don't know him."

"Oh, so he's actually a really nice guy, I just caught him on a bad day?"

His eyes dart to mine, and his lips press together.

"Didn't think so."

"Either way"—his look grows stern—"you need to rein it in around him. I hear you've already pissed him off after just a few hours. Not good, chick. He's not known for his patience, and he's got one hell of a temper." His eyes flick to my neck, which I know has now blossomed into deep purple bruises, my own personal reminder of just how short-tempered Jude is.

"Yeah, I noticed," I remark.

"Yes!" he shouts again, fist pumping as he grins at the TV.

I glance at the set and see a sea of purple and gold going nuts.

"Did they win?" I ask, because I really have no idea what is going on.

He grins at me. "I just doubled my bet and won ten grand." He rolls off the bed. "*That* is what happens when you have a bookie for a brother!"

Odds, statistics. Of course. A bookie! Oh fuck. He's legitimately a gambling mobster. Holy shit.

By the time the evening comes round I'm climbing the bloody walls. I've been pacing the small room for the past half hour.

"You want something to eat yet?" Caleb asks, stretching next to the door.

I furrow my brows. "No, I don't want anything to eat. I want to go home!"

Ignoring my request, he sighs. "You're gonna to have to eat something, or you're gonna get me in trouble. It's been three days. You must be starving by now."

I groan and go back to pacing at the end of the bed. I am not going to stay here like some fucked-up guest. I do not want to be here, and I'm sure as shit not eating their food like a good little prisoner. I'd sooner starve.

He huffs and crosses his arms over his chest. "Okay, fine. I'm going to go downstairs and get some food. I'll bring you some in case you change your mind."

He turns and walks out of the room, closing the door behind him. I hear the click as he locks it from the other side.

Guest rooms my arse. What kind of guest room has a lock on the outside of the door? These rooms are just glorified prison cells.

As soon as he's gone I scout the room, frantically searching through all the drawers, under the bed...there must be something in here that I can use as a weapon. I eye up the chair in the corner. Maybe I could smash it and snap a leg off or something. What the fuck? As if I'll be strong enough to break a chair. Who do I think I am, the Incredible Hulk?

I eventually give up. There's not a damn thing in here that can help me. I hear the lock turning again, and I look up to see Caleb walk through.

He's carrying a plate with a sandwich on it. "Okay, last chance, Ria. You sure you're not gonna eat?"

I glare at him. "No, thank you."

He shrugs and moves to the side. I spot movement over his shoulder. Glancing around him, I find Jude standing in the doorway, bracing his hands on either side of the wooden frame above his head. His hands are gripping the frame so tightly that his biceps strain from the effort. The position makes his t-shirt lift slightly, revealing a strip of tanned skin above the waist of his jeans. I can see the deep-cut V-lines dipping into his jeans.

I tear my gaze away from his body and up to his face, which is set in a mask of cold indifference as he watches me watching him.

"I think you meant to say that you were *gonna* eat," he says, his voice low and deep, rumbling over my senses and making my skin break out in goose bumps. His presence sends a shot of adrenaline through my veins as my instincts tell me to run, but there is nowhere to run.

"I'm not hungry," I say quietly. I feel like there's a bomb in the room and it's about to go off at any minute. That bomb would be Jude. He has that scary calm thing going on, and it's more terrifying than any shouting.

Jude laughs. His arms slip down the doorframe as he bows his head. Shaking it, he glances back up at me, his eyes narrowing as one corner of his full lips quirk up. "Wrong fucking answer!"

Oh, shit. I start backing up before he's even moved from the doorway.

He steps forward, quickly closing the space between us as his eyes lock with mine.

"I didn't ask if you were hungry." He steps closer to me, until I can feel the heat of his body towering over me. "Let me clarify for you. You." Another large step, and I edge backwards. "Are gonna." Then another. "Eat!" He dips his head to meet my eyes. "Aren't you?" I watch as he reaches back to Caleb's plate and picks up the sandwich.

"You can't make me eat." I stare him down, squaring my shoulders in an attempt to make my five-foot-four frame look bigger in the wake of his massive presence.

A slow laugh rumbles from his throat. "I can make you do anything I fucking want."

He keeps walking toward me, and I keep backing up until I'm against a wall. This seems to be a common theme—him stalking me until I'm against a wall.

"Jude," I warn, but it comes out as more of a plea.

"Woman, eat the damn sandwich before I shove it down your fucking throat." He holds it up in front of my face.

He wouldn't. I recoil even more, until I'm flat packed against the wall. "Fuck—"

He cuts me off by cramming the sandwich inside my mouth. Actually forces it in! Motherfucker!

"Fucking chew and swallow," he says.

Could he be a bigger arsehole if he tried?

I chew only because I'm afraid if I don't he'll actually force my mouth open and close himself, but I make sure to scowl at him the entire time.

He turns back to Caleb. "How long has it been since she's eaten?"

Caleb shrugs. "She hasn't eaten anything since she's been with me."

Jude let out a low growl. "I told you to fucking watch her!"

"Which I did...what do you want me to do? I'm not gonna force her to eat." He shrugs and leans against the far wall.

"God, you're a fucking idiot," he grumbles, before turning back to me. He leans closer to me until I can feel the heat of his body, his breath on my cheek. His hand winds around the back of my neck, holding me in place. He's so close, his presence blocking out everything. I automatically surrender under his touch as my breath seizes in my chest.

"Don't make me have to deal with you myself, *Victoria*." The way he says my name makes something inside of me tighten. What the hell is wrong with me? His thumb brushes over my throat. "I'd really hate to mark that pretty skin of yours again." His voice is guttural and harsh, but his touch is gentle. My heart hammers against my ribs like a rabid animal. What the hell is he doing to me? I'm scared of him, but part of me doesn't want him to take his hand off me. His touch is warm and, dare I say, comforting?

Oh, my god. I think I'm having some kind of psychological break! Maybe being locked in this room has made me delusional. I frown and wrench my face away from his touch. He huffs a small laugh, clearly entertained by my warped state of mind.

He turns away from me and walks to the door. He grabs the handle, then turns to his brother and takes his index finger, pressing it to the middle of Caleb's forehead. "Fucking watch her and if you have to tie her the fuck down, chew up the fucking food like a mother bird, and spit it in her fucking mouth, make her eat!"

"You are a fucking psycho!" I snap, narrowing my eyes at him.

His head snaps back around. "You have no idea, little girl."

Pointing at Caleb one last time, he snatches open the door. "Don't fuck around." Then he turns away from me, leaving the room. The door slams shut, making the picture on the wall rattle. I hear the lock click with finality.

I eat half of the stupid sandwich, because the last thing I want is Mr. Personality coming back in here. I sit on the bed with my back to the headboard, and my elbows propped on my knees.

"I did try to warn you," Caleb says, lounging on the bed next to me.

"I know," I say quietly. My hands are shaking, and I can feel my eyes welling with tears. For fuck's sake. The hopelessness of the situation is finally dawning on me. I know too much. Whatever happens, they aren't just going to let me walk out of here knowing all that I know about their criminal enterprise.

"I'm never getting out of here, am I?" I say. "He's going to kill me."

"No, he won't kill you." He shakes his head adamantly.

Several tears slip down my cheek and I lean forward, resting my forehead on my knees in an attempt to hide my face. I don't do crying. Crying solves nothing.

"Ah, shit," he groans, and I feel his arm wind around my shoulders as he pulls me into his side. He doesn't say anything, he just sits with me.

"I thought you were cool," I sniff, trying to change the subject and rein in my pathetic tears. "You sold me out."

He rolls his eyes. "Don't give me that shit. You've gotta eat, you know?"

"So you told Mr. Fucking Understanding?" I pull out of his hold a little.

I like Caleb, and, weirdly, I trust him, but I can't afford to get attached to him. He may be the friendly face of the operation, but he is still keeping me as a hostage.

He shrugs. "If you get sick, it's my ass he'll be kicking."

"Okay. I'm going to make a deal with you," I say.

He narrows his eyes. "Oh, uh-uh. No, no deals."

"But you don't even know what the deal is."

He cocks an eyebrow. "I don't *need* to make a deal with you, you're a hostage. I should be the one offering you options, not the other way around."

"Gee, thanks for pointing that out to me. As if I didn't already know," I grumble.

We sit silently for a few moments, then I hear him sigh, followed shortly by a groan. "What deal?"

"If you need me to do anything, just ask me. I would do anything, *anything*, to avoid having to deal with him."

"He scares you, huh?" His brown eyes study mine.

I nod. "Yeah."

"Okay, but, just so you know, we don't deal with women. We don't take hostages, so none of us really know how to handle this. This is not like him. He's normally more...tolerant with women," he explains. "I'll try and keep him away from you."

I flash him a small smile. "Thanks, Caleb." I don't hold out much hope, though. Jude seems to treat Caleb just barely better than he treats me.

"Pain in my ass," he mumbles, laughing.

"Please, can we leave this room?" I whine.

Four days. We've been in this one room for four days. There's a bathroom with a toilet and a sink, but no shower. Caleb gave me one of his shirts and a pair of basketball shorts yesterday, because he felt sorry for me, but I really don't smell great. Apparently hostages don't get to wash. At least I haven't seen Jude since our little sandwich incident.

Caleb takes a deep breath and throws me an exasperated look.

"Pretty please." I bat my eyelashes at him.

"Stop. You're embarrassing yourself."

"Caleb! I'm going to go bat shit bloody crazy if you don't let me out of these four walls."

"Jesus fucking Christ. You're a pain in my fucking ass, girl." He rubs the back of his neck. I can tell he's contemplating it. His eyes raise from the floor and he narrows them on me. It's obvious he's trying to make himself appear hard and intimidating with that look, and it almost works, but I've spent too much one-on-one time with him to feel threatened by him. "I'll take you out," he says, "but you have to stay close to me. Jude will fucking crucify me if he knows I let you out of here, okay?"

I nod enthusiastically. "Okay."

He casts one last semi-threatening look at me, and then signals for me to follow him out the door. We make our way through the corridor and down the stairs. I have no idea where we're going. I survey everything, trying to commit the layout of the house to memory.

He leads me into the kitchen. "You want anything to *eat*?" I don't miss the way his lips quirk as he says it. Bastard.

"Ha fucking ha."

"Just checking." He smile and grabs a packet of crisps from the cupboard before leading me back out of the kitchen. "Come on."

We walk down a hallway until we come to an entrance hall. An entrance hall with a large stained glass front door, the same door I came in through. He keeps walking, crossing the hall into a lounge. There are several flat screen TVs, all of which are switched off. Caleb picks up the remote and turns on one of the TV's. I see an opportunity, and I take it. I don't think, I just act on instinct. I will not fucking die in this house. I pick up a lamp from one of the side tables and swing it at the back of his head.

Porcelain shards spray across the room, and Caleb grabs at the back of his head.

"Fuck!" he roars.

Before he can recover, I kick him in the nuts. His hands grab between his legs as he coughs and falls to his knees with a thud.

"I'm sorry. I'm so sorry!" I shout as I'm already running out of the room.

I sprint across the entry hall and throw open the front door. I don't stop. I just keep sprinting. I catch sight of two men to the left of the door in my periphery. Fuck it. I'd sooner die trying than just give up. The gravel of the driveway bites into my bare feet, but I don't care. *Just keep running!*

"Don't fucking shoot her!" I hear Caleb's voice somewhere behind me. "Don't shoot her!" He sounds panicked and I don't know if it's because Jude is going to have his arse, or if it's because those two men have rifles aimed at the back of my head, but I don't really care. All I can focus on right at this moment is getting the hell out of here.

I can hear footsteps thundering behind me. I want to scream in frustration as I push myself to run just a little faster. I can hear them getting closer, and closer, until suddenly a weight ploughs into my back, sending me stumbling forward and crashing to the ground. My forehead smacks the sunbaked lawn, making my teeth jar together upon impact. The next thing I know some man is straddling me and pulling my arms behind my back. He holds both my wrists in one hand, and yanks me up by them, straining my shoulders until they feel like they're about to be ripped from their sockets.

"That"—the man is panting from running after me—"was a very stupid thing to do," he growls in my ear. Grabbing my hair, he jerks my head back. "Fucking walk."

He shoves me back toward the house. Caleb is on the porch standing next to another guy who is shaking his head. Caleb's face is white, and he's hunched over. Guilt wracks me instantly.

The guy marches me up the steps, and all the while Caleb glares at me. I mouth "sorry" at him just as I'm dragged into the lounge and forced to sit on the sofa.

"Someone grab me some rope," the guy holding me barks.

A few minutes later, and I'm bound and gagged. Again.

Caleb is pacing in front of me, biting his nails whilst continually shaking his head. Shit. This is so not going to be good.

Chapter 9
Jude

The blood washes from my hands, swirling down the drain. "Dumb fuck," I say as I dry my palms on my shirt. "Should've known better than to bring a fucking person to me as collateral."

I check the mirror to make sure there's no blood on any of my clothes. I don't want to walk into a bar looking like a psychopath. I smooth out the wrinkles in my shirt and leave the bathroom. On my way to the front, I find Richard still lying on the floor, groaning, his face dripping with blood. I stop next to him and nudge him with my boot. "You gonna do something stupid like that again, huh?"

A low moan bubbles from his bleeding lips.

"Answer me!"

"No."

I nod and walk to the door. "You're lucky you're my cousin. That dumb stunt would have cost anyone else their life. When you pull your balls outta your throat go do your fucking job the way you're supposed to for once."

The lull from the bar fades into the background. My head is swimming from what Marney just said.

"What?" I pause, letting his words really set in. "What?"

"I said"—he leans over his beer, his eyes cutting to the side like he's afraid someone will overhear us—"I think you've been set up."

I twist the drink in my hand, wiping the condensation from the smooth side as I stare down into the near-empty glass.

"This industry's not as tight as people like to make it out to be. You can't trust anyone."

I really just want him to shut up. I fucked up. Somehow, I missed something when checking Euan to make sure he was safe to bet with.

"You're sure he's related to him?" I ask.

Marney nods and brings his glass to his thinning lips. He grabs a fistful of cocktail nuts and crams them inside his cheek, crunching them for a few seconds. He taps his finger over the paper he's brought with him and swallows. "Records don't lie."

I glance down at the sheet and read over the names. How the hell did I miss that Euan is Joe Campbell's nephew? Out of all the damned people for me to miss something on, it would be someone related to Joe.

"Ah," Marney says as he swipes the paper from the table, folding it and shoving it in his shirt pocket. "Now, you know how long it took for me to dig this shit up? That family changes names and records like a whore changes men. Anonymity is the best way to stay under the radar. You'd only have found it if you were looking for this relationship, then it still would've taken you a week to figure it out."

I hang my head, scratching my fingers over my scalp as I stare at the worn bar top. The realization that that girl has possibly set me up crawls all over me. She has crossed a line that leaves me no choice but to take her life.

Marney clears his throat, tips his drink back, then slams the glass down on the counter. "Now, whether the girl *knows* anything is another question. Joe's smart. I wouldn't doubt if he talked the stupid-ass prep into making a bad bet with your group and then suggested he offer the girl as ransom, promising to wire him the money." He shoves another handful of nuts into his mouth. "But you can't be too careful. You're being hunted one way or the other."

I'm so disgusted all I can do is nod. I stare over the top of Marney's head, blanking out for a second. "Yeah, I know. I guess I should've just killed Joe instead of trying to make him suffer."

Marney shrugs. "Hell, nothing saying you can't still kill the bastard."

I know I could kill him. I could try, but Joe is sneaky and so it seems he already has one up on me. I know he's beefed up his personal security since the entire thing with his wife, so there's no way I could get close enough to him without a bullet going through my own skull...and he's already got someone *inside* my fucking house.

Marney sighs. "Let me just get a little more information on the prick. See if I can figure out if the girl has a clue or not, all right?"

Before I can say anything else to Marney, my phone buzzes with a text: *She got out. She's one hella feisty little bitch.*

"Aw, fuck!" I groan, rolling my eyes as I slam my fists on the counter.

"What?"

"That damn girl." I shake my head.

"Until we can find out more, *don't* trust her."

I stand, grab my coat from the back of the chair, and walk out of the bar.

The entire way back to my house, I fume over everything. I pull up to the gate and punch in the passcode, looking at the security camera as it scans the grounds.

I park the car and walk up the stairs, wondering what in the hell my brother can be trusted to do, aside from stitch up a stab wound. He's too damn nice sometimes. I want to hate him for it, but that sympathetic side of him came straight from our mother, which makes it hard to hate.

I enter the house and find only one of my uncles in the living room, and right next to him, bound and gagged, is that girl.

"Bob, what the hell?" I ask, tossing my keys on the coffee table.

He shrugs. "Your little brother's a pushover, that's how. He let her out of that fucking room, and first chance she got she clocked him one and ran." He glances down at her, then back at me. "She's got a fucking mouth on her too."

"Yeah, I know."

She's staring at the floor. Her hair is tangled and frazzled with pieces of pine straw matted in it. The clothes she's wearing are covered in dirt and grass, and her face is smeared with mud. She's a fighter, that's for fucking sure.

I walk around the back of the couch and squat in front of her. "How stupid are you? Huh?"

Her chest rises and falls in uneven draws. She's shaking, her eyes wide, and she's struggling around the gag.

"I swear to God, if I find out you're anything besides just a fucking unlucky girl..." I can't even finish my sentence because the prospect makes me so angry.

Her brows pinch together in a frown and she glares at me.

"What the hell is wrong with you? Why can't you just fucking listen and stay put until that stupid boyfriend of yours pays up?"

And then what? Release her so Joe can show up at my house? Fuck, I am beyond screwed here.

I rise, repeatedly combing my hands through my hair. I can't stand to look at her right now. "Where the fuck is Caleb?" I ask Bob.

"Fuck if I know! I've been dealing with her shit for the past half hour."

I storm off, shouting for him as I wander through the hallways.

"Caleb?" Silence. "Caleb!" I deepen my voice as I round the corner to find him sitting at the foot of the stairs.

"You fucking let her escape?" I shout. He's my brother, but his stupidity pisses me off.

He drags a hand through his hair, refusing to look up at me. "I fucked up. I'm sorry."

"Jesus fucking...how the hell am I supposed to trust you if you can't even look after a fucking girl? One girl, no weapons!" I yell, launching a vase from table. The sound of shattering glass gets Caleb's attention.

I grab him by his shirt, forcing him to his feet. I can see the flash of fear in his eyes, because he knows what's coming. "What did I fucking tell you?" I ask.

He keeps his eyes down. "Not to let her out of the room."

"And what did you fucking do?" I twist the material in my hand and pull him to my face.

"I let her out," he says quietly.

It's ingrained in me that when you get pissed, you fight. I pull my elbow back and punch him square in the jaw. His head jerks to the side, and he rears his fist to punch me back, but stops, and his hand falls to his side.

"Fuck, Caleb!" Releasing his shirt, I push him away from me.

He's holding his jaw. I know that hurt. I shouldn't have hit him, but damn. "Sorry. You fucked up." I shrug.

I don't wait for him to respond. I turn and head down the hall. "Like I said, if she has to piss, you tie her ass up. Got it? I've got a meeting. Think you can handle the simple fucking task of watching her for a few hours until I get back?"

I make my way back to the front of the house, angry as hell and late for an appointment.

When I pass Bob and that damn girl, all I can manage is a growl. "Probably best to leave the fucking gag in her mouth," I grumble as I walk out the door.

Chapter 10
Victoria

As soon as Jude slams the door behind him, Bob grabs me by the shoulders and pushes me forward. "Get the fuck back in that room."

Every few steps, he shoves me and I stumble. We come to the door and I see Caleb standing at the end of the hallway. Bob pushes me through the door and I fall against the chest of drawers.

Caleb walks in after me, and I hear the lock click shut. There's an awkward silence between us, and he can barely look at me.

I wish I could tell him I'm sorry, but I have this stupid gag in my mouth. My head hurts from where it hit the ground. My feet are cut and my knees are skinned. Worst of all, though, it was all for nothing. I barely made it fifty yards before they caught me.

Caleb looks up at me and sighs, running his hand over the back of his neck; I've noticed he and his brother both do that when they get angry.

I'm waiting for him to shout at me, but he doesn't. "It's my fault," he mumbles. "I knew not to trust you."

I shake my head, trying to talk around the gag. The look on his face nearly kills me. He looks hurt and angry and confused, because surely he knows he shouldn't feel sorry for me.

Caleb is nothing like his brother. He's kind, too kind for this corrupt shit, and I just kicked him in the nuts for it. Literally.

Taking pity on me, he steps forward. His eyes have gone all puppy dog. He sighs, shaking his head as he unties the makeshift gag.

Guilt is eating me alive.

"I'm so sorry, Caleb!" I blurt the second I can speak.

"I *trusted* you, Ria. I felt bad for you."

Oh my fucking God, could he make me feel any worse right now? His round brown eyes are gutting me.

He frowns, and a look of hurt crosses his features.

"I'm sorry!" I can feel my eyes starting to prickle. Shit, this is ridiculous. I feel guilty for trying to escape. Something is seriously wrong with this picture.

He rubs at his jaw, and I notice it's red and swelling.

"What happened to your face?" I ask quickly.

He sighs. "What do you think? I told you he would kick my ass for letting you out of this room."

"Shit." I lose my grip on whatever emotional stronghold I had in place, and the dam bursts. I start crying—like ugly crying.

"Oh, fuck!" His eyes widen and he's checking me over as though I might be hurt, lifting my chin like he's looking for choke marks or something. "What the hell did Bob do to you?"

"I can't...I just..." I cry through heaving breaths. "I miss my sister, and my job, and my fucking life, Caleb! I don't want to die here!"

His shoulders drop a little, and his eyes soften even more. "Look, I know this is in no way ideal, but I promise, you'll get that all back soon." He paces for a second. "You're not gonna die. I mean, hell, this is *not* normal. Not normal at all. Jude doesn't deal with hostages. So you"—his eyes scan over me and he shakes his head like he's sorry for something—"you are not meant to be here. Trust me."

"You don't see the way he looks at me, Caleb. He's going to fucking kill me!" I sniff through my tears.

His eyes close and he pulls his lip in. "No, he won't. I know you can't see it, but he's not a bad person. We're all fucked up. We grew up in this shit, so..." He pauses and looks at me. "But he won't kill you."

"Jesus Christ, Caleb, wake the fuck up. He is a killer. It's what he does! I'm going to die in this fucking place. My sister will never know what happened to me. I'll never become a doctor..." My voice breaks on a loud sob.

"He's a bookie, not a killer. It's just business." He pats my back, his face the image of uncomfortable. "Don't cry," he says, trying to sound reassuring, but I can hear the slight tremble in his voice. "I...it's...shit. What do you want me to do, Ria?"

"Nothing," I wail. "There's nothing you can do."

Poor guy looks like he'd rather shoot himself than deal with me right now.

"Ria, I promise I won't let anything happen to you, okay?"

I stare into his big brown eyes, and despite my inner turmoil and my fear of Jude, I actually believe that he means that. The problem is that if Jude wants to hurt me, nothing will stop him, and certainly not his baby brother.

Chapter 11
Jude

Forty minutes after leaving my house, I pull into the gravel lot outside of the lodge. As I walk toward the entrance, I watch a few drunk old men stumble out of the doors and head to their cars.

"Ah, hell, Frank," one of the white-haired guys grumbles. "You know damn well this country's gone to the Democrats."

The other man swats his hand through the air, losing his balance and falling against the side of the building.

I push the door open, and a thick haze of smoke slaps me in the face. My eyes dart around the dimly-lit room and hone in on the guy who's slumped over the bar.

I nod to a few of the other men as I make my way across the room. I lightly touch my hand to his shoulder and he groans.

"Hey, Jim. You know today's the last Friday of the month, huh?"

He rolls his head to the side, peeping up at me with only one eye. "Yeah, JP, I know."

He sits up, leaning back in the chair and digging in his back pocket. He pulls out a manila envelope and hands it to me. "I gotta stop making bets with your boss man. He's got a lot of juice for this old square."

I smile as I take the envelope. Most people think I'm a beard—they think I'm the person between them and the bookie. They have no idea I'm the person they really don't want to piss off.

"Ah, come on, now, Jim. You say that every time." I shake his shoulder and open the envelope to peek inside. "It's just for fun anyway, right?"

He snorts and picks up his glass, swirling the beer in the bottom before dumping it into his mouth. "Yeah, damn good time draining my bank account, but one of these days," he says, shaking his finger at me, "I'mma win big. Then I'll stop."

"See you in a few weeks, Jim," I call out as I head toward the door.

I climb in my car and barely get make it back onto the road before my phone rings. I answer it, and all I can hear is maniacal laughter.

"I'm busy. What the hell is going on there now?" I ask, switching lanes.

"Oh," Bob manages through a cough, "you just need to come home. See what your pussy-ass little brother's doing."

"What? Oh, for fuck's sake. Tell me he hasn't gotten his ass handed to him by that little girl again?"

There's hooting and hollering in the background from the rest of the guys. "Go, Brown. Go! Run that damn ball!" A loud eruption of screams ring out. "Looks like you're gonna have a lot of collecting to get at. Florida just lost."

"Good," I groan, more concerned with what the hell that woman has done than the money I'd just made. "Now, what the hell is Caleb doing?"

"You just need to come see this, Jude. Sad to say I don't know that he's cut out for the family business. I think he may be hiding a vagina between his legs."

I hang up and toss the phone in the passenger seat. "Damn it, Caleb!" I pound my fist over the steering wheel and swerve across the traffic to exit.

As soon as I walk in, I find a group of my uncles crammed around the kitchen table, pounding back beers and playing poker.

"Am I gonna have to beat his ass?" I ask.

Bob smiles, shrugging his shoulders. "If you ask me, I think he's probably been traumatized enough by the sound of it."

I shake my head and head down the hallway. Caleb's just a fucking kid. He's twenty-one, and at times I feel remorse that I allowed him to get involved with this shit. Sure, it's our heritage, but at some point someone has to say they're too good for this fucked-up way of living. I tried that. I tried to get out of this, but I am undeniably damaged from growing up in the middle of threats, dirty money, and vengeance. It was my job to carry on my family's legacy, but Caleb, he has no business here. He still has morals, and sometimes I hope that one day I'll be too much and he'll leave, forgetting how fucked up we all are.

I stop outside the door, jamming the key in when I hear sniffling.

As soon as the door swings open, I see him with his head on her shoulder and he's fucking crying. She has her arm around him, soothing him. She looks up when I walk in and shoots daggers at me.

"What the..." I glance at the TV and see the end credits of a movie rolling. "What the fuck? Caleb?"

He looks up, wiping the snot with his sleeve. "Dude, Jude, that's some sad shit. That's true fucking love...and the birds at the end flying off"—he pulls in a breath—"that was like their souls flying away to spend eternity together. Deep-ass, sad shit!"

My eyes bulge and my jaw unhinges. I am literally speechless as my gaze darts back and forth between the TV and the two of them snuggled up on the bed.

"*The Notebook,*" Victoria says. "I'm going to take a stab in the dark here and say you haven't seen it."

"Are you kidding me?" I shake my head and comb my fingers through my hair, trying to understand exactly what the hell has just happened.

This woman has turned my little brother into a dribbling pussy. He's watched people brutally lose their lives, and here he sits, crying over some movie, being consoled by a girl. "Fuck, Caleb!" I stomp toward them and yank him up. "Just....get the fuck outta here." I open the door, intending to shove him out into the hall, but stop.

"You know, you redefine arsehole," she snaps.

Did she really just mouth off to me? When did the weak little girl grow a pair of balls? I have to straighten this out right now. The second she's no longer afraid of me is the second my life becomes absolute hell. "What the fuck is wrong with you?" I spin to face her. "You want to die? You're going the right way about it, doll."

"Yeah, yeah." She twirls her hand in the air. "Again with the death threats." *What the hell has Caleb told her?*

Pointing at Caleb, she wrinkles her brow. "You punched him!"

"He let you out! Of course I punched him." I take Caleb by the shoulders and push him to the door.

"You're a piece of shit!" she shouts, her face turning beet-red.

"Ria..." Caleb starts, but shuts up when I squeeze his shoulders.

"*Ria?* You fucking named her?"

Caleb ignores that question, and she points at him again. "He's your brother! You don't even care about your family."

84

Oh, now she's touched a sore spot. I feel heat flood my skin, causing me to press my fingers into my little brother's shoulders. "I know he's my fucking brother. I also know it's none of your damn business. If you were so concerned about him maybe you shouldn't have kicked him in his balls."

She looks at Caleb and her eyes go all soft and mushy-looking. Oh, fuck, it seems the bitch has it bad for my little brother. I never should have left him in charge of her.

"I had to! I'm sorry, Caleb." She redirects her attention to me. "I have been *kidnapped*, of course I'm going to try to escape. What do you expect me to do, just wait for you to kill me? I do have a basic will to live, you know? You, on the other hand, are just plain mean. You don't deserve a brother like him."

I grit my teeth, open the door, and shove Caleb outside. Slamming the door shut, I turn back to her. "You don't know anything about us, so I suggest you shut your mouth if you really do have a basic will to live."

"I know that he's nice, and you're not," she says, crossing her arms over her chest

"Nice?" I laugh. "What do you think this is? A fucking summer camp? He's watching you. He's not your new friend. What next? You going to start braiding each other's fucking hair?"

She scowls at me, and I inch my way closer to her, forcing her to back up. I keep going until she's against the wall.

"Evidently, somehow you have my brother wrapped around your little finger, blubbering over some chick-flick crap, and he's apparently too *nice* to stop you from escaping. So, from now on, you'll be in *my* room, or *with* me, twenty-four hours a day, until the debt is settled or I find a better place to put you. Do you hear me?"

Her eyes lock with mine, her teeth gritting as she rises to the challenge. "Oh, I hear you," she growls. "I heard the thirteen fucking death threats. I also heard that I was supposed to be out of this shit-hole after three days. You want to kill me, then fucking get on with it already. You want to spend every minute of the day with me?" She smiles. "I'm going to make your life hell."

She's pissed as hell. She's lost her fucking mind, or is on her fucking period, because she's turned into one massive bitch. I clench my jaw, grip her arm, and yank her away from the wall, bringing her face so close to mine, our noses are actually touching. She's pulling in hard breaths, and each time she does I'm hyper-aware of those breasts of hers pressing against my chest. "You won't even so much as take a piss without me watching you. How about that?"

"I tell you what, why don't you set yourself on fire, and maybe, just maybe, you'll get to see me piss!"

I bow my head, sucking in a quick breath to try to hide the slight grin threatening to curve over my mouth. I should be livid as hell that she's being so mouthy with me, but that smart-ass mouth is hot, and that British accent could give fucking Viagra a run for its money.

"I don't even want to breathe the same air as you," she shouts. "So you might as well just shoot me now."

"Oh, trust me, I'd love to fucking put myself out of this misery, but I'm not feeling up to scrubbing blood out of the carpet today." I jerk her closer to me, bringing her forehead level with my chin. I curl my lip at the sudden whiff I just got of her. She smells like absolute shit. "Fucking hell," I cough from the stench. "No wonder Caleb wanted to get you out of this room, you smell like open ass!" I pull her behind me and reach for the door.

"That's what happens when you lock a girl in a room for four fucking days!" she says, and rips her arm out of my grasp.

At this point, treating her like a child may be my best bet. I open the door, snatch her by her wrists, and drag her into the hallway. She obviously no longer has a filter, no self-control, and absolutely no survival instincts. Maybe she's just lost her shit.

"Let go of me." She squirms. "You pikey criminal."

"Not a chance, doll." Laughing, I add, "And really, a criminal? That's a bit extreme, don't you think?" I can't help but smirk.

"You tried to fucking kill me a few days ago! If that doesn't make you a criminal then what does?" She pulls in a breath and I keep dragging her behind me as she continues to ramble about how cruel I am.

I turn at the end of the corridor and head for the bathroom.

"And you are absolutely, definitely, a massive"—she struggles against me—"fucking arsehole."

"You done?"

Her response; showing me her middle finger.

"Oh, really?" I bend, scooping her up and throwing her over my shoulder. My hand instinctually rests over her firm ass. I could move it, but seeing as how I'm such an asshole, I don't.

She screams, pounding her fists against my back. "What the fuck?" She shrieks again, and I clench my fingers into her ass, causing her to tense. "You!" I feel her fingers clawing at the hem of my shirt, pulling it up. Next thing I know, my fucking testicles are being smashed in two by my boxers. The bitch actually just gave me a fucking wedgie!

"You're a fucking bitch," I growl. She pulls harder, and I have to swallow because that shit hurts.

"Put me down!" she screams, the high-pitched squeal behind it piercing my ears.

"Oh, I'll put you the fuck down when I'm good and ready." I adjust her on my shoulder, clamping my arm around her thighs harder while I shove the shower door open. "From now on you're with me, or locked in my fucking room, which means we'll be spending some quality time together. Problem is, you smell like a fucking homeless person."

I reach over and twist the knob, then I throw her down onto the shower floor. "How about now? Is this a good time to put you down, huh?" I watch the cold water pelt down over her, fighting a smile. She looks so damn pathetic.

"Oh, you fucker!" she screams, every muscle in her body clenching as the cold water hits her.

I smirk, bracing my arms against the shower door to block her exit. She jumps up and pounds against my chest. Droplets of water splash in my face with each smack she makes over my chest. It's ridiculous that she thinks those weak pushes of hers will do anything to get me away from her.

My eyes skim down her body. Caleb's oversized white shirt is soaked, which makes it very see-through and damn near impossible to ignore those pert little nipples of hers straining against the thin material. Fuck me, she has a good body, it's hard not to notice. I swallow, and, against my will, my cock swells and presses against the zipper of my jeans. *Fucking great!*

She catches me off-guard and punches me in the stomach. "Ow, motherfucker!" she says as she shakes her fist.

I laugh as she hops around, holding her injured hand. "You done?"

I grab my crotch, nonchalantly adjusting my hard-on, which she takes note of; she swallows just before her face morphs into a scowl. She probably thinks she's about to get raped. I twist the knob to the hot water, my gaze straying back down to her perky tits before locking on her face. "You can make everything a fight, but please understand that you'll fucking lose." She is going to love this next order. "Now, take your fucking clothes off!"

Her nostrils flare and her eyes flame. "Go fuck yourself, you perverted cunt," she hisses, her expression hard, her face still red.

I laugh. "Cunt?" I ask, shocked at what a filthy little mouth she has on her. I give a half-ass shrug and cock a smile. "Have it your way." Grabbing the collar of her shirt with both hands, I shred it right down the middle, exposing her full breasts.

"What the hell is wrong with you?" she yells, and scrambles to cover herself with the torn pieces of the shirt.

"I'm done fucking around with you, so take off your clothes and clean your ass up!" I say as I raise a brow at her.

She glares at me, angry, hateful.

"Do it. Now!"

"I'll take a shower...if you get out." She's glaring at me through the wet strands of hair covering her face.

I shake my head and grin. "I don't think so. I step outta here and who knows what sort of trouble you'll get into." I lean against the shower wall, purposefully letting my eyes roam over her. I need her to feel uncomfortable and vulnerable. I have to break her down.

"There are no windows in here. I can't go anywhere except the door, which you can stand on the other side of."

Steam from the shower billows up toward the ceiling. She's trying her best to cover herself, but all she's managing to do is squeeze those fucking breasts of hers together and up, almost like a corset. I watch the water trickle between her cleavage, then down the rest of her body. The heat is flushing the exposed, pale skin of her stomach. Her matted, honey-blonde hair is sticking to her neck and shoulders. She looks fucking sexy as hell like that. I shouldn't be getting so turned on by this, but damn, my cock doesn't have morals.

"Just do as you're told for once, woman, damn!" I'm done. I can't help but think about how good it would feel to pin her up against the wall and fuck the shit out of her. This needs to stop. I need to get the hell out of here.

I shake my head, closing my eyes for a second. "Just take off your damn clothes and take the shower." I grab her tattered shirt and shred it even more, then yank it down her shoulders. The soaked material drops to the shower floor, and I grab the waist of the shorts she's wearing. She hits me and screams, but that doesn't faze me. "It's not like I've never seen a fucking woman naked, and it's not like I'm doing this to get off. I can't trust you," I say. She beats at me with her fists and causes me to lose my balance. Out of instinct, I grab onto her, my hands slipping over her wet, tight thighs. She falls silent, completely freezing in place. Quickly, she shoves the shorts the rest of the way down her legs.

Her arms tighten around her and she hunches over a little. She tries to hide her face from me, but I can still see it crumple before she peers up at me briefly. The moment her eyes meet mine, they squeeze closed.

I do feel a little guilty for doing this to her, but she really needs to learn not to test me. I reach into the shower and wrap my hand around the back of her slick neck. She flinches. Placing my lips on her ear, I growl, "Don't make me fucking repeat myself."

I feel her cower under my touch. "Please," she pleads, her voice breaking.

I skim my fingers over her skin before I let my hand fall from her neck, and there's a deafening silence.

The splatter of the water against the tiles and the frantic sound of her quickening breaths seem so loud in this moment. I stare at her. Her eyes are still closed, her hands trying desperately to cover herself. I can tell she's fighting back the urge to cry. I watch the droplets of water bead and roll down her cheek, down her neck. Her pulse is visibly thumping in her throat.

Could this woman possibly be trying to fuck me over? She's gone from terrified to outright crazy, and now she's hiding in a corner afraid again. She has no idea what she's doing.

What the hell am I doing?

I stumble back a few steps and watch her tiny form crammed in the corner, trying to hide from the crazed lunatic that put her there. I need to leave her alone so I can go punch my fist through a wall.

"Just take the fucking shower. I'll be over there." I point to the long granite countertop. "I won't look at you, but I'm not leaving you alone."

Her eyes remain trained on the shower floor as I back away, carefully shutting the glass door behind me.

I take a towel from the closet and drop it onto the mat, then lean against the sink like I promised. She's right, I could just wait outside, but I know now not to underestimate her. It's her dignity or mine.

Why in the hell does shit like this have to happen? I catch a glimpse of the shower in the mirror. I can't see her through the fogged-up glass, but I can make out the outline of her body and I force myself to look away. Two minutes ago she was looking at me like a fucking rapist, and now here I am getting aroused from a fucking silhouette of her. Primal instinct is a bitch.

A few minutes later the shower turns off and the door slides open. I keep my gaze aimed at my boots, using every ounce of willpower I possess not to glance up at her.

"Did you see the towel?" I ask.

"Yes."

When I do look up, she's wrapped in the oversized towel, her wet hair falling down her back and dripping onto the floor.

The second I walk past her, she jumps away from me. I grab another towel from the closet, and circle my finger in the air. "Turn around."

She does as ordered, her body remaining tense as she nervously glances at me over her shoulder. I gather her thick hair and place it in the towel, rubbing it to dry the excess water from it. I skim down her exposed back, stopping on the rounded curve of her ass.

"What are you doing?" she whispers.

I swallow hard. *What the hell* am *I doing?* "You're dripping all over my floor," I tell her as I twist the towel around the ends of her damp hair and toss it over her shoulder. "Take it. I don't want puddles all over the fucking place." I try to sound as annoyed as possible.

She's quiet as I lead her down the hall to my room. I stand in the doorway and point to the dresser. "Find something to put on."

I start to leave, but catch myself. *This girl's going to tear my fucking room apart looking for something to kill me with, probably.* Chuckling at the thought, I go to my closet and grab the gun stashed on the top shelf, tucking it under my arm. I move on to the nightstand and collect my pistol, then grab the gun hidden beneath the mattress. I eye her as I head to the door, smirking. "Before you get any bright ideas and accidentally shoot yourself," I say as I shut the door, locking it with the key.

"Arsehole!" I barely hear her shout as I make my way down the stairs.

Chapter 12
Victoria

He slams the door in my face, a smug smirk on his lips.

"Arsehole!" I shout after him.

I pace across the room. The last place on earth I want to be right now is in Jude's room. I swear to God, that guy is bipolar. One minute he's screaming at me and degrading me, the next he's drying my hair. I get whiplash just from being around him. Quite frankly, I'd rather he just remained an arsehole. I can take his temper more easily than I can take his kindness, not that I have to deal with it very often.

I scour his room, curious more than anything. I go to the dresser and pull open one of the drawers, half expecting to find an arsenal of weapons, but oh, no, he gutted the place because I can't be trusted not to shoot myself. Prick. I take a t-shirt out of the drawer and pull it over my head, dropping the towel. The material smells of him, without the added cigarette smoke. Clean and crisp without the taint of corruption that he carries like a bad smell. I can't find any shorts, so I settle for boxers, which weirds me out, because the only time I've ever worn a guy's boxers is after I've had sex with him.

I survey the room, looking for clues about the man who lives here. There are very few. A picture of two women sits on the bedside table, but other than that it's bare, impersonal, almost unlived in.

I move to the window, pulling back the curtain to allow some light into the dingy man cave, only to find bars across the glass. Are you fucking kidding me? Fucking bars! This place is literally a jail. I suddenly feel claustrophobic, trapped and enclosed. I'm stuck in this room, his room. What happens when he comes back? I've been in a room with this guy all of three times. The first time he strangled me, the second he force fed me, and the third he stripped me naked like the fucking pervert he is. I thought he was going to start having a wank right there in front of me. The man is an animal, a filthy, disgusting animal. Oh, God, where am I going to sleep? I'm not sharing that bed with him. What if he tries to touch me? I saw the look on his face earlier, he's going to try and touch me. My chest feels tight at the prospect. If he wants me, he can have me, and there's not a damn thing I can do about it. He's three times my bloody size, and I'm defenceless.

My eyes skitter across the room, searching for something, anything. There must be something in here. The guy has more weapons than a military regiment. I start frantically opening drawers. There must be a gun in here, a knife, something. I glance at the bathroom doorway, spotting the mirror hanging on the wall. Could I smash it? Use a shard of glass? No, too obvious. I don't want to attack him unless I have to. Weapon or not, the likelihood is that I will lose.

I storm into the bathroom and search the cabinets, until—bingo!—my eyes land on a disposable razor. I smile as I snatch it from the shelf, running my finger over it. It's not sharp, but it will do. I use the edge of the vanity to snap the plastic edge off, exposing the blade. It's not much, but if he tries to attack me, it may well make a difference. At this stage, I'll take all the help I can get.

Chapter 13
Jude

An hour after I've left her in my room, I sit in my office with Marney.

He puffs on his cigarette, then twists it between his fingers. He says something to me, but I'm too lost in my own thoughts to process it, and I guess he can tell. Marney leans over my desk, his eyes set on mine with concern. "I know you don't want to believe it, Jude, 'cause I know you don't want to kill another woman—"

"I didn't kill the first one, you did."

He rolls his eyes. "All right, but things aren't looking good for her. You need to figure out what the hell you're gonna do, son."

I clasp my hands behind my head and bend over my lap.

Marney huffs. I hear his chair creak, then I feel his hand rest on my shoulder. "I know, Jude. I know. It's not a situation you wanna be in, but you are. If she were a man, you'd kill her. You wouldn't question it, hell, you wouldn't care if you were wrong or not, you'd just kill the bastard. A life is a life, regardless what's between the person's legs." He pats me a few times and starts coughing.

I exhale and look up at him.

"David had the kid's line tapped, and he's been asking Joe when he can give you the money, Joe said he wants to give her a little more time to burn your face into her memory. Wise to it or not, that girl's gonna cause your death." He shakes his head; frail grey wisps of hair catch in the air and he quickly smooths them back out. "You gotta get her outta here. And I'm sorry to say, if you let her outta here alive, well..." He walks to the door, stopping to shoot me one last pitiful glare. "I guess if she walks outta here alive, Joe'll have you killed in a matter of hours."

The door shuts behind him and I'm left alone. This is the first time in a long time I've felt like I'm going to completely lose it. I think this may be panic. My pulse is going ninety to nothing; my thoughts are all jumbled, I can't even make sense of them; my entire body is coated in a thick sheen of sweat; and all I want to do is break something.

So what if Euan is Joe's nephew? And Marney had the dipshit's line tapped and Joe mentioned Victoria to him. That doesn't mean she knows why she's here...does it? The fact that I don't want her to be involved is concerning, to say the least, but what I really can't handle is the fact that I've been set up. That is crystal-fucking-clear. I am no longer in control of this situation, and I do not like that.

I leap from my chair and pace, dragging my hands through my hair. All I can think about is how fucked up this all is. I've been set up by the man who killed my mother and sister. I've never been outsmarted, and that's what Joe's just done. That man ruined my life once, and he's trying to do it again.

This stops right here. I need to know whether she's involved with Joe. I know that as soon as I mention this shit to the other guys, all hell will break loose. I have to be certain she is working for Joe. Without a shadow of a doubt certain. That's not going to be easy.

I stare through the thick nicotine haze. Each of my uncles' eyes are wide and set on me because of what I just disclosed to them.

Bob runs his hands down his face, his fingers scraping over his short stubble. "Set up?" He shoots out of the recliner and paces the living room. "By a fucking woman?" he yells.

Shaking my head, I clarify. "No, by Joe."

"Yeah, and a fucking woman!" He points toward the hall.

Caleb clears his throat. "You think she knows, Jude?"

Inhaling, I glare at him. What a stupid fucking question. "How the fuck would I know that, huh? I have no idea." Now *I'm* pacing, and the more I think about it, the hotter I get.

Bob blocks my path, his jaw ticking. "Every damn person knows you got a soft spot for a female." He pokes me in the chest. "You fucked up letting that be known. What better way for Joe to do you in than by a damn woman?"

I draw my arm back to punch him, but instead I turn and slam it into the brick fireplace, my knuckles splitting open against the rough stones. "Touch me again, and I'll break your fucking arm, old man."

Bob pulls his gun and heads out of the living room, mumbling to himself.

"Hey!" I shout. "Hey!" I run after him, grabbing his shoulders and jerking him back. "What the hell do you think you are doing?"

"I'm gonna fucking kill her since you're too weak to do it. Joe Campbell's not fucking with anyone else in this family...my sister and niece were enough!"

I snatch the weapon from his hand. The metal slips in my damp palm as I place the tip against his temple. "I'll handle the girl, got that?" I shout. Bob's eyes narrow in a menacing stare. I cock the gun and press the barrel harder against his skull. "Question me, and I will fucking end you. Right now, she belongs to me. You fuck with something of mine, I will blow your fucking brains all over that damn wall. Don't doubt that!"

I notice him swallow before he straightens up. "Let's be *sure* she's involved; in the meantime Joe will have us all slaughtered in our sleep!"

"Are you fucking stupid?" My finger twitches over the trigger, and I lean in to him.

"Jude!" Caleb sounds terrified. "We're just alarmed. Don't fucking shoot him."

I glare at Bob, my nostrils flaring. "Disrespect me again and see what the fuck happens." I release him, pushing him back against the wall, and he stumbles. His gaze holds mine silently for a few moments. I can tell he wants to say something, but he knows better.

"Don't fuck with me! I don't have a problem washing your blood off my hands, family or not!" I shout as I make my way down the hallway. My integrity is at stake, my livelihood, my life.

The hinges to the bedroom door creak as I push it open. She's sitting on the bed, wearing one of my shirts and a pair of boxers. My eyes instinctually travel over her lean, exposed legs, and I have to swallow hard. Fuck, she looks hot. I tear my eyes from her body and try to focus on her face. Those deep blue eyes of hers are so damn innocent, and her plump, pouty lips are the kind any man would love to see wrapped around his cock. Instinct takes over and for a split second all I can do is imagine her on her knees, those fucking eyes looking up at me. Damn. I squeeze my eyes shut and try to think of anything but fucking her mouth.

I redirect my attention to the task at hand. I start to call her name, but refuse. I'm not using her name because that will make her real. That will make me see her as a person, and I can't do that because there's a good chance I'm going to have to kill her, whether I like it or not. The business comes first. Family comes first. I need to figure out what she knows. I take a step in her direction, and she scoots back on the bed. Fear will not work in this situation, so what the fuck do I do? She needs to think she can trust me. If she does work for Joe, I need her to feel like she's in danger with him, like I will protect her. I need her to see him as the bad guy. I nod and clear my throat, not moving from the doorway. *How the hell do I do this?* "Hey…"

Her eyes lift to mine, a small frown line appearing between her brows. "Hi," she replies, an edge of apprehension in her voice as she quickly lowers her gaze back to her lap.

"Look"—I skim my hand over the back of my neck and inhale to make my tone soften—"maybe the shower thing was a bit much…"

Silence. I watch her pick at her cuticles, refusing to look up at me. "I've come to expect the worst from you, Jude. Don't worry about it," she mumbles.

I cringe at the use of my name. I don't like when she says it. At all.

"Don't fight me, then. I don't like this situation any more than you do."

Raising her head, she locks her eyes on mine. "The moment I stop fighting is the moment I become a victim and you stop being the enemy."

I shake my head. She's delusional. She already is a victim, for fuck's sake, I think she just refuses to believe that.

"Okay, well, I don't want to make you a victim." I take several steps toward the bed and stop at the foot.

"That's *exactly* what you want," she says. "I've known men like you. You thrive on power."

"Look, you don't know me, so stop psychoanalyzing what you've seen. You want me to let you out of here? You need to tell me why your boyfriend gave you up as collateral."

Her chest puffs and she shoots me a condescending look. "Because he's a fucking arsehole, obviously." And now she goes back to furiously picking at her nails.

"Yeah..." I trail off. I can't help but think that she looks so damn young. She's too fucking young to be thrown to a pack of wolves like this. She's like Daniel in the proverbial lion's den, except no angel would set foot in this house to save her.

I tap my fingers over the comforter. "All I know about you is that your name is Victoria."

"Ria," she corrects me.

I laugh. "I'm not calling you Ria. That sounds like a fucking name you'd give a bird. I think I'll just call you Tor."

"That sounds like a bloody stripper. Just don't call me anything." She narrows her eyes suspiciously, changing the subject. "We both know that you're not going to let me go, not unless Euan pays, and that hasn't materialized." She lifts a brow at me, daring me to say otherwise.

Slowly, I sit on the bed, keeping my distance from her, but even at that she presses her body harder against the headboard to keep as much space between us as possible. "I would like to, but I have to make sure I can trust you first."

Fuck, I'm not going to let her go. I'm telling her I need to trust her, and I know damned well she's not going anywhere.

"Of course, you, the criminal, need to be able to trust me, the normal, law-abiding girl you kidnapped. Makes perfect sense."

That comment of hers sends my blood pressure through the fucking roof. "I did *not* kidnap you!" I shout, my voice booming around the room. Her eyes widen at the sudden change in my tone. "I'm not into human trafficking, or taking people as ransom. Fucking stop accusing *me*. Your dumbass boyfriend gave you as collateral and my stupid lackey took you. I had no idea. You showing up here was just as much a surprise to me as it was to you."

She gets up and moves to the other side of the room, crossing her arms over her chest and staring at me. "You may not have been the one to take me, but I don't recall you apologizing and sending me on my merry way, do you?"

"At the moment, I have no other choice," I say, letting it be known I'm aggravated.

Her stare sets on mine, almost pleading with me. "There is always a choice." The softness in her eyes turns hard and her brow furrows the longer she glares at me. "Only a weak man refuses to see otherwise."

She is brave to call *me* weak. I wet my lips with the edge of my tongue, and can feel my eyes harden. "Only a weak man shoves an innocent woman to a fucking criminal to save his own ass." I cock a brow at her. "*Don't* insult me. Not a wise decision on your part, trust me," I warn.

"You're preaching to the choir when it comes to Euan and his lack of testicles. And I know well just how much not to test you," she mumbles, rubbing at her throat.

I try to shove away the memory of having my hands wrapped around her throat, and I settle back against the headboard. "How about you tell me about yourself so I'll *think* about letting you go, or you could keep on running your damn mouth and rot in here. I'm just trying to talk to you here."

She sighs and eyes me. Cautiously, she approaches the bed, her finger trailing over the foot. She perches on the edge of the bed. Her body is still tense, but at least she's not pressed up against the furthest fucking wall from me.

"Fine, what do you want to know?"

"What do you do for a living?"

Her brows pull together in a frown. "I'm a doctor. I'm...well, I *was* doing my last year of residency." Her head bows, and there she goes fidgeting with her hands again.

"A doctor, huh? You one of those wanna-save-the-world girls?" I ask, partly out of genuine interest. I don't need to fucking know her, but again, I'm curious, and that's not fucking good.

107

She shrugs. "I don't know. I guess I always wanted to be a doctor. What greater calling can there be than saving lives?"

Typical answer. That's well-rehearsed. One side of my mouth curls up and I narrow my eyes on her. "Really? That's a pretty standard answer on an application to medical school. What really made you want to be a doctor? Do you actually give a shit, or is it just the money?"

Her nostrils flare at my question. That's evidently a sore subject for her.

"Oh, I'm sorry, Mr. Fucking Therapist. Everyone needs a job. I worked hard and studied seven bloody years to be a doctor, and yes, I want to earn a fuck-load of money! Problem?"

I press my index finger against my bottom lip, trying to cover a smirk. "No, not a problem." I lean toward her, one side of my mouth lifting into a partial grin. "Earning fuck-loads of money is exactly why I do what I do."

"Except I choose to earn it by saving lives, whereas you choose to obtain it by threatening them," she says, her face utterly expressionless.

I shrug. "To each their own. Don't judge, doll." She glares at me, but the effect is completely lost. She manages to make a scowl look fucking angelic. If she's working for Joe then I give it to him, she's the perfect Trojan horse—she's attractive, intelligent, and that smart-ass mouth of hers makes me really want to fuck her.

"How do you and Euan know each other?" she asks, changing the subject. "I mean, obviously he placed a bet with you, but you must know him."

"Honey, I have never met your fucking boyfriend. I don't meet people who deal with me." I watch her carefully, looking for any subtle changes in her demeanor. The slight dilation of her pupil, a hitch in her breathing. "You are one of the few people who have seen my face and can tie me to any of the guys that do my dirty work for me." I narrow my gaze. "Which I'm sure you can see poses a bit of a concern?"

For a second, my pulse quickens, because maybe I shouldn't have admitted that to her; but then again, she's not going anywhere any time soon. If she's a threat...well, I'll deal with that when I've figured it out. For now, I have to worry about how the hell I am going to figure that out.

She frowns. "But why would you take a twenty-grand bet off a guy you don't even know?"

"That's just the way this industry works. *Most* people aren't dumb enough to fuck around and make bad bets. This isn't the fucking lottery. Gambling the way I do is illegal, and the only way to enforce the rules of an illegal business is through brutality." I force a sick smile to twist its way over my face. "Murder. People tend to take that *very* seriously."

"You say it's business, but why would you run a business like that?" she asks. "Always living on the edge. That must wear you down." She's watching me carefully, her expression curious. If she's with Joe, she already knows all this.

"It's a family thing. My grandfather did it, my father did it, and now it's in my hands."

"Didn't they want something better for you?" There's no implication in her tone, she's just asking.

"I wanted something better." I eye her. I know this next little bit will fucking floor her. "I finished a doctorate in biostatistics...but my father died, and what was I to do? I have to do my father right. Plus, it does make an ungodly amount of money."

I catch a flash of pity in her eyes. "Money isn't everything, Jude," she replies. I'm tempted to order that she stop using my name. It makes me feel...something that I don't like. I wonder what it must be like to possess her kind of innocence. I'm hardened by the violence that surrounds me, and to me, it's not just about the money, but she would never understand that. Power is a fucking bitch, and it is addictive. This job gives me power. That's the one thing she has obviously figured out about me, that I like power.

"How long have you been with your knight in shining armor?" I smirk.

"A year or so."

"Must have an outstanding family."

"His dad is the Chief of Surgery at Vanderbilt. Let's just say that Euan's life has been handed to him on a gilded platter." There's a bitter edge to her tone. "Imagine my surprise when I found out he's gambling daddy's money away."

"You close with them?

She frowns. "Euan's family?"

I nod.

"He would go to his parents every Sunday religiously. Sometimes I would go with him. I guess they're okay. A bit pretentious for my liking."

"Hmm. He from a big family?"

Her brow wrinkles. I'm sure she's wondering why the hell I care about that. "Not really. Why?"

"You ever meet any of his family?" I arch a brow. "An uncle, perhaps?"

"Uh, I met one of his uncles once."

"What was his name?"

She shakes her head as a frown masks her expression.

"What was his name?" I demand.

"Um, Joe. I think. I don't know. I didn't really speak to him. He kind of just ignored me and spoke to Euan the whole time. Apparently they're close." She crosses her arms over her chest. "Why are you asking me this? Is the whole family in on this shit?"

"That's none of your concern," I snap, trying to keep my jaw from twitching. She drops her gaze to her lap again. Damn it. I raise my voice one time, and she withdraws. I need to keep a lid on my temper.

I trail my gaze down to her neck, landing on a necklace with a tiny silver bird attached to it. A fucking hummingbird? I hate those damned birds because they remind me of my mother. At that thought, my eyes automatically drift to the framed picture on the side of my dresser.

"Did your guy give that to you?" I ask, picking up the tiny charm.

She stiffens and her breath hitches as my fingers graze the skin at the base of her throat. "No," she breathes, refusing to look at me. "My sister did."

I drop the charm, and swallow. "You have a sister?" *Fuck! This is making her a person, Jude. Fucking stop talking to her.*

She looks up slowly, her big, round eyes locking with mine for a moment. I can see the indecision cross her expression before she speaks. "Yeah. Lizzy."

"I miss her so much." She's talking to herself, not to me.

"That's mine in that picture over there, with my mother." I point to the frame. My pulse picks up and heat washes over my face. *Why the hell did I just say that?*

She stares at the photograph for a second before moving to the dresser and picking it up.

"They're beautiful. You look so much like your sister, more so than Caleb," she murmurs.

I don't normally talk about them, but the words fall from my lips before I can stop them. "She died fifteen years ago, along with my mom. Caleb was only five at the time." I tighten my fists and inhale as an uncomfortable feeling settles in my chest.

"I'm sorry," she whispers. "My mum died three years ago. I felt like my whole world imploded. I wouldn't wish that on anyone." I don't want to feel anything, but her words have a sincerity about them that make it hard not to feel something. I have to look away because her eyes are fucking bottomless, and I feel stripped bare when she looks at me. It's like she knows the weakness that's festering inside me, only she doesn't see it as weakness because, in her world, it isn't. Having a fucking heart in her world is normal, whereas in mine, it will get you killed.

"Mine were murdered. And this right here"—I wave my hand around the room—"it's all I have left. You asked whether I wanted something better for myself; I do. I want to be the man who fucking makes that guy pay back everything he cost me. Call me a criminal if you want."

For the first time, she doesn't look at me with absolute disgust. She nods. "I can understand that." Her voice is barely a whisper. "If there were someone to blame for my mum's death, I'd want revenge."

I release a tense breath. I can't do this. This is too real. This is not the situation I need to be in. I fucking feel sorry for her. Fuck! This is the last thing I should be doing, talking to her, connecting over our fucking dead mothers.

Her eyes meet mine. She looks hurt, and my natural instinct is to console her. No wonder Caleb gave in to her. There's something about her that makes me instinctively want to protect and shelter her. The longer I study her, the more real she becomes. I know she has a family that's worried about her; she has a life she's worked hard for. She has dreams, and I'm about to crush every fucking one of them. I have no choice. I may make my living from gambling, but when it comes to my own life, I don't take chances. My pulse is throbbing in my neck and my mouth is completely dry. I have to swallow, then force my eyes away from hers. Shit. I just need to get the hell away from her before she makes me pity her even more, or worse, she begins to pity me.

"Okay, well. I'll see what I can do about getting you back to your boyfriend as soon as he fucking pays me my money."

She presses her lips together, shutting down again. Without another word, I stand and cross the room. This shit just got far too real.

I'm standing on the porch, mulling over everything when Marney's truck pulls into the drive. He opens the door and grabs a paper grocery bag from the cab of the truck, whistling as he leisurely makes his way up the stairs. "Smith's money," he says, handing me the bag. It's heavy, about twenty grand. I drop it to the porch and lean over the rail. He glares at me, tilting his head inquisitively. "Little shit hasn't paid, has he?"

"Of course not." I trace my fingernail along a groove in the wooden rail.

"Mmm." He thumbs over his stubble. "It's been four days, Jude. What you waiting on?"

Shaking my head, I groan. "I don't fucking know." I've thought about how to handle this for hours. I know when I send someone to collect from Euan, Joe's guys will most likely be there. And I know that the moment I hand her back to him, I'm fucked. Whether she works for him or not, he *will* get information from her, and she knows far too much already. She knew too much the moment she set foot in my house.

Marney leans over the railing next to me. He squints against the sun and raises his brows. "You can't treat this differently than you would any other situation. I know you don't *like* it, none of us do, but she doesn't belong here and she's gonna fuck everything up as soon as she gets back to Joe." He inhales, then leans in closer to me. "Even if she has no idea why she's here, Joe will do whatever it takes to find out what he wants. To know what your face looks like...he'll gut her."

We stand in silence, staring out into the woods.

"Jude, she's gonna die either way. Think of it that way. If you don't kill her, Joe will. At least you'd be more humane about it, I'm sure."

I swallow because I know he's right, but the thought of killing her sickens me. I feel this irrational need to protect her, for God knows what reason. If Joe's intention is to use her, then kill her, surely I should save her? That would fuck up his plans.

I push off of the railing and pull my phone from my pocket, selecting Euan's number from the directory.

It rings several times, and just when I'm about to hang up, he answers. "Hello?"

"Where's my fucking money?" I growl through my teeth.

"I...I've got about five thousand, but I can't...I haven't been able to get the rest yet, but I will. I can in a few more days, please, just..."

"Not good enough!" I pause, my mind clouded by thoughts of Joe, my mom and sister...Tor. "You had three days, and unfortunately the thing of yours closest to me is that girl you so idiotically sent to me."

"Don't hurt her, please!" he pleads like the pathetic piece of shit he is. For fuck's sake, is he really begging *me* not to hurt the girl he willingly sent to me, knowing damn well what I'm capable of?

"For each day that you don't pay me, I will mutilate a part of that perfect little body of hers. If I don't have everything in full, plus another ten grand, I will kill her in three days. Got it?"

There is no sound aside from his sniffling and stuttering over the word "please."

By now anger has set in. I've been set up, fucked over, and this little shit thinks I'll take pity on him. My jaw is ticking, my breath labored. "And you tell that fucking uncle of yours he made a very bad decision to fuck with me." I hang up the phone, clenching it in my fist.

I can feel my face heating as I turn to Marney. "Look, I know I've been set up. That's not the issue right now. The issue is whether or not she's part of that set-up, because if she isn't, that makes her an innocent victim. I will *not* kill an innocent girl."

"Your job is to protect this"—Marney waves his hand at the house—"not worry yourself about 'innocent victims.' You're not a knight in shining armor. You're a bookie." He huffs out a harsh breath. "You protect number one, no matter what the cost."

At what point does the cost become too high? Where do you draw the line? Even a man with no morals has to have a line he will not cross.

I stare at him; there's not one ounce of remorse on his face. If it were up to him, she would already be dead. This life is all he's ever had, and it's left him soulless and bitter. Is that what I look like to her? Like a heartless, bloodthirsty bastard?

He shakes his head like he can't understand what my hang-up is. "You think she's innocent, but you can't guarantee that. Are you willing to bet your life on it? Caleb's life? Because you need to be that sure. If you can't put your hand on your heart and say that, then you do what needs to be done."

"Fuck!" I slam my hand against the wooden rail. Is she really worth the risk? Why the fuck can't I just do the logical thing here?

There's only one way to be sure someone is telling the truth, but my mind doesn't want to go there. If this were a guy, torturing him for information wouldn't be a problem. Hell, I'd do it myself. So now I'm left with very few options: shoot her, in case she's working for Joe, or do whatever it takes to drag the truth from her in the hopes of proving her innocence. Fuck, she may prefer the option of a bullet.

"I'll make sure," I say without looking at him.

He claps his hand over my shoulder as he moves past me. "I know you'll do what needs to be done." There's doubt in his voice, and he stops on the stairs, glancing up at me. "You killed Joe's fucking wife. It's your life or hers, remember that."

I swallow, unable to even say anything at this point. My pulse thumps hard in my chest, and all I can see are brutal images of Tor beaten and bloodied, crying and begging for me to stop, and my stomach knots.

I watch him climb into his truck and back out of the drive. I pick up the bag. "Fuck!" I shout as I open the door to the house. I walk into the living room and Caleb tosses his head back over the couch to look at me. "What the hell's wrong with you?"

I shoot an angry glare at him and toss the sack on the table. "Oh, I don't know, Caleb. Maybe I'm fucking pissed because I've been set up, and I've got a possible bug locked up in my goddamn bedroom?"

I watch his eyes glaze over, his face growing pale. "She's not a bug..." He swallows.

"You don't know that. We've gotta be sure."

His jaw tightens. "She's just a girl. I swear, she's got nothing to do with Joe. Are you losing your mind? Are you that paranoid?"

"You spent three days locked in a room with her, and you think you know her. You don't know the first fucking thing about her." I groan, frustrated at the situation. "She spins you a few lines, bats her eyelashes, and that's it, you believe every word that comes out of her mouth. It's too much of a coincidence. She's too much of a risk."

Caleb jumps from the couch and stomps toward me. His face blood-fucking-red, his eyes narrowed. He's fucking angry. "You're not gonna kill her!"

I drag a hand through my hair and cock a brow. "I'm running out of choices here, Caleb. If she works for Joe and I let her go, we're fucked. So, I either kill her now just in case, or I prove beyond a shadow of a doubt that she's innocent."

Caleb falls back onto the couch, holding his head in his hands. "What are you gonna do to her?" It's evident by his tone that the thought of harming her makes him sick too.

I inhale. "Whatever it takes to make me believe she's innocent...or not. It's her or us."

"Fuck, Jude." Caleb's head is still bowed. I think he can't stand to look at me right now.

"And you're gonna have to help me."

"No."

"It wasn't a question. You *will* help me. You're the only person here that's not a fucking monster."

His eyes rise to meet mine, and they are angry. "I won't hurt her."

"I know. That's why I need you. It's your job to make sure I don't kill her."

Chapter 14
Victoria

I wake up to the sound of the lock clicking. I open my eyes and watch the door swing back, throwing light across from the room.

Jude's enormous frame is silhouetted in the doorway before the door closes, blocking out the light once more. I hear him kick off his boots and the rustle of clothing as he undresses. Then I feel his weight dip the mattress. I go rigid as I feel the heat of his body near mine. I can smell the scent of whiskey and cigarettes that is all Jude. I shouldn't like it, but, weirdly, I do. He barely seems to notice my presence as he rolls over. His breathing evens out and within a few minutes, he's out cold. I lay there, every muscle in my body tense as I stare at the ceiling.

I move my hand underneath my pillow, my fingers curling around the plastic handle of the razor. I eye the door. I didn't hear him lock it. This should be easy. Just slit his throat and run. Fuck! If only. Can I really kill a guy in cold blood? He'd do the same to me given half the chance, but what if I get caught? What if I don't kill him and just hurt him? My chest starts to tighten, and my pulse hammers in my veins as adrenaline floods my system. If he catches me, he will kill me. Honestly, I would rather die fighting than just take this like some pathetic victim. I need to do this.

I pull the razor from under the pillow and slowly sit up, trying to make as little noise as possible. The bed creaks slightly as I move. I stare at Jude led on his back, one arm thrown over his head. I can just make him out in the darkness. His chest is bare, the broad muscles rising and falling steadily. My eyes trace the lines of ink that wind across his chest and down his arm. He's power personified, and although he terrifies me, I'd be lying if I said that there isn't a part of me that is in awe of that power. He exudes it with every breath, every small action; he lives and breathes it.

I take a deep breath and steel myself, moving onto my knees over him. If I'm going to succeed in doing this, then I'm going to need to use what little body weight I have.

My hand shakes as I move the razor blade toward him. I eye the line of his throat, imagining what it will look like when I slit his jugular. I have the blade millimetres from his skin, when I hesitate. *Fucking do it!* My mind is screaming at me to man the fuck up and save myself. That's all it takes, that second of hesitation. I'm staring at the blade, willing my hand to move, when I feel his fingers slowly wrap around my wrist. I want to cry. I'm not even strong enough to kill the guy who might kill me. I don't even move or try to fight him. He's going to kill me, and it's my own fault because I fucking hesitated to kill a murderer, a criminal, a heartless bastard.

He pulls the razor closer to his throat. "What are you waiting for, Tor? Do it." My eyes meet his, glinting in the dark. "Do it," he repeats more aggressively, pressing the blade into his skin.

"I..." I can't, I can't do it. What is wrong with me?

He suddenly moves, grabbing my hips and flipping me onto my back. His enormous body hovers over mine, pressing me into the mattress. "You want to kill me?" he whispers, his face is so close I can feel his breath on my lips, the scent of whiskey and cigarettes overwhelming me. "Well, here's your chance, *Tor*. Slit my fucking throat." I still have the razor to his throat. I can do this. His eyes lock with mine, holding my stare, daring me. There's a deafening silence as we both wait and see whether I will do this, kill a man.

His hand slowly wraps around my wrist again, and he forces my hand above my head, pinning it to the pillow. His face drops to my neck, and he inhales along my throat.

"You can't do it because you're not like me," he whispers. My body temperature skyrockets as his lips barely skim my neck. "You save lives, I take them." I don't want to be affected by him. I hate him, I want to kill him, but the way his body is pressed against mine, the way he touches me as if he owns me, it has my heart trying to escape my chest, and my lungs struggling for breath. I hate myself more than I thought possible in this moment.

"Are you going to kill me?" I manage to gasp.

He moves his face from my neck as his fingers release my wrist and wind into my hair, pulling it almost to the point of pain. "I haven't decided yet," he murmurs, so close to my lips that I feel his brush against mine. My breathing accelerates, and he huffs a laugh. "Scared?"

"Should I be?" I breathe, my voice shaking. Yes, I should be, and I am, but not as much as I need to be with a murderous psychopath pressed between my thighs and a razor blade inches from my head.

He tightens his fingers in my hair, wrenching my head to the side. His lips move to my ear, making me tremble beneath him. "Definitely," he growls.

Oh, God. I can't breathe, I can't talk. All I can feel is him. I don't want to feel him, and my mind is screaming a thousand questions at me; namely, *what the fuck are you doing?* My body, though, my body is a traitorous slut evidently.

His teeth gently nip at my earlobe, and I lose my shit. I drop the razor blade and my hand flies to his hair, pulling at the short strands. I don't know whether I'm trying to pull him away from me, or bring him closer. He laughs and his hot breath blows across my neck.

"Not so innocent now, are we?" he mumbles as he rolls his hips against me, teasingly.

His hand moves from my hair to my jaw, gripping it roughly. His lips are so close, and every hormone in my body is screaming at him to kiss me. I'm a mess. Just when I think he's going to, when I can feel the brush of his lips over mine, he pulls away and rolls away from me, climbing out of the bed.

I hear the rustle of clothing, before he opens the door. "You fuck with me, I'll fuck with you," he says, and slams the door shut behind him.

Fucking prick. All I can hear is my pulse hammering in my ears as I attempt to come to terms with what just happened. What the hell is wrong with me? If he had kissed me then, I would have let him; hell, I might as well have just stripped fucking naked for him and laid out a welcome mat. I feel like I need to jump in a bucket of bleach just to wash the whoreishness off me. There are times in life when you have to seriously question your own sanity, and this is one of them.

Chapter 15
Jude

I slam the door behind me. My fucking dick is throbbing, my pulse is hard and heavy. That bitch just tried to slit my throat, and it fucking turned me on. The way she felt pinned underneath me, my leg pressed between her warm thighs, my bare chest against her full breasts...*Fuck!* I stop at the top of the stairs and swipe my hands through my hair. I glance back at the door. She was fucking willing, had I tried to fuck her, I am damn sure she would have let me. What kind of fucked up shit is this? *Shit! She's trying to seduce me. Make me want her, feel like I can trust her so she can fuck me over and sell me out to Joe...*

I shake my head, and make my way down the stairs. I can't think about that right now. All I know is that I need to get away from her. I pass through the living room and Caleb is sprawled out on the couch watching TV. "I'm going to check on the titty bar."

He glances back at me, his lips curving into a smile as he grabs the remote and flips the TV off. "I'mma come with you."

The doors to Elysium swing open and the loud bass rumbles through my chest. We weave our way through the crowd toward the bar.

The bartender looks up, shaking his head. "Vincent called in. I'm sick of this shit."

I make my way behind the bar, clasping my hand on his shoulder. "I just own the fucking club. Bitch to Chris about shit like that would you?"

I grab a bottle of Maker's Mark and pour two large glasses. I hand one to Caleb as I round the bar, and make my way past the stage. One of the half-dressed waitresses struts by and I pop her ass. She doesn't miss a step. I tip the glass back, sucking back the chilled liquor as we shove our way through the thick crowd of men gathered around the stage, tossing bills at the dancer. The music fades as we walk down the hallway. I stop in front of the door that says "staff only", taking another large swig before turning the knob. As soon as the door opens, we are greeted with squeals.

"JP!"

"Caleb!"

Crystal glances up from her dressing table, each side of her full lips flipping up into a grin. She tosses her makeup brush down and slowly stands, sashaying over to me. She's wearing black, sheer lingerie and a silk thong. Her perfectly round tits bounce with each heavy step she takes, and it makes my dick throb like a motherfucker. Stopping in front of me, her eyes trail up my body.

"I've missed you" she purrs, her fingers brushing over my crotch. The other girls leave, flashing me seductive smiles on their way out. I arch a brow in amusement.

"Have you?" I ask and take another large gulp of whisky.

"Looks like you missed me too." She bites her lip, her fingers already undoing my fly. She yanks my cock out. Her nails gently trail over the tight skin.

Out of the corner of my eyes, I see Tara approach Caleb and shove him down onto the couch. I tip the glass back again, staring down at Crystal as she drops to her knees. This is why I like her, no fucking around, just straight to business. She slowly drags her tongue over my dick before she shoves it in her warm mouth. I inhale and place one hand on the top of her head, guiding her. Her fingers wrap around me, twisting up as she forces me to the back of her throat. I yank her hair, groaning as I take another swig of whisky. She's working me over, but not damn near hard enough. My hand slides down the back of her head, fisting her hair as I force her down on me as far as she can go. She gags and tries to pull away.

"Fuck that!" I laugh. "You can do better than that, can't you?"

She groans and pulls in a breath as she swallows more of me back. She grabs the waist of my jeans, yanking them down with my boxers while she eye fucks me. She aggressively cups my balls, her eyes slamming shut as she goes down further on me. I feel her tongue press under the tip of my head then circle around it. Her teeth gently scrape over me, she moans and rolls my balls in her palm....and... I can't get off.

I widen my stance and exhale. I'm not even fucking close. She's growing frustrated, working over me harder, deeper, rougher. I feel her finger creep under my balls and slip over my taint, putting pressure on it. I grit my teeth as I pull her hair and lean my head back. Tara moans, and the slapping noise from Caleb fucking her does nothing but distract me. I close my eyes, and, against my will, I imagine that the warm, wet sensation enveloping my cock is Tor's mouth. My hips thrust forward, groaning as my fingers clench in her hair. Her nails dig into my thighs. The more I think about Tor, the more I fuck the shit out of her mouth, every few seconds causing her to gag and attempt to pull away from me, but I won't let her.

"Fucking take it, Crystal." I pull in a breath, picturing those steel-blue eyes of Tor's glaring up at me.

Crystal deep throats me, her finger pressing on me in just the right spot as heat spreads over my body. I hold her in place. I feel my balls tighten, my muscles stiffen, and I pull out of her mouth, furiously beating off on her face.

"Shit! JP!" she yells, her hand wiping over her cheek.

I fall back on the couch, some of the whisky sloshing out of the glass I'm still holding onto. I suck the last bit down. I sit, my pants around my ankles, and think about how fucked up it is that I just had one of my stripper's deep throat my shit while I fantasized about a girl locked up in my room as collateral for a debt.

Women don't do that to me. They don't get to me...but she does. There's no room for sentiment in my world. She's involved with Joe, of course I want her, I'm supposed to want her, which only makes me fucking angry that I do. Joe's a fucker. It's hard to kill something you want, bastard knows that. I can't let him fuck me over. I won't let him fuck me over, and I'll fuck up any intentions he had. I have no choice in the matter. My hands are literally tied behind my back. I'm either going to kill her, or save what's left of her once I'm done with her.

Chapter 16
Victoria

When I wake up the next morning and my vision comes into focus, I find two massive men standing beside the bed, staring at me.

"What the hell?" I croak. "Who are you?"

They say nothing, and without warning, one of the guys grabs my leg, dragging me from the bed. I hit the floor hard, hitting my elbow as I go down.

"What the fuck? Who are you? Where is Jude?" I try to crawl away from him, my heart slamming against my ribs. I never thought that I would wish for Jude, but suddenly I wish he were here. He scares the shit out of me, but I trust him not to deliberately hurt me. These guys, though...these guys look like they would rape and kill me just for shits and giggles.

The two men scoff at each other. "Oh, he had to go take care of some business." One of them grabs my shoulder and yanks me to my feet. "He asked us to *handle* you while he's gone. Get you ready for when he gets back."

He shoves me toward the door. "Now move it."

I stumble, grasping for anything to get me away from these ogres. "I need to wee," I blurt. He scowls at me. "Please."

"Fine. Fucking hurry up."

He stands in the doorway with his back to me. Shit, what am I going to do? This is it, I know it is. I don't know if Jude's in on this or not. I know he's an arsehole, but I've always taken him as the kind of guy that handles his dirty work himself. If he wants me killed, the least that bastard could do is pull the trigger himself.

I wash my hands, keeping my eyes down, not wanting to look at him. I can smell him from here. He smells like cheap whiskey and sweat.

"Time's up. Move your ass." He grabs my arm, dragging me out of the bathroom and across the bedroom. His grip on my arm is so tight my fingers are growing tingly from the restricted blood flow. He doesn't let up as he moves through the house. I can hear the other guy behind me, but he does nothing to help me. We pass what looks like a living room, which has at least four different televisions playing various sports games.

I'm lead to a door. Once it opens, I'm staring down a set of stairs. "Walk," the guy hisses, shoving me forward.

I stumble down the wooden staircase, my pulse becoming more frantic with every step. At the bottom, my bare feet hit what feels like rough, cold concrete.

I hear the click of a light switch, and a fluorescent light flickers to life overhead. I'm standing in a plain room. The floor is concrete with tiled walls. There are various cabinets on the walls, and a gurney in the middle of the room. I guess this is a criminal's version of a medical room.

The brute keeps shoving me across the room and to a door on the far side. He opens it. Another fluorescent light buzzes on. I involuntary push back against him as he pushes me forward. I don't want to go any further into this room. There are guns and knives everywhere. Jesus, this looks like something out of a mafia film.

Wooden racks are stacked with assault rifles. Strings of bullets hang from the walls. There are boxes labelled with explosives. Shit, what are they going to do? Start a fucking war?

"Keep walking," he snaps at me, pushing the back of my head.

I step toward the next door. Everything in me is screaming at me to run, but I can't, or at least I wouldn't get very far.

My hands are shaking, and my heart is banging against my ribs. My chest seizes, and for a moment, I feel as though I can't breathe. The only thought I can muster is the thought of what the hell am I about to walk into? Why am I down here? What are they going to do to me? I just hope they make it quick.

He opens the door, pushing me through it. My entire body freezes. I can't breathe. I can't move. I'm going to die.

It's so cold in here I can see my breath in front of my face. The walls are covered in plastic sheeting, and the room is empty except for a single aluminum chair in the middle and a metal trolley set against the far wall. I can't see what's on it, and I'm pretty sure I don't want to. Right underneath the chair, set into the concrete, is a drain.

This is the point where I freak the fuck out. I turn on my heels and I try to run. I make it to the door before I'm grabbed by the hair.

I fight.

I fight with everything I have left in me. I claw at his face and bite the grimy arms restraining me. I scream, begging for someone to save me, although I know no one will. I bite him again; this time, the cooper taste of blood trickles into my mouth, and the man holding me growls. He swings his arm back, smacking me across the face and sending me sprawling across the floor as blood fills my mouth.

"Fucking bitch," he roars, shaking his bleeding hand.

I don't have the strength to even save myself. I've never felt so helpless in my life. Tears of frustration run down my face as my chest heaves in desolation.

"Get the fuck up, slut!" he shouts at me.

I don't move, and he strikes me again. I feel my lip burst, and pain explodes through my face as blood streams down my chin. My head is spinning from the force of the blow.

"I said, get the fuck up," he says in a threatening voice. I can't get up, my vision is dipping in and out. I think I'm going to pass out. I groan and brace myself on my hands and knees. The next thing I know, I'm hit with ice-cold water. All the air leaves my lungs in a rush. My heart almost leaps from my chest as I scream. Fuck!

"Up. Now!" He tosses a bucket to the side of the room.

I can't move. My limbs won't respond. I start to shiver, and my teeth are chattering.

"What the fuck, Bob!" A glimmer of hope blossoms in my chest at the sound of Caleb's voice. He appears in the doorway, wearing a smart shirt and suit trousers. He steps closer and drops to a crouch in front of me. He grabs my chin and his eyes lower to my swollen and bleeding lip.

"Ria." He draws in a heavy breath. "I'm sorry."

I peer through the wet strands of hair hanging in front of my face. My eyes lock with his, and I can see nothing but regret swimming in them. I trust Caleb, but right now, I'm realising what a mistake it was to ever trust anybody. He helps me up and tells me to sit on the chair. The cold metal bites against the backs of my bare legs. It's so frigid in here I can't stop shaking.

Caleb takes my wrists, pulling them behind my body and fastening them to the back of the chair with rope. His thumb brushes over my wrist gently, and I hear him release a soft sigh. I can't take this. I hang my head, shaking as tears stream down my cheeks. I don't want to die. At this moment all I can hope for is pity.

"Please, help me," I murmur.

"I'm sorry," Caleb whispers, sweeping his hand over my back before he joins the other guy.

"He told you not to fucking touch her," Caleb hisses, his voice deepening. He looks so scrawny standing in front of the brute of a man, but he projects some of his brother's power.

"What the hell does it matter? Not like she's getting outta here," the guy grumbles, still inspecting the bite mark on his arm.

Caleb glances over at me, and with one look at his pity-filled eyes I know I'm not getting out of here. No one can save me now. I will never be a doctor. I will never get married, or have kids. This is my shitty destiny, to die in a freezing cold room, surrounded by people who couldn't care less about me. Surrounded by utter monsters. I drop my chin to my chest. I'm shivering so hard it's causing my muscles to ache.

Long minutes drag by, and no one says a word. They're just standing there, staring at me. They seem to be waiting for something. The longer I wait, the more anxious I grow, and the colder I get. Shivering turns to full body convulsions. My teeth clench so hard, they feel like they might break.

Just when I think I can take no more, I hear footsteps. I glance up just as a figure steps into the doorway. Jude.

His eyes instantly lock with mine. He clenches his jaw, as he drags his gaze over my body. They're stone cold, unfeeling, remorseless. If I thought he would help me, I was wrong. He looks exactly like the cold killer I know he is.

Chapter 17
Jude

She's sitting in the middle of the room on a chair, soaking fucking wet, and her lip is split. There's blood trickling down her chin. Torture a fucking woman? It's sick. But what choice do I have? What fucking choice do I have when everything is at stake?

"What the fuck is this?" I growl at Caleb. "I told you, no one fucking touches her until I get here!" I shout.

"She was like this when I got here. Apparently Bob couldn't control himself for two fucking minutes." He glares at Bob, and my gaze follows.

"The bitch bit me!" Bob sulks, showing me his bloodied hand.

I can't look at her. I clench my fists hard, wondering if I can actually go through with this. I inhale deeply. The longer I stare at Bob, the shallower my breathing grows. From the corner of my eye, I can see her shaking.

Taking several steps into the room, I tighten my fists. "I told you..." I can't even finish my sentence. I slam my fist into

Bob's face and grab him by the shoulders, throwing him to the ground. "Get the fuck up!" I shout, my voice echoing around the concrete room. He clamors to his feet.

"You can't follow directions worth a shit." I take a second to calm my breathing. "You know what's been discussed. You veer from that plan and I will fucking gut you."

I go to look at her, but can only manage for a moment. Her teeth are chattering violently, her skin's pale, almost grey, and her lips are tinged a light blue. She almost looks like a corpse. "Victoria." I say her name in as stern a voice as I can manage, but she doesn't respond. "Victoria!"

I pull the gun from the waist of my jeans and cock the trigger. That sound rebounds off the walls. I swallow because honestly, what I'm about to have to do to her sickens me to no end.

I close my eyes as my hand grips the handle of the gun. "Bitch!" That comment causes her eyes to slowly rise. She blinks; the slow flutter of her lashes tells me she's barely coherent. "I know why you're here, and I have to tell you, it really, *really* pisses me off."

Her brow wrinkles. "Why I'm here?" she says through her chattering teeth. "You took me." Her words are slurred and weak.

"No, you showed up here, remember? I had nothing to do with that." I raise my hand back like I'm going to strike her, the gun clenched tightly in my fist. She flinches, and I lean in closer to her. "This was well-played, I'll admit, but now the game is over. You made a mistake coming here, little girl, and you're about to learn just how much of a mistake that was. Woman or not, you step up like a man, you'll be treated like one."

"What are you talking about?" Her voice wavers, tears trickle down her pallid cheek.

"Who sent you here?"

"Euan," she says, her voice snagging, and her body convulses. I watch her eyes drift in and out of focus.

"If you won't tell me, I can *make* you tell me, I promise you that." I draw my hand back a little more, then snatch her chin; her chilled skin sears through my fingertips. I force her face up to look at me. "I will have no choice but to hurt you if you don't answer me." I swallow hard, then place the barrel of the gun underneath her chin, dragging it across her damp skin, and that action is harder for me to manage than I thought. My hands are shaking. My nerves are on fucking edge. She doesn't say anything, and I squeeze her jaw. "I will break you, and I will end you. You are fucking with the wrong people."

I drop her chin and stand, moving to the side of the room and leaning against the wall. My heart is hammering in my chest, my stomach knotting. Deep down inside, I don't think she has anything to do with this, but to be sure I'll have to break her like I would any other enemy. I will have to utterly destroy her, and if she really is innocent, I don't know that I will ever be able to forgive myself for what's about to happen.

I shrug at my uncle and brother. "She's not gonna cooperate, she doesn't understand what the fuck that word means."

Caleb glances at me. His expression is hard, his nostrils flaring as he glares at me. I shake my head at him and he pulls in a hard breath, silently mouthing the words "fuck you" to me as he walks toward her. Bob grabs her by the hair, jerking her head back while Caleb cuts her hands loose and stands her up.

"Ria, just tell us. You can make it stop if you tell us." Caleb is pleading with her, not demanding; he is begging her to tell us so he can stop.

"I don't know what you're talking about." Her chest swells and the next sound that comes from her is a loud sob. "I don't know. I don't know. Please, Caleb," she begs between sharp breaths. "You're not a monster," she whispers. "You promised."

I watch Caleb flinch as though she just inflicted a physical blow to him. His eyes move to mine. "Jude..."

"Do your fucking job, Caleb," I growl at him. I don't have time for his bleeding heart bullshit.

Caleb takes a deep breath and clenches his jaw as he motions for Bob to move to the side. He takes her by the shoulders, tilting her chin up like he's begging God for forgiveness before he throws her to the ground. Water splashes up from the concrete when her body hits it. He hovers over her, panting. I know he wants to kill me for making him do this, but you can't befriend the enemy, and this is a lesson to him. Bob takes her legs, pinning them down beneath his spread knees.

Caleb glances back at me, once more silently pleading with me to let up, but I nod. "Fucking do it," I growl.

He grabs the collar of the shirt she has on and rips it from her. I expected her to fight, to scream, something...but she's just lying there weeping and shaking uncontrollably. Her muffled cries damn near cripple me.

She's a person...I close my eyes for a second, trying to separate myself from this entire thing, and when I open them, Bob has torn the boxers from her. She's lying naked on a cold concrete floor with icy water puddled underneath her.

"Do you work for Joe, or did you come as a favor to Euan?" Bob asks.

She turns her head away from Bob, and her eyes squeeze shut as she tries to cover her chest with her arms. She's violently shivering from the cold temperature of the room; each ragged breath she manages to let go of comes out as a white cloud.

I just want her to answer him. I want this to be fucking over. I need to push her far enough to be sure, but this already feels too fucking far...and it shouldn't. I've done far worse than this.

Bob crawls off her and crosses the room, lighting a cigarette before he grabs the edge of the metal cart, the rusty wheels squeaking as he pushes it over beside her.

I swallow. My heart's banging around in my chest and up into my throat; sweat collects in the palms of my hands.

There's a loud thud on the thick door behind me, and I flinch as the door crashes against the wall.

"Jude, we got a problem. There's two men sneaking around in the woods in the back of the property."

"What? How did they get past the fucking security?"

"Fuck if I know. But they're armed."

"Fucking Joe!" I look at Victoria. "If I find out you have *anything* to do with this, I can promise you I will show no mercy!"

I motion with a quick jerk of my neck at Caleb. "Come on."

Caleb looks back at her, then up at me with a worried look.

"Come on!" I growl.

I step out, holding the door as I peer back into the room at Bob. "You fucking touch her, and I will strangle you with my bare hands."

Bob nods, standing up and pulling in another drag from his cigarette as he leans against the far wall.

"Do you fucking hear me?" I shake my gun at him. "Don't touch her until I get back!"

"Yeah, yeah. I won't. Cross my heart hope to fucking die."

The door slams shut just as she lets out another loud sob. I weave through the rooms and up the stairs, my gun clutched tightly in my fist as I follow the rest of the guys onto the deck.

"Two guys in the woods over there." Paul points to the back of the lot.

I don't wait. I feel like everything is collapsing around me. I've got her downstairs, these guys on my property. I feel like I'm being come at from all directions. I sprint toward the tree line, Caleb following close behind me. The rest of my guys swarm in, guns drawn. I hear one of the trespassers shout, and then I see them dart through the thin pine trunks.

I get one in my sight and pull the trigger. The loud explosion from the gun rings through my ears, momentarily muffling the noises around me. Seconds later, a shot fires back at me. At that instant, the entire group exchange shots. Bullets ricochet from the trees, bark splintering off and spraying through the air.

I can no longer see the men, and I pick up my pace, my eyes scanning through the thick woods. "Do you see them?" I shout, gun still cocked and ready.

"No," Caleb yells. "I don't see anything. Shit! They must have gotten hit."

I comb through my hair, still searching for signs that they were shot. I take a few more steps in the direction I saw them flee, and I find bright red blood trailing over the dried leaves. "Well, there's blood." I squat, inspecting the leaves. "Not a lot." I scan the woods once more. I see nothing. I hear nothing. I have over fifty acres; these men could be anywhere.

"Find them!" I order, and head back to the house.

Chapter 18
Victoria

I watch Caleb leave the room, and any hope that I might actually survive this leaves with him. The door slams shut, and a deathly silence fills the room. The only sound is the steady trickle of water as it flows down the drain.

I'm freezing, and my body convulses violently. I can't feel my limbs. I can't feel anything except fear and desperation.

Bob goes into a coughing fit in the corner of the room. I refuse to look in his direction. I just lay here, naked, in a puddle of freezing water, and stare at the fluorescent light flickering overhead.

"You're fucking with his head," I can barely hear him mumble that over the rattle of my teeth. "You know he has a soft spot for you, huh?"

Again, I lay silent. His face moves into my line of sight, a sick smile on his lips. He blows a ring of smoke in my face, making me cough weakly. His teeth are nicotine-stained and his gums are tinged grey. Everything about him repulses and sickens me.

He rests the cigarette on his lips again and inhales. "You make him weak." I hear him move across the room, his boots squeaking against the concrete.

A few seconds later, he leans over me, holding out a blade. The light catches it, glinting off the steel surface. My mind is racing, panicking, but my body...my body can't react. A frustrated sob breaks from my chest. It's one thing to go down fighting, but to be unable to fight, this will not only destroy me physically, but also mentally. I only hope that whatever he's going to do, he does it quickly.

He brushes his finger across the sharpened edge of the knife. I close my eyes and when I open them, he's crouched down next to me. He grabs my face. His fingers are rough and reek of cigarettes.

He shoves the sharpened blade in front of my face and whispers, "I'mma do things to you that'll make sure he's not weak for you. Hard to be weak for a bitch that's got her guts hanging out of her."

My breath catches. I shake my head. His eyes are black, his face hard, except for a small flicker of excitement that crosses it when he stares at that damned knife.

"Damn"—Bob takes a drag of his cigarette, gripping it between his lips as he continues—"such a shame to fuck up a body as nice as yours."

He takes the knife, barely touching the tip to the skin between my breasts.

I want to scream, but the cold is overwhelming me. I can feel my breathing getting slower, and my vision starts to blur. If Bob here doesn't kill me, then the cold will.

He takes the cigarette and smashes the hot butt out on my breast. The heat is searing and I make a weak attempt to scoot away, but he grabs hold of me and yanks me back. My bare back slips against the cold, wet concrete.

"Has he fucked you yet?" He rolls his lip underneath his teeth and chuckles. He gropes my breast, pinching my nipple hard between his fingers. "Has he fucked you the way a dirty whore like you deserves to be fucked?"

I shake my head, a pitiful moan slipping from my lips. He presses the blade harder into my skin. "I'll be doing him a favor by killing you. 'Cause I don't think he's got it in him to do it himself."

My chest is heaving. I can't breathe. I feel the sharp edge slicing through my skin and pain erupts across my chest as he drags it down my body, inch by inch, stopping right before he reaches my belly button. I feel warm blood oozing down my sides. I close my eyes, and tears trickle down my temples.

He grabs me by the throat, and leans his body weight into me, his face inches from mine as he growls, "I will cut up every"—he places the blade under my throat—"fucking inch of you, and enjoy each second."

He moves the knife from my neck, and the next thing I know, his fingers brush the inside of my thigh. I feel the slight scratch of the blade as he trails it lightly over my skin. He moves higher, until he's almost at the apex of my thigh. My vision swims, and I fight the urge to pass out. I cannot pass out, I cannot let this happen, I think to myself frantically.

"How 'bout I fuck you with this knife?" He drags the blade over the juncture of my thigh, laughing as I whimper.

I can't stop the sob that slips from my lips. I want to die. *Please kill me. Please kill me.* I silently plead over and over again.

He strokes my face with his fingertip before pressing the tip of the blade into my cheek. I don't even care anymore.

"Kill me." It's all I can say, all I want. I am done. I'm not strong enough for this nightmare. These are the monsters that other monsters fear. They will break me beyond reparation. Black spots dot my vision. I'm so tired. I'm so cold. I just want to sleep.

His smile deepens into a maniacal grin as he places the blade against my throat. "Not yet, sweet thing." His eyes trail over my naked body, and he chuckles. "Not until I get *exactly* what I want."

He palms my breast again. His harsh movements pull at the cut on my chest, and I wince. His hand trails over my stomach. "How about I finger-fuck this pretty pussy of yours." His fingers dip between my legs, brushing against me. I squeeze my legs closed, trying to scoot away from him, but

I'm too weak. Bile rises in my throat, even as my consciousness tries to slip away. Everything in me recoils violently at the thought, battling through my foggy mind and demanding I fight this. This man has stripped me, beat me, cut me, but he will not fucking rape me. I would rather die a thousand times over.

I grab his wrist and use the last of my energy to thrust myself off the floor. The sharp edge of the knife bites into my neck. I instantly feel the hot blood rush down my throat, and I smile, falling back against the concrete. I'm so cold. My body is broken and my soul is shattered. I welcome the blackness as it consumes me.

Chapter 19
Jude

I open the door and hear Bob's gruff voice. "How 'bout I finger-fuck this pretty pussy of yours?"

I feel a growl work its way up my throat as I throw the door to the freezer room open.

Rage consumes me. She is sprawled on the floor, still naked, only now, her bare skin is coated in blood. Bob has a knife to her throat, and his filthy-ass hand is sunk between her thighs.

Red. That's all I fucking see. I'm going to rip his fucking head from his shoulders.

I watch her fingers wrap around Bob's wrist, and in that moment, everything seems to slow down. She violently jerks her shoulders from the floor, forcing the blade of the knife against her throat. Blood spills from the cut. Her eyes flutter closed, and she slumps back against the concrete floor.

"Fuck!" I shout, and grab Bob's shoulder, shoving him away from her. "Get the fuck away from her!"

I look at the gash on her throat. There's so much fucking blood. It's trickling down her neck in a steady stream and pooling beneath her. The adrenaline jolting through me makes my head swim. I press my hand over the wound in an effort to slow the bleeding, and red liquid wells up through my fingertips.

"Tor!" I shout at her, panicking. I take my free hand and pat her face. "Victoria?"

I rip my shirt over my head and place it over the wound. It quickly soaks with blood. I trail my eyes down the long, jagged cut on her stomach. If I thought I could remove my hand without her dying, I would take that knife and slit Bob's throat right now. He's just standing behind me, watching her die, and that pisses me off. He knows this isn't how we planned this. This is not what was supposed to happen.

"Get me some fucking blankets, you worthless shit!" I scream, and he calmly leaves the room.

Slipping my arms underneath her back, I pick her up and cradle her limp body in my arms.

Her lips are deep blue, her skin a listless grey. She's so fucking cold. *Shit.*

Guilt consumes me. *What the fuck have I done?*

I rush into the medical room and lay her on the gurney. I hear footsteps running down the stairs, and Bob hurries in a few seconds later with an armful of blankets, followed by Caleb.

"What the *fuck*"—Caleb's wide eyes dart up to me—"did you do to her?" He's already at the foot of the gurney, tearing open one of the medical kits. "You're a fucking asshole," he growls as he throws my hands away from her neck. The bloody shirt falls from the bed, making a sickening splat when it hits the ground.

"Watch the way you fucking talk to me." I shove my finger in his face. "She's not fucking dead!" I yell. "Fix her!"

He shakes his head as he mumbles something under his breath. "Hold this to her neck," he says, passing me a handful of gauze. "And put the blankets on her!"

I take the gauze, pressing as hard as I can over her throat. *Shit. She looks dead.* I can feel my pulse in the back of my throat, and I realize I'm panting.

"Shit! She has hypothermia!" He's pacing, his tone frantic. His eyes widen and shoot up to mine. "We need to warm her up, *right* now." He gathers her in his arms.

"Warm her up? What are you gonna do, throw her in a fucking tub?"

"No, you fucking idiot! You'll send her into cardiac arrest. She needs more blankets and body heat." He lays her back down, running his hands over his head. "Fuck, Jude! Just fuck!" He punches the wall, then leans over his knees shaking his head. I can tell he isn't exactly sure what to do, which makes me uneasy. He straightens up and inhales. "Okay. We've got to warm her up. And we've got to stitch that cut on her neck."

My gaze darts to the weeping wound on her abdomen. Blood is every-fucking-where. It's never bothered me before, but this...this makes my stomach turn. "The one on her stomach? You need to stitch that!" I shout at him.

"Shut up and just let me think." He grabs his head, pacing again as his eyes shoot back over to her. "That can fucking wait. It's not that bad."

I stare at her, and I swear, she's growing paler by the second. "We need to get her out of this damn basement. It's too cold."

Caleb picks her up, and I immediately snatch her out of his arms, bundling her in the blankets. I nod toward the door. "Come the fuck on. I can't stitch her up."

I'm taking several steps at a time with her clutched to my chest. I kick my bedroom door open. The doorknob crashes through the sheetrock.

"This is a fucking mess!" Caleb flips back the comforter. "A fucking mess, Jude," he shouts.

I lay her on the bed and touch her cheek, hoping some heat has returned to her, but she feels even colder to me. "Why isn't she warming up? Why's she still so fucking cold?" I scream, pointing at her. "She's got blankets. She's colder than she was without them." I can't stand to look at her any longer. I don't want her to fucking die.

"She can't generate her own body heat. Someone else has to do it for her." He's calmed down a little, and is already laying out items from the kit he brought with him. "You're gonna have to do it. I need to sew her up."

"Do what?"

He glares at me as he pulls thread out. "Warm her up...this is a little fucking far...don't you think?" Caleb's threading the needle, but his eyes are locked on me. "Are you gonna give her some body heat or what, Jude? I'm not gonna stitch her up if you're just gonna let her die anyway."

"Shit." I yank the comforter back to crawl in the bed next to her.

"Skin-on-skin," he says. "It needs to be skin-on-skin to work."

"Seriously?"

"I'm not gonna watch her die, Jude! Take your fucking clothes off and warm her up!" he shouts. Caleb's on edge, and I can't really blame him. This is fucked up, even for us.

I strip down to my boxers and pull the comforter over us both. I drag her lifeless body to mine, wrapping my arms around her. I immediately cringe away from the chill of her skin.

Caleb kneels beside the bed. He pulls the gauze from her neck and tosses it to the floor, then shakes his head. "You're gonna have to lay on your back and pull her on top of you. I can't reach her throat this way."

I do as he says and roll over, pulling her body on top of mine. He tucks the sheet up over her shoulders to cover her breasts. "This is all your fault!"

"Shut the fuck up and stitch her."

He sweeps her damp hair to the side, and it falls onto my shoulder. I feel ice-cold water drip down my bicep. "I told you this was bullshit, Jude. I told you she didn't know anything." He jabs the needle through her skin. She doesn't flinch. She doesn't move.

His face grows redder with each passing second. "She's innocent, and you knew that, deep down inside." He works the thin black thread in and out, quickly sewing up the wound. His brow is furrowed in concentration, his disgust with the situation all over his face. "I've spent the last week locked in a room with her, remember? I think I would have had an idea!" he shouts, his voice slightly shaking.

I adjust her on top of me, tightening my hold around her to provide as much warmth as possible. "You can't ever be too sure. You should know that."

"Well, looks like you got what you wanted."

"I didn't want this, Caleb. She's linked to fucking Joe. *Joe!* There was a chance she was in on it. I had to find out."

He pulls on the thread and cuts it. Then he lifts the covers and stitches her stomach. Once he's finished, he pushes himself away from the bed. Leaning down to me, he narrows his eyes. "There was a chance. A very small chance. Hell, you're a fucking genius with numbers, how small was that chance, huh?" He straightens up and wipes his bloody hands down his shirt. "You think everyone is a threat, why not just go on a mass killing spree? She's *just* a girl." He points at her. "A girl who was taken against her will. And I told you that. But guess what, now she's a girl you almost killed because you're paranoid. She's gonna be fucked in the head for the rest of her life because you had to be *sure*!"

"You need to shut your mouth right now," I slowly say, my tone calm and collected and deep.

He turns to make his way across the room, but stops at the foot of the bed. "I know we have fucked-up lives, but everybody needs a limit. *This* should have been yours!" He can't even look at me now. His eyes are locked on her. "You're fucking soulless."

He's right. I close my eyes and exhale. "You may be my brother, Caleb, but tread fucking carefully. It's me that keeps this business and this family alive. Everyone outside of this house *is* a threat."

"Right now"—he points to her—"I trust her more than I trust you. You better hold her until she comes to. I've done all I can fucking do." He opens the door and slams it closed.

I stare at the wall, holding her so damn close to my body that the cold is bleeding into me. "Bring me some clothes to put on her, do you hear me?" I yell, my voice straining from the volume. I want to scream until my throat fucking bleeds.

I roll her onto her side and slide up behind her. I rest my chin on her shoulder and breathe over her neck to try and warm it. She's not near as cold, and her breathing is growing less shallow and erratic. I pull her closer, my palm slipping over the mutilated flesh on her stomach, the thread coarse against my palm. I have to swallow down the acid rising in my throat. Her blood is all over my hand. *Shit.*

I grew up in the middle of violence. This life has been all I've known. I can't count the number of times as a child that I watched my father rough someone up. Violence surrounded me, and the only pure things in my life were my mother and sister. In my family, women were respected, worshipped almost. They were like a forgiving light that shined through the hell that surrounded us, and then that light was smothered by Joe.

This life will damage and ruin anyone I become involved with. It's an evil that seeps its way into things, and this right here just proves that to me. I watched her try to kill herself. Out of all the people I've seen die, I have never seen someone beg for death. They beg for life, they plead, they bargain—but she saw death as a better option. What the fuck have I done to her?

She moves her arm, and a muffled whimper escapes her lips. I know she's in pain. I've never felt remorse like this for hurting someone, and I'm finding the guilt slamming its way over me right now to be fucking unbearable. This right here has fucked me in a way I've never been fucked. She was good and pure. She was everything I'm not. I took that innocence from her. This girl makes me have a fucking soul, and I can't have that.

It's late. And here I sit, slumped against the wall, staring at her asleep in my bed. I feel a need to protect my family, my business, but, for whatever reason, I also feel the need to protect her.

Bob defied me; he went against my orders and he hurt her. What he did to her will be permanently marred across her body, and fuck knows what it's done to her mind. He's made me no better than Joe. Every time her hands brush over that scar, she'll see Bob's face, and she'll hate me for leaving her, for allowing it to happen.

I bite down on my lip as anger slowly swallows me like a black void. She turns in the bed, the pain causing her to cry out in her sleep. That sound flips the switch in me.

I jump up and leave the room, storming through the house. "Bob?" I shout. "Where the fuck is that piece of shit?" With each step I take, I feel my pulse behind my eyes. I can't get the image of him on top of her out of my head, and it's making me enraged. "Bob!" I yell, balling my fists.

I come into the living room, and he's sitting on the sofa.

"What did I tell you I'd do if you disrespected me?" My fingers dig into my fists, and tension courses through my muscles.

His eyes hone in on me as he takes a sip of his beer. "If I didn't know better, I'd think you liked the bitch."

I feel my eye twitch, and I inhale. Gritting my teeth, I slowly cross the room. Without thought, I raise my hand back and slap the beer from his hand. Frothy white foam spews through the air. Bob's eyes fly open and he attempts to stand, but I grab him by the throat, jerking him to his feet.

"You don't deserve to live after what you did." I squeeze my hand around his thick throat. The tendons pop beneath my grip as my fingers dig into his sweaty flesh.

His fingers clench into my arms, clawing at me to let him go. He strains his neck to the side, managing to choke out, "You're no better."

I shake him, my hold tightening. He's thrashing around, trying to fight me. In a moment of strength, he grabs my shoulders and manages to force me back. My legs bang into the coffee table, and we both crash down on top of it. I hear the glass cracking beneath me, and before I can stand, the glass shatters, sending us both crashing to the floor.

I lose my hold on Bob, and he attempts to roll away, crawling on his hands and knees as he pants for breath.

I go at him, grabbing him by his hair. "Family or not, I'll teach you to fuck around with me. Blood holds little meaning when you can't trust a person."

I pull him to his feet and drag him down the hallway to the basement door. He's screaming like a bitch the entire way. "Caleb! Paul! Help!" he shouts. "He's gonna kill me. Help!" He's pleading, groveling; his voice has a prominent tremor behind it.

I open the door to the stairs and pull him behind me. His body bangs down each step. He's scratching at my hands to let him go. When we get to the bottom I hear footsteps running down the stairs.

"The fuck, Jude?" I hear Caleb mutter behind me. "Jude!" He tries to get my attention again, but I just keep walking to the door leading to *that* room.

"Jude!" Caleb keeps shouting after me.

I open the door to the room Bob tortured Tor in. The cold air rushes around me as I step in. I pull the thin, worn string that hangs above my head, and the dim light buzzes on. The floor is still covered in Tor's blood and a thin layer of water. "Cut the temp up to sixty, Caleb."

He says nothing, but I hear him fumble with the dial outside the room.

I eye Bob, my nostrils flaring. "Get me some chains."

"Jude, man, you can't be serious."

"Did I fucking stutter, Caleb? Get them. Now!" I growl.

He turns, and I glance down at Bob. "You will be sorry for what you did to her. You will regret disobeying me."

Bob tries to shake free from me and I twist a fistful of hair, jerking his head back. "Don't fucking fight me. I will win. *Don't* fuck with me."

His body falls limp and he releases a long breath of surrender. The rattle of chains breaks the silence when Caleb drops the heavy metal on the floor beside me.

"Chain his arms and hang him up." I point to the ceiling.

Caleb's gaze locks on Bob as he closes the handcuff around his wrists. He unfolds the step stool, the worn metal legs scratching against the floor as he climbs up to hook the chains to the ceiling.

My gaze is fixated on Bob. "You will stay here until you realize how wrong you were."

Bob laughs while his body is raised slightly from the ground. "You're the one who's wrong. You're the one that's fucked up."

I can't stop myself. My vision goes red from the amount of blood coursing through my body. I slam my fists across the bridge of his nose. Warm blood splatters over my forearm and the front of my jeans. I want to fucking kill him, but I have something else in mind right now. I stand, glaring at him, angry as hell, and have to force myself to leave.

"Come on," I say to Caleb

On the way out of the room, I catch the glint of something on the floor. *Tor's necklace.* I pick it up and continue out of the room.

"He shouldn't have done that to her," Caleb says.

I nod, shoving the necklace in my pocket. "We shouldn't have done that to her. I should have let her go the second she got here," I mumble, climbing the stairs, my chest tightening with regret and guilt.

I feel responsible for her, and in that moment, my mother and sister flash through my mind. I need a fucking line, and Tor is that line. I draw in a labored breath as we step onto the landing. "Every fucking piece of shit that put her here will pay, I'll see to that."

I floor the accelerator, the momentum forcing my head against the leather headrest. I've had an entire day to mull over what happened, and all the anger has festered into full-on wrath.

I know Tor's here because of Joe. That bastard never should have put an innocent woman in that situation, and I will not let him use her the way he planned. She's mine now, and I *will* fucking kill him. I will torture him, then kill him in the most brutal way I can think up. He made me choose between my business, my life, and my dignity. He made me realize what kind of person I really am—he made it apparent that I'm just like him. I am exactly like the man I fucking hate. And I will fucking murder him for that.

I'm going a good fifty miles over the speed limit and coming up on traffic. I swerve around an eighteen-wheeler, my tires losing traction for a moment, and the car fishtails across the lane.

"Get the fuck outta my way!" I shout, clenching my jaw and gripping the stick shift.

I pull up to the apartment complex and park the rental car by the exit. The ground is covered in a thin layer of snow, which crunches underneath my boots as I make my way toward the apartment. The tendons in my neck tighten, and my breath grows more heated with each hard step I take. I check to make sure my gun is secured in the waist of my jeans, then stop in front of apartment 3C.Tapping my fingers over the door, I wait.

Nothing.

I pound my fist over the door, but not too hard. I don't want to give away that the person on this side of the door is ready to fucking kill someone.

I hear movement inside and pull the mask down over my face as I move out of the peephole's view.

Footsteps stop right on the other side of the door, and I hear him breathing nervously.

"Your uncle sent me. There's been a problem."

He clears his throat but doesn't say anything.

"Come on, Euan."

Silence.

"They killed her. She's dead, and now they're after you. We've gotta get you to a safe place. Joe sent me to get you."

There's a loud sigh and then the knob turns. The door barely cracks, then I shove my way in, grabbing the dumb bastard by his throat and knocking him to the ground.

"You fucking worthless little shit," I hiss.

His eyes widen, pupils dilate, and his skin washes white.

"Who the fuck do you think you're messing with, huh?" I roar as I tighten my grip on his neck, squeezing so hard I can feel the delicate bones crush underneath my fingertips. He chokes. His arms flail. His fingers dig into my hands, trying to pry them away from his throat. He's so small compared to me, barely what I would call a man.

"Ah, ah, ah." I shake my head. "You calm the fuck down right now, or I'll just go ahead and end your pathetic life right here."

His eyes widen more and he struggles beneath me, managing to nod his head. When I loosen my hold, he pulls in a desperate breath.

"You answer every last question I ask you, or I will kill you fucking slowly. Understand?"

He frantically nods again.

Out of all the questions I can ask him, out of all the information I could actually use to my advantage, the only thing I want to ask him is why he gave her away.

"Why?" I swallow and try to regulate my breathing. "Why did you hand her over?" The thought of it and of everything that ensued once she arrived at my house flips through my mind. An angry heat consumes me. Leaning over his face, I shout at him, "Why would you do that to her?"

Euan closes his eyes. Like that can make any of this go away. "Did they really kill her?" he chokes out.

My fingers claw into his throat again. "What the fuck do you think? You handed her over to low-lifes. She's gone."

I watch tears trickle down his face, and I can't help but to jerk his head up and smash it onto the floor. "Don't fucking cry, you worthless shit. It's your fault." I slam his head into the floor again and he whimpers. "You're a murderer, Euan," I hiss.

I pull the gun from my pants, and push the barrel against his temple. My hand shakes from anger. "I should blow your fucking brains all over the place just for that. For crying like a little bitch about something you did."

He's still crying.

"Get up!" I twist the tip of the gun against his head as I stand, leaning over to drag him to his feet. "Get"—I yank him once more—"up!"

I move the gun to the back of his skull and watch the end of it disappear in his hair. I shove him toward the kitchen. "Face the corner." Using the gun, I push him against the wall. "Put both your hands behind your back, cross them over one another."

He doesn't move.

"Do it now!" The command echoes from the cabinets.

His arms come behind him, noticeably trembling as he crosses them as instructed. He's not even fighting me. He's this pathetic that he won't even fight for his life.

I place my face close to the back of his neck and growl, "You move, and I swear to God, I will make you suffer." I exhale and wet my lips with my tongue. "I want to know every last person that works with your uncle."

"Uh, um, I...I don't know them."

"Okay," I nod and grab onto his scrawny bicep, burying my fingers into his flesh. "You sure about that?"

"I don't," he whines. The fear must really be setting in now.

Holding onto his arm, I slam my entire body weight into him, pushing against his shoulder until I hear a crack. Euan screeches as his shoulder pops from its socket.

I glance around the kitchen, my eyes honing in on the large chef knife. I snatch it from the counter, wielding it in the air. "Maybe I should do to you what they did to her?"

He won't open his eyes. He's just repeating please over and over again, still crying like a pathetic little bitch. "You want me to show you what they did to that pretty little girlfriend of yours?" I take the knife and lay it over his t-shirt, pressing it through the material until I see bright red stain the fabric. I slowly carve 'P' into his chest. He's screaming, shrieking, trying to jerk away from me. "Shut up!"

Next I cut a 'U'.

Between yells he shouts, "Dan—Daniel."

"Not good enough," I say, and focus on the letters I'm slicing over his chest. Blood stains his shirt, dripping from the tattered pieces. I watch some of it splatter onto the toe of my boot before I finish carving the 'Y.' I lean in and point the knife under his chin. "That's what you are, a pussy," I whisper into his ear.

"Daniel. Daniel Capes," he shouts.

"Oh, so you *do* know?"

"Yes. Daniel's his hit man. And then there's Fisher, I don't know his first name, but he's a cop, and the only other one I know of is Simon DeLucas."

"So," I say as I lock my eyes with his and feel a coldness creep through me, "why did you give Tor up?"

His brow scrunches. He doesn't know who Tor is.

"Victoria, you dumb-fuck. Why would you do that?"

His face crumples and he shakes his head. "Joe said he'd kill her if I didn't."

Hanging my head, I mutter, "She was dead no matter what you did." I look up at him. "You didn't even try to save her."

"Did she suffer?" he asks. I have to shut my eyes at that question.

"What the fuck do you think?" I ask as I wipe the bloody knife over my jeans.

His eyes slam shut and tears pour down his face. "I loved her."

That comment enrages me. He loved her yet he gave her up, he bowed to the wishes of his uncle?

I grit my teeth. "How hard did you beg for her?"

He opens his eyes, regret swimming in them as he stares at me. He didn't beg for her. He didn't fight for her. He is a coward. A selfish pussy.

I shake him. "How hard did you beg for her?" I scream at him. I'm frantic. My pulse is hammering through my temples, my forehead is dotted with sweat. I feel damn near insane.

His gaze drops to the floor, and my hold on him tightens. "Let's see how hard you beg for *your* life, and you tell me if you begged for hers like that, you little shit!"

"Please," he pleads pathetically.

I smile, chuckling as I grab his hand. Taking a single finger, I snap it backward, my grin deepening when the bone cracks and he screams in agony. I take the next finger and slowly bend it, waiting for the bone to splinter. "Please!" he yells.

"You consider *that* begging?" I growl, forcing two more fingers back toward his knuckles. "Pathetic!"

I trail the knife over his throat and he sobs, his lips quivering. I've never wanted to make someone suffer as much as I do him at this very moment. I place the blade behind his ear, pressing on it with my thumb. I bite down on my lip then jerk the knife forward. Euan howls in pain as the knife slices his ear off. He doubles over. Blood pours down the side of his face and over his neck. I step back, pacing in front of him. He's still screaming and sobbing, pressing his un-maimed hand against the gory stub that was his ear. The louder he wails, the more my blood boils.

"Please. I'll do anything," he pants, "anything, just please, don't kill me."

"Stand up."

He remains bent forward, the blood continuing to flow.

"Stand the fuck up!"

He slowly manages to pull himself upright, and as soon as he does, I punch him in the gut as hard as I can. His back slams against the wall, and he groans as he plummets to the floor. I kick him over and over: in the stomach, the shins, his balls, his face. Visions of my mother and sister flash through my mind, the house burned to the ground and smoldering, Joe's wife pleading for her life. I swear, there's a moment of externalism. It's like I jump out of my own damn body. I smash my fist over his face, grab his head and slam it against the floor. And now, all I can see in my mind is Tor bloodied and crying. The thought of *that* makes me beat him harder All I can hear is my pulse in my ears, the labored breaths my lungs force out, and the weak wails of Euan as I take all my aggression out on him. When I know he must think he's close to death, I walk to the side of the room, folding my arms as I lean against the wall. "Go!" I growl.

He moans and attempts to roll onto his hands and knees. With each small movement, loud sobs rack his body. There is most likely not a single bone in him that hasn't been cracked, broken, or smashed.

"I said, go!"

He can't support himself. Every time he tries to pull up, he collapses to the floor in a pathetic heap. I watch as he uses his elbows to drag his useless body across the floor toward the door. A trail of cardinal red blood smears the floor behind him. When he gets about a foot from the entrance, I push off the wall, and he freezes. With each loud step I take, his breathing grows more labored. I squat next to him and fist his hair, yanking his head back. "Changed my mind," I whisper as I flip him over.

I straddle his chest, the blood quickly soaking through my jeans as I pin his shoulders down with my knees. Forcing his jaw open, I manage to grab his tongue and use the sharp knife to saw through the thick muscle. He screams hysterically as he jerks his head from side to side.

"Stay the fuck still," I say, and put the blade back to the mangled piece of flesh, finally severing it. The scream he lets out is guttural and riddled with pain, but even that's not enough to satisfy me.

"I want you to lie here in agony. I want you to feel the fucking blood drain out of your pathetic body. I'm gonna let you drown in your own fucking blood, and I'm gonna watch you fucking suffer."

I force his mouth open, blood spilling from its corners, and cram his tongue far back into his throat. He gags. His mouth opens and closes like a fish out of water, and I just lean against the door to watch him struggle. "This is what you fucking deserve," I growl. He fights the inevitable for a few more seconds and then falls still.

I step over him and put my hand on the doorknob. I hear him gurgle from the blood pooling in his throat, and I twist the knob. "You were wrong," I say as I slam the door closed behind me.

Chapter 20
Victoria

Even in the darkest situations, I like to think that you can find a glimmer of light.

I can't.

Not this time.

There are some things that can break a person, break them to the point of wishing for death with every fibre of their being.

I've never understood how anyone can get to the point of contemplating suicide. Turns out that point comes pretty bloody quickly when you're faced with the possibility of something so horrific you would do anything at all to escape it.

I can take pain. I can take fear. I can take a lot. I can't comprehend being raped, violated, degraded. I would rather die.

Every time I close my eyes I see Bob's face, feel his hands crawling over my body, the knife biting into my skin. Whenever I fall asleep I wake up screaming and crying. Each sound, each click of that lock makes me jump. I never thought I would be this person. They made me this person.

Never in my life have I felt so utterly alone, so betrayed, so hurt. I have nothing to live for, because even though I survived this time, he *will* kill me eventually. He has to. I know it, and so does he. He may have found some trace of a soul this time, but he's a ticking bomb just waiting to go off. I'm living on borrowed time and I'm never getting out of this.

I slide out of the bed. My legs shake beneath my weight as I make my way to the bathroom and close the door behind me. I turn on the shower, twisting the knobs to the hottest they'll go before I turn to the vanity and carefully pull my t-shirt over my head. The material brushes against the stitches, making me hiss in pain.

It takes me a few minutes to muster the courage to look in the mirror, and when I do, I wish I hadn't. I don't recognise the girl looking back at me. I have to pretend that reflection is someone else, some stranger I don't know, because this girl is broken and unsalvageable in every way. She's skinny and frail, her skin sallow. Her skin is a map of bruises and cuts. An ugly red line runs from her chest to her stomach, matching the stitched five-inch long cut across her throat. Her lip is split and face bruised. The part that scares me the most, though, are her eyes, they're completely lifeless. She looks so sad, so desolate.

Victoria Devaux died three days ago when a man tried to violate and torture her, and she willingly slit her own throat, praying for death. She did that because she was strong, because she was a fighter who took control of her own fate.

The girl I'm staring at is not strong. I'm nothing anymore.

I step away from the mirror until I feel the cold, tiled wall against my back. Sliding to the floor, I hug my knees to my chest. The dry wound on my stomach crinkles, and I flinch from the sudden pain, but I don't cry.

I'm past crying.

I've accepted my fate in this hell.

I don't know how long I stay like this; it may be minutes, it may be hours. All I can hear is the sound of the shower running, the water splashing against the floor as the bathroom fills with steam. It's hard to accept that my life has been stolen from me, and that even if I could be handed freedom, at this point, I wouldn't want it. I've nothing left.

Eventually there's a soft knock on the door. I don't move. I just keep staring at a spot on the wall across from me.

My stomach clenches at the sound of his voice, and my nails dig into my shins. I taste bile rise up my throat.

I remember too late that I didn't lock the door. The door cracks, and I hear his heavy boots move across the floor.

He comes in and rummage through the drawers, mumbling to himself. "Are you okay?" he asks, then I hear him stop beside me, and I look down to see his brown boots with what I assume is dried blood on the toe. I don't answer him. I don't want to talk to him. I have nothing to say. All has been well and truly said and done. Some things are just beyond words.

I feel him looming over me and then he crouches down in front of me. He gently lifts my chin and examines the wound on my neck.

I look straight at him. A frown etches between his eyebrows as he studies my face. I blankly hold his gaze for a few seconds before pulling my chin out of his grasp.

I get to my feet slowly, and turn to face him. I stand in front of him completely naked and watch as his eyes skate over the long cut down the centre of my body. He closes his eyes and tilts his head back before dragging his hands through his hair. It's then that I notice the blood covering his shirt, evidence of his last victim. The monster in all his glory. I can't even find it within myself to be scared. I'm not scared of him. I don't fucking care anymore.

His eyes dart down to the blood stains, then back up to mine. "You don't need to be scared of me. There's a lot you don't know."

"I'm not," I say. "Can you leave? Please."

He looks at me again and nods. He turns to leave, but stops. "I shouldn't have left you. I'm sorry."

I don't care what he has to say. The door clicks closed behind him and I get in the shower. I turn the water up as hot as it will go and stand underneath it. It burns my skin, and I relish the feeling of it.

When I step out of the shower, there's a fresh towel as well as some jeans and a tank top left on the vanity. I've almost forgotten what normal clothes look like. I dry and change into the clothes.

When I walk into the bedroom, I find Jude sitting on the bed. His elbows rest on his knees, and his head is in his hands.

He's topless, his eyes fixed on the bloodied shirt in his hands. The tattoos winding around his biceps seem to pop against his olive skin. He glances up when he notices me and drags a hand over his dark hair. "I thought you might want clothes," he says quietly.

All I can do is stare at him.

"Are you not gonna talk?"

"What would you like me to say?"

He shakes his head and picks away some of the dried blood from his nails. "Something." He hops up from the bed, putting his face close to mine. "You tried to fucking kill yourself, Tor. You should have something to fucking say."

I watch him for a few seconds as he clenches his fists and a muscle in his jaw ticks.

"I have nothing to say to you," I say quietly.

"Fuck!" he yells, turning away from me and stalking to the far side of the room. He slams his palm against the wall, keeping his back to me as he breathes heavily. There's a long beat of silence. I don't move. I don't know what he's going to do next.

"The man that killed my mother and sister," he says, so quietly I barely hear him, "was Euan's uncle. He wants me dead." He turns to face me, leaning against the wall and lifting his eyes to mine. "I don't believe in coincidences. I thought you were working with him."

I frown. I should feel nothing for him and yet, my heart aches for him, for all that he's lost. The loss of a mother is a tragic and heartbreaking one. "I'm sorry." I whisper.

He shakes his head and drops his gaze to the floor. "He and my father had a ...disagreement, so he burned our house down with them inside it. On the one year anniversary of their death he sent my father a video of him raping and torturing them before he set the house on fire. I passed by my dad's office when he was watching it." *Oh, my God.* He's breathing is heavy, his fists clenched. He can't look at me. "I fall asleep every damn night hearing the screams from that video." He speaks the words as though they are a dirty secret, an unwanted weakness.

I press my hand over my mouth as a choked sob escapes my throat. I should hate Jude. I should want nothing more than to kill him right now, but I don't. I try desperately to cling to my rage, my hatred, the pain, because suddenly I feel sorry for him, and I don't want to. I want to cry for the two women that are strangers to me. I feel as though we are bound in some way, victims of these monsters who pretend to be men.

"I will kill anyone that works with him, I promised my father I would, but you..." he swallows as his eyes rise to mine. "I never *wanted* to kill you, Tor. I just...I needed to be sure." He pulls in a heavy breath and pushes off the wall, closing the distance between us. I take an uneasy step back and he holds his hands out; slowly, gently brushing a strand of hair away from my neck. His eyes flick to the ugly mark across my throat and he squeezes his eyes shut. "I never should have left you." his voice breaks.

His fingers brush across my cheek. "Joe is trying to use you, whether you know it or not." I watch as anger masks his face, his green eyes becoming turbulent and volatile. "I will *not* let him do that. Not to you."

I drop my gaze from his, unable to look at him. "You already did it." I whisper. His hand slips from my cheek, and his head falls forward as his shoulders tense.

"I'm not like him." I don't know who he's trying to convince more, me or himself.

"What happened to your family is horrible, but that doesn't justify you doing the same to someone else. An eye for an eye. Is that how it works in your world?" My voice shakes as I try to control my emotions. I thought I was done feeling. I thought I was broken beyond repair, but I'm not. I'm still fucking here, and his bullshit justification for his actions isn't enough.

He takes a slow step back. "Don't you fucking dare compare me to that fucking bastard!" He shouts, pointing at me. He clenches and releases his fists, attempting to rein in his temper. "I didn't fucking touch you! And I would never rape a woman. Ever." His breathing is audible, his chest heaving.

My cold numbness is giving way to a very real, very feral anger. "No, you're worse, because you ordered someone else to hurt me, and then left me!" I snap. "If you wanted me tortured, you should have at least had the balls to do it yourself. You're a fucking coward and you're weak."

He takes a predatory step toward me, glaring at me. He grabs me by the shoulders and pushes me back against the wall. Panic grips me as I feel his fingers creep around my throat. I flinch as he brushes against my stitches. His breathing is ragged, his hand shaking. He squeezes his eyes shut, his fingers twitching against my neck. I turn my face away from him and close my eyes, waiting for the inevitable. There's a tense beat of silence before he shoves himself away from me.

"Fuck!" he growls as he grabs the closest thing to him which is the picture of his mother and sister, and hurls it across the room. Glass scatters across the floor. Taking his arm, he swipes at everything on the dresser, sending it crashing to the floor. "Fuck!" He freezes and clasps his hands behind his head, breathing heavily. He hangs his head forward and drops his hands, slowly moving to the broken picture, and he picks it up, removing the remaining glass.

He places the frame back on the dresser and leaves the room. For the first time since I've gotten here, I am alone and there's an open door in front of me, but there's no point in running. I walk to the door and softly close it.

Sometime later there's a soft knock at the door, followed by the creak of it opening. I'm lying on my side, staring at the wall.

"Ria?" Caleb says.

I feel the mattress dip slightly as he sits on the far side of it.

"I need to check your stitches." This is the third time in two days that he's been in here to check on my stitches. They don't need checking. I'm a doctor, for Christ's sake. I don't need a trainee paramedic telling me whether or not I'm okay. If it weren't for him and his brother, I wouldn't need checking on.

"They're fine," I say. I have to hand it to him, he did a good job of stitching my throat. It will scar though, and so will my chest and stomach. A permanent reminder of this nightmare.

He sighs. "Ria..."

"I'm a doctor. I'm fine."

"Damn it, will you please talk to me."

I sigh and roll over, sitting up against the headboard. I pull my knees to my chest and wrap my arms around them.

"Talk and then leave," I snap.

He drops his head forward into his hands. "I'm so sorry. You know I didn't want to do it." He's already said this, but I've refused to acknowledge him, and so he keeps coming back.

"You did, though, Caleb," I say blankly.

"Please, you know I would never..."

"Cowards hide behind excuses. A weak man blames his actions on others. You let it happen, and if you believed it was wrong, then you should have stood up for what you believed was right."

His eyes meet mine, begging me to hear him, to understand, but I don't understand. I don't understand how you could bind a girl and watch a man tear her clothes off and let her almost freeze to death, without acting against it.

"Ria," he whispers.

"No!" I snap out. "You disgust me as much as your brother." He recoils as if I had physically slapped him. "Please, just leave."

He looks up at me like a puppy that's just been kicked. My heart gives a little squeeze because I've lost the only friend I had in this place, and his betrayal hurts worse than any physical pain I've endured.

He sighs heavily. "You have to come with me."

"Where?"

His eyes lock with mine. "Jude wants you. He has something for you. Something that might make you feel better."

I glare at him. "Tell your fucking brother that this can't be fixed with shallow gifts."

"Trust me, Ria, I think you'll want this."

"I don't trust you, or him."

"Please," he begs.

Call it curiosity, or maybe I'm just bored shitless of looking at these four walls, but I get up and follow him out of the room. We don't speak on the way down the stairs. I think Caleb finally realises that no amount of apologising will ever make this okay.

Chapter 21
Jude

I haven't been able to sleep, hell, I'm barely able to shut my eyes without seeing her all bloodied and split open. It's taken me three days to calm down enough and rationalize how to handle this, because at first all I wanted to do was kill Bob, but that would do nothing but grant me a fleeting moment of satisfaction.

Drumming my fingers over the worn edge of my desk, I wait. There's a cigarette smoldering in the ashtray. I haven't smoked it. I'm just watching the thin white swirls float in front of my face as I try to even out my breathing. What he did to her was unjustified, sick, and shows a complete lack of respect for me, and for her.

I listen to the footsteps coming down the stairs, and seconds later there's a knock on the door. The hinges of the chair creak as I rise to answer it, and the door swings open before I can get there. I see Tor's tiny frame behind Caleb. Her eyes lock with mine, and I can barely look at her. They're empty, hollow. That spark that I admired so much has vanished. She really is gone.

"Come on," I say hoarsely as I make my way down the hall.

She and Caleb follow me, and the second I reach for the door that leads to that room, I hear her breathing pick up. I know she thinks I'm bringing her here to kill her. I push open the door and stop, not bothering to glance back. "Tor, I'm not gonna let anyone hurt you again. This is for you."

I place my hand on the small of her back and guide her through the door. I can feel her muscles tense as she braces herself. She takes one look around the room and spins to face me. "What is this?" Her voice is quiet, barely above a whisper.

I briefly divert my gaze from hers. The light from the doorway casts a faint glow over the room. Bob dangles from the metal hook in the ceiling, groaning, his feet barely touching the floor. Dried blood stains his chin, and his bare torso is covered in large, black bruises.

I manage to maintain my calm when I look at him. I have to strain to keep control of my voice. "You had no right to touch her, you sick piece of shit!" I direct my attention back to Tor. "He was wrong, and you're gonna make this right. This is the only way I know to help you."

I yank the thin cord to the light and the bulbs flicker and buzz. I can hear each breath I draw in rumble with a growl as I circle by him. I walk toward the corner of the room and pull open a drawer on the small metal cabinet. I stare down at the assortment of weapons and grab a hunting knife. I slam the cabinet shut with a bang, and everything inside rattles. Within seconds, I've grabbed Tor's hand and placed the blade inside her damp palm. She's trembling, her eyes blanketed in confusion as her eyes dart from me to the knife to Bob.

Her gaze sharpens on the knife, her brow creasing. "I'm not a monster, Jude, not like you, not like him." Her voice is soft, uncertain, as a look of disgust crawls over her face.

"Maybe you *weren't*"—my eyes narrow on hers—"but you are *not* the same person you were when you were brought through those doors. When someone hurts you, the only way to take that pain away is by taking revenge. He didn't just steal something of monetary value, Tor." I can feel my pulse thumping in my temples. My teeth grind against each other from the anger bubbling to the surface. "In this world, when someone fucks you up, you fuck them up, or you will never survive." I take a few steps toward her and close my palm around her tiny hand in an effort to tighten her grip on the handle. "Make him *feel* what he made you feel," I growl, my eyes tearing into hers.

I want to help her. I want her to feel vindicated. And after what has been done to her, the only way she will ever feel that is with bloodshed.

Chapter 22
Victoria

My heart hammers against my ribs and my palms are damp as I grip the handle of the knife. Jude's fingers cover mine, tightening my hold. I look up into his eyes, and he holds my gaze. Part of me fucking hates him, part of me would sooner plunge this knife into his chest and just be done with it, but the other part, well, in his own sick and twisted way, he's trying to make amends.

In his world, this is how justice is served. I can feel how much he wants this, how much he wants to give me back something that was taken, but he can't. All that's left is this anger and hatred that's festering inside me. I don't want to be this person.

"He will pay for what he's done." Jude lowers his face to mine, his eyes intense, intimidating. "Do you hear me, Tor?" I've never actually been able to *feel* someone else's anger before, but at this moment, it radiates from him like an inferno, and if I don't get away from him I'm going to be consumed by it.

I hear the chains rattle, and a weak groan echoes through the room. I can't look up at Bob.

"I was only thinking of you, Jude," Bob rasps. "She makes you weak. We're family!"

The room seems to drop by five degrees, and it has nothing to do with the temperature. Jude goes deathly still, and that is far scarier than any words he could possibly say. He moves toward Bob with a deadly grace that has me in awe of him. He stops in front of him and grabs his jaw.

"You disobeyed me." His voice is a low rumble, full of menace. "And you disrespected me. Family or not, you will pay."

"She'll ruin you!" Bob whispers, his chains clanging together once again.

"Shut the fuck up!" Jude snarls, clenching and releasing his fists. He turns and I think he's going to walk away, but suddenly he spins around, his fist smashing into the side of Bob's face. I instinctively recoil from the show of violence and power, but I'd be lying if I said that I don't want Bob to suffer; I do.

He turns away and moves to stand in front of me. His large frame towers over me, blocking out everything but him. He holds my chin gently between his fingers, and it's such a strange sensation—amidst all his rage, his touch is gentle.

"Sometimes two wrongs make a right." His eyes narrow, and it's as though he's trying to convince me of this. "Trust me, nothing is more healing than making someone who hurt you bleed. Justice doesn't know how to play fair." His eyes flick briefly to the blade in my hand. "This is the only way I know how to help you, Tor," he whispers, and there's remorse in that statement, I can hear it.

There's the slightest vulnerability in his eyes, and despite my instant revulsion at his methods, I almost understand them. He wants to help me, he just doesn't know how. I don't know if I can even be helped at this stage, but the fact that he wants to try touches on something that it really shouldn't. Maybe my mind is so fucked up that I can't tell right from wrong anymore, enemies from friends, because right now, Jude doesn't seem like the enemy, and that's dangerous.

A low moan floats through the air. "I would have been doing you a favor by killing her," Bob pants.

Any softness in Jude's eyes disappears, and an icy rage covers his features. He grabs my hand, taking the knife from me. Every step he takes echoes off the walls in the empty room.

"Unchain him," Jude orders, and Caleb scurries over. I watch as he unfastens the shackles and Bob drops to the concrete floor with a muffled thud.

Jude circles around him, literally stalking him like a wounded deer. The blade every so often glints under the flickering light.

"Get up!" Jude shouts hoarsely.

Bob lays there.

"Get"—Jude reaches down and yanks Bob to his feet—"up!"

Bob languidly shrugs. "What ya gonna do? Kill me? Your father would be disgusted with you," he spits.

The guy must have a death wish. Maybe he already knows his time is up, no point in dragging it out, I guess. I can relate to that. I've felt that. He made me feel that.

Jude shakes his head and slashes the knife across Bob's stomach in one quick movement. Blood pours from the wound, and Bob screams. I usually shun away from violence, but somehow I find myself fascinated by the blood, reveling in Bob's screams. I want him to suffer and I want him to die, because that's the only way I will ever be able to close my eyes and not see his sick, twisted grin as he butchered my body.

"You gonna fight me?" Jude asks. "Or do you realize you're just that fucking worthless?"

Bob says nothing.

Jude grabs his hair, violently jerking his head back. He's walking him over to me. *Oh, my God! What is he doing?*

"You tell her you're sorry." Jude shoves him in front of me, and Bob falls to his knees, Jude's hand still gripping his hair. "Tell her you are a worthless piece of shit!"

Bob's groaning in pain. The blood is pooling right in front of my bare feet, and I take a step back.

"Tell her!" Jude shouts, his voice booming around the room.

"I...I'm, I'm sorry," Bob grovels.

"Tell her how worthless you are."

Bob inhales several times. "I'm worthless..."

Jude kicks him in the back and Bob falls forward, his face smacking the cold concrete. "Do better than that!"

"Jude!" I shout. He looks up at me, his lips pressed into a hard line. "Stop," I say quietly. I shake my head, but he's too far gone. This isn't about me anymore. This is about him, and whatever demon he has riding his back.

He wipes his hand down his face, pacing behind Bob as he nods his head. He drops to a crouch beside Bob and flips him over, pinning him to the floor by his throat. His face is focused and determined as he squeezes Bob's throat, watching as the man coughs and fights him. This is when Jude is at his most terrifying, not because he looks crazy, quite the opposite; he's so controlled, fully aware of what he's doing.

"Tor," he grates. His voice makes all the hairs on the back of my neck stand up. He looks up at me and gestures me over. The angry and abused girl in me wants to hurt Bob. The rational side of me says it won't help, but I'm so fucking tired of feeling like a victim, of feeling weak in this place where monsters pretend to be men. So I take the first step toward him.

"Ria..." Caleb starts. I glance at him, and his expression is filled with pity. I don't want his pity. "You don't have to do this. Let me do it for you."

190

"Caleb, out!" he snaps. I focus on Jude's face, on his dark green eyes that always seem so bottomless. Something passes between us, an understanding, a matching need for revenge, an outlet to purge the rage and hate. I've been blaming him for what happened, but I know it wasn't him. His only crime is leaving me. The man currently choking and gasping for breath, he's the animal here.

I close the distance to Jude and kneel down beside Bob's thrashing body. Jude's eyes never leave mine as he carefully places the knife in my palm with a nod. He may be violent, he may be a criminal, but he understands what I need, and he's giving me the means to take back my own power. He can't give it to me, though, I have to take it.

My pulse speeds as I shakily hold out the blade toward Bob's chest. My hand won't still, and I close my eyes as I try to control my nerves. I feel warm fingers wrap around my hand, stilling it. When I open my eyes, Jude is right there with me. He guides my hand to Bob's chest, pressing the tip into his skin before slowly dragging my hand down, and the blade with it.

Bob screams, and there's a certain satisfaction in it that both thrills and scares me. I feel as though by inflicting pain on him, I'm being relieved of my own; it's almost cleansing.

Blood wells and spills down his sides. I want to hate myself for this, I want to hate Jude for turning me into this, but I can't. I didn't do this, I became this.

When Jude lifts the knife away from Bob's skin, I release the breath I didn't realise I had been holding. He lets go of my hand, and I numbly drop the knife, watching it to clatter to the floor. Suddenly, Jude grabs onto Bob's throat, squeezing to the point that it literally looks as if his eyes will pop from his skull at any moment. "Caleb!" he shouts.

The door cracks open and Caleb pokes his head around the door. "Take Tor outside," Jude grates through gritted teeth.

"Jude," Caleb starts.

"Take her the fuck out!" he shouts. I glance between the two of them as a tense, silence takes hold. Caleb breaks first, gently wrapping his fingers around my arm and pulling me from the room. I glance over my shoulder, looking back at Jude as his eyes fix on Bob who is still struggling against his hold.

The door slams shut behind me, and all I can hear is the echo of my footsteps. I'm halfway to the next door when I hear a loud gunshot ring out behind me, followed by another. I flinch, and my hands start shaking. I know Jude just killed Bob. One look at his face and I knew there was no way Bob was getting out of that room alive. Jude is not someone to double cross. Bob hurt me and he killed him for it. Part of me knows that he doesn't deserve my gratitude, and yet I can't help but feel some towards him. I'm no longer just veering from my path, I'm crashing and burning, and like the masochist he makes me, I'm reveling in the flames.

I don't know who I am anymore or what I'm becoming. I just took a knife to a man, and I *liked* cutting him. It felt cleansing to me, and that's depraved in so many ways. By the time I reach the door at the end I'm shaking, my knees threatening to buckle. I glance down at my hands, and they are covered in blood. For the first time in my life, they are covered in blood because I was harming someone, not saving them.

I small sob rips up my throat, and tears slip down my cheeks. I've become the very thing I've always feared, because as of this moment...death no longer affects me. I feel nothing except the loss of myself. My knees give out and I drop to the floor.

"Ria!" Caleb rushes to my side, but I push him away.

"No." I whisper. I don't want Caleb to see this. He still sees good in me, and his faith is so misplaced. I glance up at him and meet his concerned eyes. "I'm sorry. You're not a monster," I cry. How could I ever think he was a monster? He's just a kid.

His hands stroke over my face. "I'm sorry." "Shh, it's okay." He smiles. "You have nothing to be sorry for."

I nod and sniff as he wipes tears from my face.

"Caleb. Go." Jude's rough voice rumbles behind me. Caleb rises to his feet, flashing me one last look before he turns away.

"Tor," Jude says my name quietly.

I meet his eyes, and he studies me for a long while. "I'm...I can't..." My voices trembles as I try to process what just happened.

"Tor," he says, more sternly this time. "Look at me." I can't look at him. "Look. At. Me," he demands.

I drag my eyes to his, expecting his anger, but instead understanding. "It's okay," he whispers.

I nod, and whatever emotional barrier that I had in place snaps as tears stream down my cheeks. I don't know what's happening to me. I don't know whether I'm losing myself or finding myself. The old me would never have taken a knife to someone, she would have recoiled in horror. This damaged version needed to cut Bob, needed revenge and Jude could helped me with that. I close my eyes as shuddering sobs wrack my body. One minute I'm falling apart, and the next, strong arms are wrapping around me, holding my broken pieces together.

I shouldn't let him hold me, but I do.

I shouldn't like the way his warm chest feels pressed against my cheek, but I do.

This should feel wrong, but it doesn't.

Maybe I'm more broken than I thought.

Chapter 23
Jude

I sit at my desk taking bets, but I'm distracted. I can't get her out of my fucking head. I start to light a cigarette when the phone rings and I answer it.

"Go ahead."

"That missing person's report came in," David pauses. I can hear the muffled noise from his police radio on the other end. "I cancelled it twice already. Can't do it again. You're gonna have to do something to make this disappear."

I twist the cord between my fingers, scraping a film of nicotine from it. This is all I've been able to think of. What I'll do with her. I can't let her go because I fear Joe will kill her. To me, there's only one logical solution. I inhale. "I need your help."

"Yeah?"

Cradling the phone with my chin, I bury my face in my palms. I'm tired. I'm worn out from dealing with this shit, from all the fucking guilt I've had over her. "I need a body," I say.

I hear David draw in a long breath. "A body, huh? How tall is she?"

"About five four..."

"She have anything on her that could ID her?"

"A necklace." I bend a paperclip, then drag the end along the edge of the desk. "We've still got her boyfriend's car too."

"All right. You're gonna have to help me though. Shit's a lot of work."

"Yeah, okay."

"I'll go around to some of the abandoned houses on the North side. Give me a few days and I can probably find a dead transit we can use." I hear static from the radio calling for back-up, which causes David to groan. "I'll handle it later. I gotta go," he says quickly, and hangs up.

I open the desk drawer and pull out her necklace. There's still dried blood in the tiny crevices of the chain. She'll never really appreciate why I'm doing this, but that doesn't matter.

Three days later, David and I cart the corpse through the pitch-black abandoned lot. I tuck the legs under my arm as I open the door to Euan's BMW, and we set the body behind the wheel. David found her early this morning when he was on patrol, and by the look and stench of her, she's been dead for a few days.

"This is sick, even for me," I mumble, my fingers trembling as I pull Tor's necklace from my pocket. I loop the chain around the dead woman's neck and fumble to fasten the lock. A light breeze blows, causing the rancid smell of rotting flesh to waft up to my nose, and I gag. I have to step away to catch a breath of clean air before finally clasping the lock.

David tosses me a pair of pliers. "Pull out her teeth."

"Are you serious?" I furrow my brow, then glance back at the corpse. "I'm not fucking doing that!"

"Dental records won't match. You want them to believe this is her, the only form of ID you can leave is that necklace," David pats the hood as he leans against the car, "and this car. You want to make people think she's dead, this is what you gotta do."

I catch another whiff of death and feel my stomach churn. I swallow the bile eating its way up my throat as I lean into the car, placing my palm on the woman's chilled forehead. What's underneath my palm no longer feels like skin; instead, it's wet and waxy. I gag and cough, spitting out mouthfuls of saliva as I clamp the pliers over one of the few teeth in her head. It takes more force than I think to wiggle it from the socket. Each time I pull, the cracking noise it creates nearly makes me vomit.

I pull the last tooth and get out of that fucking car as fast as I can. *This is fucking sick!* I pace as David douses the body in gasoline. I hear him strike a match. I don't look back. I just walk straight ahead to David's patrol car. The entire drive back to my car, I fight the urge to throw up. I can smell death on me, and I don't know that any amount of washing will get rid of the stench. I stare out the window and I wonder how in the hell I got to the point of desecrating bodies, but above anything else, I wonder why in the hell she's been put into my life.

I fold the newspaper and pick up the phone.

I hear the lull of the TVs in the background before anyone says anything. "Yeah," Rich groans.

"Send Caleb down with the girl."

"All right."

I set the receiver down and light a cigarette. Leaning back in the chair, I take a long pull from the smoke and train my eyes on the door.

Within a few minutes, I hear footsteps on the stairs, and then Caleb walks into the room with Tor. Just looking at her causes a reaction in me: anger, guilt, need. I don't fucking like that she makes me feel anything, and I try to look anywhere but her face. I trail my eyes over the pair of jeans she's wearing, over the loose shirt that hangs from one shoulder. I cringe when I notice the long pink wound across her throat.

"Sit down." I point to the chair in front of my desk.

She silently does as asked. There is nothing in her eyes. No fight. No fear. There's a fragility about her that makes me want to protect her, and that's some fucked-up shit right there.

"I need to tell you something." I pause and look her over. What I'm about to tell her is going to send her over the edge. She looks so frail, and this is going to be hard for her to process. I am pretty much ripping away any sliver of hope she may have left. This will make her hate me even more than she already does because she won't possibly understand that the sole reason I'm doing this is to protect her. Why would she believe that a man who held her captive would ever be trying to save her?

"If I could, I would protect you from this..." I trail off, waiting to see how she responds.

Her eyes set on me, cold and hard. "It would seem that the only person I need protection from is you and your family."

I tried to help her the only way I know, but I guess revenge doesn't work the same for everyone. She still blames me, still hates me. I narrow my gaze. "You think?" I arch my brow and shake my head. "Because I can assure you that Joe is a much bigger threat to you than I am."

"Fine, enlighten me."

I glance over to Caleb. "Get out," I say. I don't want anyone else in here because I know this is going to be awful.

He looks nervously at Tor before walking out of the room. The door softly closes behind him, and I rise, walking around my desk.

"You know...I visited Euan the other day."

"Oh, did you have fun?" A wry smile pulls at her lips, and I can't help but grin at the slightly sadistic glint in her eyes. Hell hath no fury like a woman scorned.

"Tor," I lean over her chair, gripping the arms, inching my way closer to her until the only thing I see are her gun-metal blue eyes. I gently sweep a stray piece of hair behind her ear. I trail my finger down her jaw, and her muscles stiffen, but she doesn't pull away. My gaze drifts over her full lips before slowly rising back to meet her eyes. "Trust me, when someone fucks with something that's in my possession. I. Am. Brutal." Those last three words come out so low, so hoarse, I almost don't even recognize my own voice.

Her eyes hold mine. I know she wants to ask me if I killed him, because there's not much more that comment could have insinuated, but she remains completely silent. There's no reason to tell her Euan's dead, because in a moment that won't even matter.

"I just want you to remember that I did this to protect you from Joe. He will kill you if he finds you because this didn't go the way he planned." I inhale as I slam down the front page of the Vanderbilt newspaper in front of her. "I've done what I had to do to ensure your protection."

She eyes me before glancing down at the article. Her brows pinch in confusion, then her face washes white. "What...is this?" Her voice is a breathless whisper.

"You are dead as far as the rest of the world is concerned."

She snatches the paper from the desk, her eyes frantically skimming over the write-up detailing her grizzly death.

"My sister," she breathes, and in that moment I feel sympathy for her.

"I'm sorry. It had to be done. I had no choice."

She sits there staring at the paper, and I wait for her to fall to pieces. The more she reads, the heavier her breaths become. She frowns, her lips forming a thin line. "You didn't even tell me what you were going to do!" she shouts at me.

"Why would I?" I shrug. "You didn't have a say in the matter?"

"You know what? Fuck you, Jude!" She stands and throws the paper down on the desk.

She's angry as a hornet, and she has every right to be. I wet my lips with the edge of my tongue and reach for the cigarettes on my desk. Just as I pull one from the pack, she swats it from my hand.

"Fuck you!" she growls again. Her stance widens as she balls her fists by her side. She looks like she may be about to punch me. "*You* have cost me everything, and now you've cost me my life."

I shake my finger at her. "No, I *saved* your fucking life!" I'm growing agitated, not necessarily at her, but at the fact that I've had to damage her even further.

Her entire body is shaking. "You have taken everything from me, including my freedom."

I pick up a loose cigarette from the floor and light it. I hold the smoke inside my lungs as I glare at her. Letting the thick cloud roll from my lips. My chest tightens, I feel sorry for her, I feel guilty, and those are not emotions I'm much accustomed to. I pull in another drag from the cigarette and wait for her to completely break, because it's coming.

Her expression morphs instantly from despair to rage. Rage I can deal with, tears not so much.

"Why would you do this? Have you not taken enough from me? You're a selfish bastard!" she screams at me.

I put the cigarette in the ashtray. I lean against the desk, bracing myself with my arms. She doesn't get why I did this. "I told you—"

"I'm not interested in your bullshit excuses! You have ruined my life. My sister thinks I am dead because of you! This was all just to protect yourself, so do me a favour and stop with the fucking lies."

"If I hadn't you would have ended up dead, and if you think what I'm capable of is fucking deranged, you don't want to know what Joe would do to you! If you want to blame anyone, blame that shit-poor excuse of a man who handed you over to criminals in the first place. This is all his fucking fault. *He* ruined your life!" I shout. "And he made a fucking mess of mine."

"Fuck. You!" she screams, swinging her arm back.

Her palm hits the side of my face with a loud clap, and my head slams to the side. Heat floods my cheek where she struck me, stinging like a motherfucker. I inhale as I close my eyes, trying to breathe. I will fucking take it this once.

"Tor," I growl in warning; my jaw tightens, my fists clench.

"How has this messed up *your* fucking life? You're not a dead girl walking!" She grabs the ashtray from the desk and chucks it at the wall. Soot flies everywhere. We've skipped the crying and gone straight to irrational, apparently.

She stomps across the room. "*You* don't have to think of your sister crying over your fucking closed casket." She rips the painting off the wall, and smashes the frame over the desk. I jump to the side of the room as she hurls the mangled frame at me. "*You* haven't just lost the career you worked eight fucking years for!" She takes the crystal decanter of whiskey and throws it against the wall.

"And you don't have a foot long scar down your body, and a slit throat! I fucking hate you!" she screams manically, throwing the telephone at me.

This is how I would react, not how I expected her to react. I expected her to fall into a sobbing heap on the floor, not destroy my fucking house. I stand to the side of the room, lighting another smoke as I lean against the wall and watch her. If this is what she needs to come to term with things, so fucking be it. Eventually, she's run out of things to break and grabs the cushions from the sofa, giving them an exaggerated throw in my direction.

There's nothing left to throw. She's standing in the middle of utter destruction, chest heaving and tears pouring down her face. Her knees buckle and she falls to the floor, sobbing. She looks so small and broken, and it pulls at something inside me that I thought had long ago been lost. *Fuck, I should do something.* I'll be honest, I have no idea what to do here. I haven't done anything aside from fuck a woman in the past ten years.

I toss my hands up. "What do you want me to do?"

"Leave!" Her chest is heaving. "Let me leave." She looks utterly broken.

I drag my hands through my hair and pace. I glance at her, tears are streaming down her face. I don't need her here, because she is a weakness. If Joe finds her, so be it. She doesn't belong to me, but for some reason part of me feels like she should. Exhaling, I point toward the door. "Leave then. If that's what you want, then leave. I won't stop you."

She stares at me, her expression falling blank.

"Believe me. You can leave, but Joe will find you. What are you gonna do, huh? Go to the police?" Laughing, I shrug. "You've no idea how corrupt everything is. If I have the police in my back pocket, believe you me, so does fucking Joe. The second you go to them, he'll find you." I fall silent, thinking of the shit he did to my mother and sister. "And the things you've unfortunately experienced here will pale in fucking comparison to what he will do. So if that's what you want, just go ahead and leave. I'm not fucking keeping you prisoner. The fucking debt has been paid. Go!" I realize I'm shouting.

She nods, walking past me cautiously, like at any minute she expects me to grab her and force her against a wall. As soon as she gets to the door, she runs.

I exhale, my eyes dropping to the floor. If she really leaves, she's as good as dead.

Chapter 24
Victoria

Leave. It's one word with so much meaning. Freedom, escape, liberation. His eyes bore into mine, daring me to go.

I turn on my heel and walk out the door without a backward glance. My pace picks up as I climb the stairs and run along the hall to the front door. I throw it open, half expecting an armed firing squad to appear at any second. Nothing. I watch a handful of dead leaves blow across the gravel drive.

I jump down the steps and start running, the gravel crunching beneath my feet.

I hit the tree line and keep going. I run until I realise that I don't know where I'm running to. I stop in a clearing, my chest heaving as I try to catch my breath. I have my freedom, but what is freedom when you have nowhere to go. You can release a bird from its cage, but if you've clipped its wings then its freedom is merely a false kindness.

I have nothing. I believe Jude when he tells me that Joe will kill me. Any man who would kill Jude's family and risk his wrath is not a man that I want to risk provoking.

I could go to the police, tell them I'm not dead, but the second I do that, Joe knows I'm alive and it will only be a matter of time.

I could run away, but I have no money, no friends to help me anymore. I'm completely alone, more alone than I have ever felt in my life. Its one thing to be lonely, but quite another to be a dead girl walking. I don't exist anymore. I don't exist outside the boundary of Jude's property. Jude and Caleb are all I have left, and isn't that just tragic?

Tears stream down my cheek as I realise what a broken mess my life really is. My former life seems like a distant dream, and like a dream that you can barely remember, there seems to be no way back to it.

If I run now, the likelihood is that I will die.

I lean against a nearby tree for a second and listen to the birds chirping happily in the trees. I remember when I was little, I always used to climb into my mother's bed early in the morning and she would tell me to listen to the bird song. I always took that sound for granted, but now I can't remember the last time I stopped and listened to it. Sometimes it's the small things in life that make it worth living. She would want me to live. She would want me to make the best possible choice for my own survival, because when this is over, and I have to believe that it will be over, life will go on.

Jude is my only option here, because he will protect me from Joe. For some reason I trust him, I trust him to do as he says. If he says he'll protect me then I know that he will. He has no reason to lie to me, and everything that he has done, he did because of Joe. Joe has taken everything from me, and he destroyed Jude's family. In a way, we are united over a common enemy.

I need Jude's protection, but this is only for now, not forever.

I turn around and make my way back to the house. I can already imagine the smug expression on his face as I trample through the undergrowth.

When I break through the tree line, I glance at the front of the house. The house that has been my prison for the last two weeks.

There's a lone figure sitting on the porch, and a steady stream of smoke billows around his face, catching on the breeze.

As I approach the porch, Jude looks up at me, taking another slow drag of his cigarette.

"I..." I don't know what to say. "I can't...I have nowhere to..." I choke on a sob as tears once again prickle my eyes.

He takes one last drag on his cigarette, then tosses it to the ground with a flick of his wrist. "Hmmm." He presses his hand over his mouth, his fingers brushing over his stubble as his eyes fix on me. "You can't what?"

"I can't leave." I say quietly.

He pulls in a heavy breath. "Then don't." His gaze narrows on me, and he stands.

I drop my gaze to the floor, and nod, more to myself than him.

He rises from his spot on the step and steps towards me. "You may fucking hate me," he reaches out and cups my cheek, "but I *will* protect you from that bastard." He pauses, drawing in a deep breath. "For as long as you want me to. I owe you that."

I burst into tears. God, I'm such a mess. Jude watches me for a second, looking distinctly uncomfortable. Then he steps forward, wrapping his arms around me. He stiffens for a moment before he lowers onto the step and pulls me into his lap like a child, cradling me against his enormous chest. His massive presence making me feel safer than I have any right to feel with him.

Chapter 25
Jude

I sit with Tor, not really knowing what the hell to do. Her fingers twist into my shirt, clinging to me like I might try and leave her.

I know how she feels in this moment. Everything she's known has been destroyed, taken. And that is exactly how I felt when my mother and sister were murdered. It is a helpless feeling, and the thing that fucking guts me the most is the fact that, even though it wasn't my intention, I did this to her. I pull in a hard breath. I cannot abandon her. I will not let life fuck her the way it fucked me. Her entire body convulses as she weeps for what she's lost. And in this moment I have nothing to say. I know no way to help her, and that pisses me off. I am the person who ruined her, and I hate myself for that. I inhale, my fingers combing through her thick hair. "I really am sorry, Tor, I had to," I whisper into her hair, my fingers sweeping through the tangled strands.

Without warning, she buries her face in my shoulder. I can feel her tears on my skin, her heart beating against my chest. She's clinging to the person who has taken everything from her because I am all she has, and that's just fucking tragic. Her fingers dig into my shoulders as loud, pitiful sobs break from her. I hold onto her, burying my face in her hair as my hands clasp the back of her head. I know this should feel wrong, because it is—this brings a whole new meaning to the term fucked-up—but part of this feels right. She feels right to me, and I know that's dangerous, but I can't help it. I give in to the way this feels and lose my bearings. "I will make this up to you," I whisper in her ear.

What the fuck has she done to me?

We stay like that for what feels like hours, and I don't know that she will ever truly come to terms with the fact that she's lost everything she's ever had, but given the choice, I would do the same thing again.

Chapter 26
Victoria

I cling to Jude, because if I don't, I feel like I'm going to fall off the figurative cliff edge that I'm desperately holding onto. None of this is right or fair. I just want to go back. I want to erase the last couple of weeks.

I can't help but picture my sister burying the body of some poor girl whose family will never even know she's dead. Life is so fragile. Everything can change in a heartbeat.

Jude holds me close, everything about him strong and powerful, yet the way he touches me is gentle, almost reverent. I pull my face away from his neck, sniffing away the last of my tears. As his eyes lock with mine, I can't remember a single bloody reason why I should push him away.

I want to hate him. This place has broken me, unleashing horrors that I could only dream of in my worst nightmares. But in the aftermath of those horrors, at a time when I would have broken, when I wanted to give up, he made me fight. He made me take back my power. I may have become tainted in the process, but better to be a tainted survivor than a victim.

What doesn't kill us makes us stronger, and sometimes life doesn't play fair. You have to evolve to survive, and that's exactly what I'm doing. I've evolved. I've become who I need to be in order to survive this, and this girl wants vengeance, she wants blood, and Jude is the very embodiment of both.

"Joe needs to pay for what he did." I hear myself say quietly.

"He will." He nods, brushing a finger across my cheek. A small smile pulls at his lips. "I promise." I nod, because if Jude makes a promise, especially when it involves killing someone, I know he'll do it. "Did you kill Euan?" I whisper.

"Would you prefer me to be a murderer, or a liar?"

"He wasn't dead when I left." He shrugs casually as he glances at his watch. "Pretty sure he's fucking dead now." His voice is utterly cold.

"Good." I hate Euan for what he did to me. I find it ironic that the man who was supposed to love me gave me over to criminals without a second thought. It's warped because at this stage, I think Jude might actually be the only person who gives a fuck about me.

Life is so twisted. Everything's not always as it seems.

My heart is pounding against my ribs as adrenaline courses through my veins. A strong hand wraps around my throat, pinning me to the hard, unforgiving ground.

Hands grope at my naked body, violating me in every way. Tears roll down my temples as a ragged cry slips from my lips.

I can't make out the face of my attacker. I turn my head to the side, instinctively seeking him out. Knowing exactly where he will be, because it's the same place he always is. He stands watching me, but makes no move to help me.

He looks so beautiful, like an angel of death, without mercy or a touch of kindness. His green eyes lock with mine.

"Jude!" I scream at him, begging him to help me.

His lips pull into a cruel smile just as I feel the stabbing pain in my chest. I scream as the pain increases, spreading down my chest and across my stomach. All I can hear is the deep rumble of his laughter, a vicious backing to my agonised screams.

Screaming, I jump awake, sitting bolt upright and dragging air into my lungs frantically. My hands are trembling as I drag them through my hair and hunch forward, pulling my knees up to my chest. I focus on my breathing, deep breath in and out.

I hear footsteps outside the room. The door creaks, and a sliver of light from the hallway breaks the darkness. I see Jude standing in the doorway.

I wordlessly slide out of the bed and make my way to the bathroom. I pull the door closed behind me and rush to the toilet as bile rises up my throat. I swear I can feel Bob's hands on me, his rancid breath on my face. Tears stream down my face as I wretch uncontrollably. I press my hand over my mouth and try to quiet my loud cries. I hate that I've become this pathetic. I stop heaving and slump back against the bathroom wall.

I hear the door click open and glance up to find Jude lingering in the doorway.

"I'm fine." I wave him off.

He sighs and crosses his arms over his bare chest. "Screaming in your sleep sure seems fine," he grumbles.

I glance at him. A loose pair of trackies hang from his narrow hips, and his hair is messy as though he just rolled out of bed. I don't even know where he's been sleeping. He just started sleeping elsewhere...*after*. He steps into the room and drops to a crouch beside me. "Come on. Up."

A frown marrs his features as he grabs my arm, helping me up. He places his hand on the small of my back and guides me to the bed. I pull the duvet up to my neck as Jude perches on the edge of the bed. "You okay?" he asks without looking at me.

I can tell this entire thing makes him uncomfortable. He's not used to asking about anyone else, because he doesn't care. He doesn't care now, but I guess he must feel obligated.

His face turns toward me, his eyes studying me in the dim light from the bathroom.

I roll onto my back, staring at the ceiling. I can feel his gaze burning into the side of my face. "Yeah," I croak. "It's just a bad dream."

I see him nod in my peripheral vision. He moves to get up, and I don't know why, but I panic. I reach for him, wrapping my fingers around his thick forearm. He twists around, glancing over his shoulder at me.

"Wait. Don't leave," I whisper.

He runs his hand over his chest, staring at me for a few seconds. Nodding, he sits on the edge of the bed, eyes locked on the floor. The thought of staying in here by myself makes me panic. "Just...stay in here."

I watch him in the dark. His brow creases as he sighs, settling back against the headboard. He stays there, not saying a word and staring at me for what feels like hours. I feel safe with him, and how twisted is that? Eventually, he lays on his side, propping his head up with his hand and looking down at me.

I close my eyes, suddenly exhausted. I'm tired. I'm tired of the constant internal war that I'm waging with myself, as the old Ria fights to maintain even a shred of the person she used to be.

He gently brushes a fingertip over my cheek. "You *are* stronger than this."

I roll my head to the side and look at him, barely able to make out the outline of his face. "What if I'm not though?" My voice breaks.

His eyes narrow, glinting slightly. "You are." I feel his fingers brush against mine, and I reach for him, for whatever reason...I *reach* for him. He winds his fingers through mine. It's such an innocent gesture for him that, for a moment, I freeze, waiting for the penny to drop. He moves his thumb in circles across the back of my hand, and to my surprise, that feeling eases some of the tension.

"If I could take it back, I would." His voice is so quiet, I'm almost not even sure if I heard him properly.

"I know," I whisper into the darkness, and he squeezes my hand tighter.

"Go to sleep, Tor."

I fall asleep with my hand still entwined with his, and for the first time since the day I was plucked from my perfect life, I don't close my eyes to images of knives and sick, twisted smiles.

I wake the next morning with my face pressed against something hard and hot. I lift my head and glance down at Jude's very bare, very muscled, and very male chest. *Shit*. I try to slide away from him slowly, but his arm is wrapped around my waist. When I try to move, he groans and tightens his hold possessively, pulling me back to him.

I glance down the length of his body and can't possibly miss the bulge tenting the front of his boxers. My thigh is barely a few inches from his package. Oh, my God. I'm wrapped around him like a fucking vine. A slutty vine. I feel my face heat up like a furnace as I try and slowly pull my leg back. His cock twitches and he groans again. He rolls over and bends his knee, pressing his thigh between my legs in his sleep. I squeeze my eyes shut as I try to control my hammering pulse. He moves again, pressing *everything* against me, *everywhere*. My body lights up like a fucking traffic light.

His arm moves across his chest and cups the side of my face, his fingers winding into my hair. Part of me gravitates toward him instantly as that weird pull he has over me kicks in. It's a primal reaction. My hormones are overriding rational thought. At least that's what I tell myself. Yeah, that's it.

He's holding me so close, and his body is like an open flame. I'm burning up. I try to move again, but fucking hell, he's strong. In the end I resort to poking him in the ribs. He grunts and stirs underneath me. I just need to separate my body from his as soon as possible.

Chapter 27
Jude

My eyes slowly come into focus. I squint against the bright sunlight pouring in through the window and realize my fingers are tangled in hair. Tor's warm body is pressed against mine in a death grip. Her legs are draped over me, and her lace-covered pussy is pressed up against my thigh. *Fuck!* I grit my teeth and try to think of anything else, but all of my blood has already shot to my dick, which is so fucking hard it hurts.

She wiggles, trying to free herself from me, and it's really, really not helping matters because every movement just rubs over my skin. Parts of her that don't need to be touching me are all over me, warm and firm. My fingers clench against the soft skin of her neck. I release my hold on her as she presses her palm into my chest to push herself up. Her face is flushed, her eyes wild—a look I find hard to resist. I have to bite back a groan.

I need to move before I do something stupid like fuck her seven ways from Sunday. She sits up and looks away from me, embarrassment written all over her face.

I grab the comforter and pull it over my lap in an attempt to hide the raging erection currently trying to make bail out of my boxers.

"You sleep okay?" I ask, attempting to make this less awkward, but I'd say nothing is going to help that.

She nods quickly, but stays silent.

"Good." I hop up and go to the bathroom. I eye the toilet. There's no way in hell I'm ringing the toilet with a hard-on like this. I stumble to the shower, push the door open, and piss, trying to take a second to calm my dick the fuck down. When I come back in the room she's laying in the bed, staring up at the ceiling like she's horrified. I skim over her body, unable to avoid the perfect little dots hiding beneath the thin cotton shirt she's wearing. *This is fucked up.* She's turned on by me, I'm turned on by her. How much more twisted and warped is my life going to get? She notices me staring at her and quickly yanks the covers over her chest.

She huffs, her face blushing a pale, sex-flush pink.

I run my hand over my bare chest and tap my fingers over the muscle. Her eyes follow my hand, and she swallows hard before slamming them shut. At this point there's no reason to try and hide the fact that I was just staring at her. "Sorry. I've got a fucking dick, you know?" I shrug and shoot her a cocky grin. Her cheeks darken even more as she dips her chin and stares at the comforter.

There's an awkward silence. What the fuck am I supposed to do with her? She doesn't belong in this fucked up shit I call my life. What the hell is she going to do? Stay here, in this house for the rest of her life? What the hell am I doing here? Sleeping with her, fucking making small talk...*just fuck me*. I'm not made to handle a woman. It's foreign to me. Am I just going to cart her around with me every-fucking-where? *Shit*. This entire thing makes my fucking head hurt.

Somebody needs to fucking say something. I narrow my gaze on her. "I've gotta go check on something tonight, and I'm not fucking leaving you here."

"I don't want to go with you to kill people," she grumbles.

"I'm not leaving you here with the other guys, so you don't really have a choice."

I open the passenger side door, and a chilly breeze swings it back just before she steps out. She looks so confused. Like this is the first time she's been outside, and I guess, in a way, it is her first time. This is the first time since she was taken that's she's been off of my property, the first time she's been anywhere since she no longer has anything to call her own.

Grabbing her hand, I squeeze it as a reminder of how serious I am. "Now, like I said on the way over here, if anyone asks, you're a date."

"Yeah," she flattens out her shirt. "Great!"

The gravel crunches beneath my boots as we walk across the dim lot. The light from the sign flickers, and she glances up as she swats her hair from her face. "A bloody strip club? *This* is where you take girls on dates? Wow, keeping it classy."

"You've no idea how classy I am." I wrap my arm around her waist and pull her into me. She shoots an unnerved look up at me. "Well, gotta make it believable," I say with a shrug.

The steroid-enhanced bouncer manning the front door nods as he sees us approach. "JP. Haven't seen you in a while." His eyes dart down to Tor and his lips curl up. "How come you always have attractive women with you?" Leaning in to her, his voice lowers. His eyes meet mine, and I stare him down as I possessively pull her closer into me. "Don't you know what a piece of shit he is?" he chuckles.

She feigns a laugh. "I keep telling him he's an arsehole."

"A sexy voice too," he groans, his eyes seeming to reassess her.

I usher her in and we're swept up by the rumble of dance music. Men whistle and shout as half-naked women twist around poles. I pull her through the group of overweight, middle-aged men gathered around one of the booths toward the hallway leading to the dressing rooms. I push open the door and Tor yanks back on my hand. "Come on," I say and drag her in the room, pulling the door shut behind her.

The group of nearly naked girls primping and standing in front of the mirrors look over at us. Every last one of them glares at Tor, eyeing her before trailing their gaze over to me and smiling.

"I need you to watch her," I say and step toward the door.

Ginger tosses her blonde curls behind her shoulder. "What in the--"

I cock a brow. "Just watch her."

Ginger shrugs, tapping her brush against her palm as she cocks her hip to the side.

"I'll be back in a few minutes," I say, stepping out. I walk out into the club and take a seat in front of the stage, settling back as I glance at my watch. The lights flicker and one of the dancer struts out onto the platform, spotting me and winking.

I keep glancing at my watch as girl after girl comes out on stage. The fucker I'm supposed to meet is thirty minutes late. With each passing minute, I'm growing more agitated.

Just as a song comes to an end, I feel a tap on my shoulder and look over it to find one of the club bouncers.

"The guy's here. Up at the bar." He points. "Red shirt."

I glance back at the bar and spot the man I'm supposed to meet. He's leaned against the bar, nervously bouncing his leg. He's scrawny and dressed in a golf shirt and slacks. He looks like a fucking tool. I exhale and rise, squaring my shoulders as I push through the crowd.

I stop behind him, and he must feel my presence because he slowly turns, his head tilting up to look at me. "Uh...I'm, I'm..." he stumbles over his word and swallows. "JP?"

"Yeah." I feel my jaw twitch.

"I'm Big Ole' Boy--"

I shake my head and glower at him. "Don't ever use your handle like that, dipshit."

His eyes widen and he quickly nods. "Yeah, sorry."

I clasp my hand over his shoulder and squeeze harder than I should. "You got my money?"

He reaches into his pocket and pulls out an envelope. I sit on a barstool and drag the envelope across the bartop. I pull the flap open and dump the cash onto the counter. The man's eyes nearly bulge out of his head as he nervously glances around the bar like he expects a SWAT team to swarm in at any second.

"Relax," I groan as I spread out the cash and count it. I lock my eyes on him, glaring. "You fuck around like that again and make me wait on my money and I'll cut your fucking balls off. Got it?"

He nods, cautiously backing away from the bar.

"And don't run late to another appointment with me," I continue to hold his stare as I pull a cigarette from my pocket and light it. "It's fucking rude," I snarl, smoke billowing from my lips. The guy's just standing here frozen in place looking at me like I'm the fucking Wizard of Oz. "Fucking go!" I shoo him with my hand and he quickly turns to leave.

Pinching the cigarette between my lips, I mumble, "Dumbass," as I stack the bills together, I glance up to the stage and watch one of the girls swing around the pole as I pull my wallet from my pocket. I take another puff and cram the money inside as I make my way back to the dressing room.

I have the cigarette halfway to my lips when I open the door, and I freeze in place. Tor's sprawled out on the sofa, legs draped over the arm, with a near empty bottle of tequila clutched in her hand, and a drunk grin plastered to her face. She glances up at me and rolls her eyes as she waves her hands through the air. "Dum, dum, duuum!"

I pull in a long drag and arch a brow at her. "Really?" I ask stepping toward her and snatching the bottle. "Who the fuck gave her liquor?" I look accusingly around the room at the girls who are all giggling. I drop my smoke into an empty glass and shake my head.

One of them shrugs. "Coco thought it'd be fun to see a British chick drunk."

Slapping my palm over my forehead, I groan. "For fuck's sake."

"You need to improve your vocabulary." Tor slurs. "It's always fuck this, fuck that. So angry." She shakes her head.

Coco walks past me, swaying her hips and smiling. "She's funny. I like her, she's got some spunk," she says as she leaves the room.

Tor grins. This is going to be a fucking ball ache for sure. "All right. Come on. Time to go."

She staggers to her feet and stumbles away from me. "Nooo!"

Is she trying to fucking run? Fucking hell

I exhale, preparing to throw her over my shoulder and cart her drunk-ass out, when the announcer comes over the speakers. "And please welcome the lovely Miss Coco Chanel to the stage."

Tor jumps up, squealing. "Oh, I promised Coco I'd watch her dance. I need some money to put in her *panties.*" She darts to the door, her shoulder slamming into the frame as she runs out.

"What the..." I walk out after her, shaking my head.

She makes a beeline for the stage and plops down in an empty seat. Tor glares at me, looking around before her eyes fall back on mine. A guy near us turns and drags his eyes over her body before winking at her. He's blatantly undressing her with his eyes. She scowls at him.

"All right, let's go." I reach down to grab her hand and she snatches it away from me.

She rolls her eyes. "I can't believe that *I* am having to try and convince *you* to drink and watch strippers."

"Fine." I shrug and take a seat in the chair next to her.

226

The guy gawking at her whistles. "Hey, sweet thing, you gonna crawl up there and show them girls how it's done?" he slurs, swaying in his chair.

Tor nervously laughs and scoots her chair closer to me, and the guy keeps staring. He stands and she immediately hops up and drops in my lap. I frown and tilt my head to look at her. "Excuse me?"

She leans in close to me, her hands flat against my chest. The smell of tequila nearly knocks me out of my chair. "That guy is creepy," she whispers, her breath blowing over my neck. The fact that I am now her safety is beyond fucked up. I shift her weight in my lap.

I place my hand on her leg and glare at the guy. His eyes immediately redirect to the stage. Her eyes drop to my hand. "Would you get your hand off of me?"

"Relax, Tor." I lean in to her ear. "You put yourself here, don't blame a guy for taking advantage. I promise I won't bite." I whisper teasingly as I place my hand on her thigh. "Try to relax, maybe even enjoy yourself."

She eyes my hand on her leg. "I'm pretty bloody sure that's something the devil says to you when he welcomes you to hell." She huffs then glances back over to the guy still eyeing her. "And just so you know, I'm only sitting on you so I don't get raped."

Smiling, I sweep her hair to the side. "Well, at least you think I won't do that." I hold my gaze with hers, watching her.

A giddy squeal comes from behind me. "JP!" I turn, coming eye level with a pair nipples at attention.

"You don't come around as much as you used to. It makes all us girls sad." Tara leans over and presses a kiss to my cheek as her eyes fix on Tor. "Is this your new girl?"

"Not exactly." I angle my head to look at Tor and catch her roll her eyes.

"Oh, Crystal's gonna be *so* mad at you!" Tara bats her fake eyelashes. "Want some drinks?"

Tor hiccups, and I pull in a breath. She's fucking drunk as piss, and I'm going to *need* a drink to handle her for the thirty minute drive back home. "Get me a whiskey, would you?"

Tara nods and trots over to the bar. Tor glares at me, crossing her arms over her chest. "Where's my drink?"

I cock a brow at her. "You already had your bottle. You don't need another drink. You'll just throw up."

"I haven't had nearly enough," she grumbles. "At least not enough to deal with this hell hole."

Just as Tor mumbles that, Tara leans in with a tray of drinks. She looks Tara over from head to toe. "Tell Caleb to call me, would you?" Tara says.

"Yeah, sure."

She struts off, shaking her ass as she makes her way over to a man holding out a fistful of cash. "Oh, bloody hell no! Not Caleb." Tor shakes her head. "Please tell me he's not sticking his dick in that nasty shit."

I laugh and squeeze her thigh, allowing my eyes to drift up to the girl on the stage. "Oh, come on, now. All men fuck strippers."

"Gambling, murder, and whores. Might as well complete the repertoire, I guess."

I direct my attention back to her. "Would you expect any less of me?"

She shrugs, slowly moving my hand from her leg and placing it on the arm of the chair. "My expectations of you are extremely low, Jude."

Ain't that the fucking truth?

"So"—I arch a brow at her—"how's *hell* treating you?"

"Hell has tequila. It could be worse." She shrugs and pets my cheek like a damn dog "You're an arsehole, but you're a really pretty arsehole," she slurs, the scent of tequila blows across my face.

Fucking hell. She's soused.

Chapter 28
Victoria

"You're drunk."

I toss my head back, laughing. "Shit, I need to be drunk around you. Hell, someone just hook me up to a fucking drip. Make this shit permanent."

He slumps back against the chair, running his fingers through his short hair and sighing. "Fuck. I have a feeling you're gonna be even more annoying drunk than sober."

"Nope." I pop the 'p' at the end of the word, and that causes him to narrow his eyes on me, almost condescending. "Drunk Ria is finding *you* much more tolerable."

I try to focus on what I know will be a scowl on his face, but my vision is still blurred. Fuck, I'm more pissed than an owl in socks. Not my brightest idea.

"Let's see how long it takes drunk *Tor* to throw up." The bastard is smirking over his glass at me.

A waitress, if you could call her that, prances over, stopping behind us. She tosses her bleached-blonde hair behind her shoulder and wiggles her hips. I can't help but watch her boobs. They're bigger than my bloody head. I place a hand each side of my head and try to compare it. Jude cocks an eyebrow at me. *What?* I mouth at him.

"Would you like some more drinks, JP?" she asks.

"Yes!" I shout, at the same time as Jude growls no. I shove my erect middle finger in his face as I smile at the waitress. "Tequila!"

Another annoyed groan rumbles out of him, and he's rubbing both his hands down his face. I swear to God, he sounds like an animal, like an actual growling, snarling animal. The waitress scurries away, fake boobs bouncing as she goes. I don't blame her. Cheery here isn't exactly the best company.

He points at me. "*You* don't need another fucking drink, woman. Your fucking eyes are crossing already!"

"I can still see and hear you, which means I haven't had nearly enough to drink." I smile and turn up my empty glass.

"Oh," he nods, one brow arching, and I can't tell if he's angry or challenging me. "You want to get drunk? I'll get your ass drunk." He grabs a waitress passing by. "Six shots of tequila."

I watch the waitress nod and prance off. "Fina-fucking-lly," I drawl. "You're so....gnarly all the time."

I catch a slight grin flicker over his lips. "Hmm," he laughs. "Don't really know any other way to be, doll."

Two hours and fuck knows how many tequila shots later, and I'm so pissed that even arsehole extraordinaire over here isn't seeming that bad. In fact, he's looking pretty fucking hot. I squint and focus on his bulging biceps, the ink of his tattoos bringing a whole new level of sexy badass to the table.

"You're really hench," I slur as I hang off Jude's arm. We're leaving apparently, but it's slow progress. I can't feel my legs...or my face...or anything, really. I'm beautifully numb, and everything just seems so much better.

"Hench?" He glares at me, dragging me toward the door. "Would you speak fucking English?"

"Muscley. Pretty." I grope at his arm. "You're really pretty."

He's so pretty. I want to touch him. I reach out and stroke his face.

"Okay." He jerks his head away. "I'm not a fucking dog," he says, and then proceeds to stumble into the wall.

I laugh, and point at him. "You are definitely a dog...and a rat. A drunk rat." *What am I even talking about?*

He slumps against the wall, mumbling as he pulls his phone from his pocket. "Fuck, I can't drive." He fumbles with his phone and drops it onto the lobby floor. "Shit."

I bend down and pick it up, dropping onto my arse. I squint at the bright screen, trying to get my eyes to focus. "I can't see! Fuck!"

He eyes me, his gaze narrowing. "That voice of yours..." he groans, taking the phone from my hands and placing it to his ear.

"Hey, I need you to come get me." There's a brief pause. "Just come get me. I'm at the titty bar." He groans and shoves his phone back in his pocket. He shakes his head and looks around. "You can't be all sprawled out on the floor of my club." Bending over, he picks me up and slings me over his shoulder. "You need fresh air anyway." He carts me out of the doors and into the parking lot.

"Jude." I try to struggle, but I can barely lift my own arm. The air is cold, but I can't feel it. I have my alco-jacket. I have to close one eye to see straight. The club gets farther away as we move deeper into the shadows. His breathing is ragged and with each step his grip on my thigh tightens. He stops under the shadow of a tree. I can't see anything and I have to squint in the dim light from the club. We're far enough away that no one can hear us. No one can see us.

He puts me down, my body sliding over every inch of his on the way down. I wobble slightly and his arms tighten around me, pulling me against him. He says nothing for what feels like forever. His eyes are locked on mine, a dim green in the fading lights of the car park. His hand moves, his fingers inching under the hem of my top to brush the skin at the small of my back. My skin prickles under his warm touch. I'm drawn to him like a moth to a very sparkly, very pretty flame. *What the fuck?* I frown as I try to work through my tequila-induced fog. *What am I doing here? How did this happen? Shit. How much did I drink?* You know it's too fucking much when the murderous psychopath is starting to look appealing. *Well, technically he's my protector now. Does that make it okay? Fuck knows.* My drunken mind can't work this out right now.

He bends forward, his lips brushing my earlobe as he speaks. "I can practically hear you thinking, Tor." Brushing his index finger across my forehead, he smooths out the frown lines. His breath blows across my face. The scent of tequila and tobacco invade my senses, causing my head to spin. I cling to him, not because I'm drunk, but because I want to, and that right there scares the shit out of me.

He pulls back and his eyes flick down to my mouth. He closes his eyes on a groan as though he's struggling with something.

"What am I thinking?" I blurt, my voice husky, like some kind of bloody sex phone hooker.

His lips pull up in a wicked smile. My breath hitches in my lungs. Oh, God, that smile makes my heart stutter and then break into a sprint.

His hand moves to the nape of my neck, grabbing a fistful of my hair. "I'll tell you what I'm thinking." He slams me against the trunk, the rough bark scraping against my skin. His breath touches my neck and I shiver violently. His teeth skim over my pulse before he bites down.

I groan, and my back bows away from the tree, scrambling to get closer, demanding more.

I can't control myself. I just want him, and I don't care about the complications or the consequences. I gasp as his body presses against mine. He releases my hair and his fingers skim down my neck, gripping it lightly, dominating me with every breath. My pulse skyrockets as my body basks in his dominance. I can feel every hard inch of him, the heat of his body through his shirt, his warm breath touching my lips, his fingers digging into the skin of my throat. He's everywhere. I can't escape him. I should be scared of him, but I'm not. I could blame the tequila, but can't deny that he affects me.

His hand creeps down my chest, skimming over my breasts, gliding down my stomach. He grips between my legs, squeezing through my jeans. I roll my hips into him, desperate for some pressure. *Something!* His breath caresses my neck as he kisses over the place he just nipped. My nails dig into his skin, raking over the back of his neck as my skin breaks out in goose bumps.

With a growl, he grabs a handful of my hair, wrenching my head back. He tightens his arm around my waist and pulls me up on my tiptoes, crushing his lips to mine. My fingers tug at his shirt, in a desperate bid to get closer to him. I want more. I need more. My body feels like it's on fire. I can't breathe properly. His tongue teases my lips, and my lips part.

"Fuck," he growls against my mouth before I feel his teeth bite my bottom lip. He tugs at it gently and pushes his body harder, if that's even possible, against mine.

I moan and claw at him like a bitch in heat. *Fuck me.* I have no shame right now, and I can't even be embarrassed about that.

He rolls his hips against me, grinding his erection against my stomach. "Damn it," he hisses over my lips. He grips my waist, lifting me and pinning me to the tree with his hips.

My legs clamp around his waist and his fingers grip my thighs, digging into my skin. He buries his face in my neck, his lips working down my throat, kissing, nipping, and licking as they go. My head falls back as my hands seem to find their way into his hair, pulling him in, wanting more. I can't seem to get close enough to him. His lips continue their journey until he's biting the tops of my breasts.

"Jude, where the hell are you?" I hear a deep male voice shouting. "Jude?"

Raising his head from my chest, he glares at me. "I'm not done with you. Do you hear me?" he whispers, slamming his lips to mine one last time before slowly releasing me.

I don't answer him. I can't answer him. Shit, I can barely breathe. My heart feels like it's trying to escape from my rib cage, and my knickers are in dire need of replacement.

He takes my hand and pulls me toward the parking lot. I stagger after him on shaky legs. The combination of tequila and Jude's lips have really done a number on my equilibrium. I can see a figure approaching us in the dark, and I instinctively cling to Jude.

"What the hell were you doing?" It's Rich.

"None of your fucking business," Jude says, still pulling me behind him.

I follow him to a truck and he opens the door.

Rich glances at me. "She better not puke in my truck," he groans.

He can go suck a big one. I flick him the bird, feeling very brave with Jude half-sheltering me from his view. I cling to his arm, trying not to sway like the intoxicated mess that I am.

"Just fucking shut up and drive," Jude demands.

As soon as the truck starts moving, I feel myself drifting. I've hit the figurative wall, and I need to pass out. I lay down across the back seat, and let my eyes close. I can hear the low rumble of Jude's voice as he talks to Rich, and some country music playing through the radio. The last thing I hear before I pass out is Jude calling my name.

Chapter 29
Jude

"Tor." I shake her, but she's passed out cold.

"You want me to carry her?" Richard asks.

"No!" I'm too quick with that reply, but I don't want him touching her. "No, just go. I've got this." He's a fucking idiot and would probably come in his pants if her tits rubbed over his shoulder the right way.

He shrugs and turns around, heading to the house. I drag Tor across the back seat by her ankles. She's like a rag doll. Her limbs sway as I scoop her up and throw her over my shoulder to carry her inside the house.

What in the hell am I doing? I take the stairs two at a time until I reach my bedroom. I open the door and throw her unconscious form on the bed.

She groans as her head rolls to the side. "Jude?" she mumbles, her brows pinching together as she squints at me.

I fucking love the way she says my name. I swallow. *I shouldn't have this soft spot for her. I shouldn't be thinking the things I am.* "Yeah?" I sigh.

"Where am I?" She presses her palm to her forehead. "Oh, God, the room is spinning."

"And of course you're gonna vomit, right? Only makes sense." I sit her up, draping her arm over my shoulder as I help her up and cart her dead weight into the bathroom. I flip the light switch and she grumbles. Using her hand, she shields her eyes from the harsh light as I plop her onto the floor in front of the toilet.

"Oh, God," she moans, resting her forehead against the toilet seat. "Why did you let me drink that much?"

"Let you?" I shake my head, starting to argue with her, but why bother? "Fuck, woman, you were necking tequila like it was a damn sport."

"Fuck you," she grumbles.

"If you throw up, then no fucking thank you." I smile. *Jesus, she's a damn mess.*

"Oh, God. I feel so ill." Her knuckles grip the edge of the toilet so violently they turn white.

I hear her sniffle. *What the...is she crying?* I angle my head to look at her. Her face is scrunched up, eyes closed, lip quivering. She's fucking crying; she hasn't even been sick yet...and she's crying.

"Why the *hell* are you crying?" I try not to laugh, but honestly, this shit's funny.

"Shut up. I hate being sick, okay?" Her entire body shakes and her shoulders lurch forward as she heaves.

I lean against the wall and watch her, not exactly sure whether to leave her or stay. After a few moments of retching, she stops, and resumes crying. When she dry heaves again, she dramatically throws herself over the toilet and her hair falls in her face. I roll my eyes, huffing as I step toward her.

"Jesus." I squat down as I pick the sticky, damp hair off her cheek and wrap the rest of her loose hair around my wrist in an attempt to keep it out of the way. "You don't make *anything* easy, do you?"

"Just—" She heaves again. "Just leave," she pants between deep breaths. She tries to push me away, but her movements are weak. Her face is still practically in the toilet.

"If I leave, you'll probably drown."

"Oh, God. I think I'm dying!" She wails, tears streaking her face.

I plop down on the floor and stare at her in amusement. *Is this how all fucking woman are? Dear God. They're fucking insane.* "You are not *dying*. Chill the fuck out."

"I am fucking dying!"

I rub my temples. She gets nearly gutted, and this—vomiting from one too many tequila shots—has her in tears and fearing death is imminent? "You're not fucking dying, not *yet*, at least," I groan. "What kind of fucking doctor were you? Jesus. Since when has tequila been a fucking death sentence?"

Her face doesn't budge from the toilet, but she does wave her middle finger at me. "What would you know?" She spits into the toilet a few times. "You're a cunt!" Her voice echoes from the bowl.

I laugh. That word on her prissy British lips turns me on every damn time.

She sits back on her heels and snatches her hair away from me.

"You done?" I raise a brow at her, tapping my fingers over the floor. She looks like shit glaring at me with bloodshot eyes.

"Come on. Up." I pick her up and flush the toilet before walking her to the sink. I turn the water on and point to the basin. She's stumbling around like she's about to fall over. "You gonna wash the puke off your face or what?" I ask.

I open one of the drawers in the vanity and rummage through, grabbing a toothbrush. I run it under the water, slather some toothpaste on it, and hand it to her. "Is this what it's like to have a kid?" I groan. "Damn. Here. Brush your teeth too."

She takes it from me, swaying back and forth while attempting to flash me a scathing look. It's more of a drunken squint. She holds the toothbrush in her hand and stares at it like she has no clue how to fucking use it.

I wave my hands at her like a fucking orchestra conductor trying to teach a bunch of idiots to play Bach. "Aaaand brush..."

"Why are you still here?" she moans. "I can brush my bloody teeth. Get out!"

"Just brush your teeth, Tor." I walk to the toilet and pull out my cock to take a piss. As soon as the piss hits the water, she slowly turns her head, blue foam all over her lips.

Her eyes widen and her jaw drops. "*What*...are you doing?"

I step back farther from the toilet, still aiming the steady stream as I smile at her. "Taking a piss. See?" I shake it, then put the seat back down. "My bathroom. I piss when I feel like it. I'm going to bed." I grin as I peel my clothes off, making my way to the bed and flopping down.

"You're repulsive, you know that, right? I cannot believe you just got that thing out in front of me."

I crumple the pillow up underneath my head. *Will she ever shut the fuck up?* "God!" I groan.

She stumbles into the room a few minutes later with her top wrapped around her neck and her arms in the air. Is she serious right now? I shouldn't laugh, but fuck. She's like a damn kid when she's drunk. I sigh and get out of bed, yanking the top over her head.

"I had it," she grumbles.

"Uh-huh. Looked like you had it." I pull a t-shirt from my dresser and toss it at her before climbing back into bed. "And don't worry. I'm not watching you." I roll over, facing away from her, and hear her stomping around as she tries to get dressed. She's mumbling to herself. God only knows what the hell she's saying.

A few seconds later, the other side of the bed dips under her weight. I lean over and switch the lamp off, plunging the room into darkness. Within minutes her breathing evens out and becomes heavy and I'm...wide awake.

Every tiny movement she makes is magnified. I'm hyper-aware of her presence, and so is my dick. What the actual fuck have I done? I must be a masochistic fucker to sleep next to the woman that only hours ago had me so hard-up I slammed her against a tree, ready to shove my cock in her as she dry-humped me like a two-dollar hooker. She's hot, plain and simple, and my dick seems to feel the need to remind me of this fact...often. The longer I think about having her against that tree, the harder I get. *This is fucking ridiculous.* My eyes trail over to her. I watch her chest rise and fall in deep swells, and I'll be damned, every time those fuckers move, her tight little nipples poke through the thin undershirt she's wearing. That sight makes my dick twitch like it's going to explode.

I lay in the darkness, just staring at the ceiling. A few minutes ago I was dog tired, but now...now, sleep is the *last* thing on my mind. I reach down and rearrange my dick. Just that brief touch has my cock begging for more. *Fuck this.* I climb out of the bed, my boxers pitching a tent as I stumble toward the bathroom. I leave the door cracked just enough to see her. Fuck it if she wakes up. It's her fault I have this hard-on.

I lean one hand against the wall, peeking out at her as I sneak my hand beneath the elastic of my boxers, fisting my hard cock. I imagine her thighs wrapped around my waist as I viciously grind my cock against her pussy. I can almost hear the little moans she makes, practically taste the tequila on her tongue. I run my thumb over the head and it glides over the drop of pre-cum. *Fuck.* I can only imagine how damn good it would feel to actually have my dick *in* her. I give myself one long stroke and immediately feel everything in me relax. Picking up the pace, I push off the wall, turning to lean my back against it as I reach down and grab my balls. I tug harder and faster, massaging my balls as I think about how damn good it felt having her all over me.

I imagine what she would look like on her knees, with those fucking lips wrapped around my cock, my hand fisted in her hair while I fuck her face until she gags. I'm frantic at this point. My hand is loudly slapping against my lower stomach. The fact that she's completely unaware that I am beating my shit like it owes me money makes me even more frantic.

I barely hear her talking in her sleep. "Jude," she whispers, followed by a soft, feminine, incredibly sexy moan. And that's it; I feel my balls tighten and my entire body tenses like a coiled spring. I go off like fucking Mount Vesuvius. It's been awhile since I've been teased like this, which means shit goes every-fucking-where. *Holy shit!* My body tenses and jerks with aftershocks, my head slamming against the wall as I try to catch my breath.

"Jude..." she mumbles, which snaps me out of my fog. "Please..." Her voice trails off and I can barely make out her begging, and not the good kind of begging.

I grab a towel and wipe myself off. She mumbles my name again and whimpers. I step back into the room, and climb across the bed, brushing her hair from her face as I lay down next to her. She quiets and turns into my neck.

I don't know what the fuck I'm getting into here. I just have this unexplainable urge to fix her, which is fucking ironic, because I'm usually the one to fuck shit up. It's unnatural for me to care, and I have no idea how to handle it.

I close my eyes, my mind racing. I glance at the clock and minutes fade to hours. Every damn time I close my eyes I see my mom and sister; I hear the screams, my mother begging Joe to not hurt my sister, to let her go. I see Tor crying and bleeding, Euan pleading for his life. For the first time in my life I allow myself to realize that I am the monster in other people's nightmares just like Joe is the monster in mine. I have brutally taken the lives of people, leaving their families with nothing but a fading memory. The people I kill know damn well what they're getting into when they decide not to pay me my money, but their families...that gaping wound ripped into their souls from that loss...that affects me. Since when have I had pieces of me that give a fucking damn? I don't want to give a damn, but Tor fucking makes me. Her being here has chipped away at me, caused me to re-evaluate everything. I roll onto my side, and instead of an empty space, there she is. She's like a physical fucking conscience that I can't ignore. I stare at her silhouette and my mind comes to a gridlock. This woman has changed everything in my life. In a matter of weeks she has created a fucking war inside me. She makes me question who the fuck I am.

I trace my fingertip over her arm. She's something I'm not used to, something that almost doesn't seem real. She is light in this pit of blackness. She's an angel surrendering to the unforgiving flames of hell, and in no way is that right.

She sighs and tosses in her sleep. She is so much more than what she's been reduced to. She's in my bed because she's afraid to be anywhere else; really, because she has nowhere else to go. She's been given freedom, but she's chosen to remain captive. She's that wounded that a heartless bastard like myself seems like a haven. I draw in a heavy breath, the scent of her drowning me.

I am all she has.

Having one person, that's a shitty destiny.

I will keep her safe, and I will fucking slaughter Joe. For my mother, for my sister, for Tor. Right or wrong, I don't fucking care.

Chapter 30
Victoria

Oh, my fucking God. What the hell happened last night? My head feels like somebody just smashed it into a wall. I groan as I roll over, and my stomach follows suit. Ugh, my mouth feels like a badger took a shit in it. I try to open my eyes, but I can't. *Holy shit, I think I'm actually blind! Maybe I've had a stroke. Oh, God. Why is the bed moving? Wait, that's not the bed.* I rub at my eyes and blink. My vision is blurry, but I seem to have an in-depth knowledge of Jude's chest now, and I know that's exactly what is moving beneath me.

I manage to pull away from him without yesterday's limpet display. I groan when I stand up, swaying slightly. I feel gross. I can practically smell the tequila seeping from my pores. Ugh, tequila. Just the thought of it makes my stomach turn.

I wobble to the bathroom and lean over the loo for a few minutes because I'm pretty sure I'm going to hurl. Eventually, though, my stomach calms its shit. A shower, that's what I need. Everything will seem better then. Hell, at least I don't have anywhere to be. Silver lining and all that.

I turn the shower on and let the water warm. I glance at the vanity. I should look awful this morning, but I don't. As always, my eyes drop to the long scar across my throat, only this time, there are two purple marks to the side of it. I touch them gingerly and step closer to the mirror to get a better look. Bite marks, they're bite marks! I remember Jude's body pressed against mine, his lips at my neck, his teeth...My lips are swollen, and my bottom lip is raw.

While part of me is screaming *what the fuck,* there's another part that's like a giddy bloody girl. What the hell is with that? This is Jude I'm talking about here. Giddy should not even be a possibility around that man. He's a killer, a criminal, a man with no morals and few loyalties.

What happened last night should never have happened, so why, when I think of it now, does it make my skin flush and my stomach tighten? I'm so fucked.

I jump into the shower, hoping that the water will strengthen my resolve and give me the will power I need to face Jude this morning...think of the devil, and he shall appear. I hear the bathroom door open, and he steps in. For one awful yet somehow hopeful second I think he might try to get in the shower with me, but he doesn't. I hear the taps turn on, and I think he's brushing his teeth. Then there's the unmistakable sound of him pissing. I roll my eyes. Really? Why can that man not urinate somewhere away from me? I'm

really hoping our drunken bonding ha.
weird barrier whereby we're suddenly .
pissing. Some things are just sacred.

The entire time he's in here, he never says a
my God. Maybe he's ashamed too. I stay in here for ong
time, trying to wash away my shame. There's not enough
water or soap in the world for that, though.

I eventually step out and wrap a towel around me. *Okay,
be brave, Ria*. It's no worse than a one night stand...except
for the fact that I have to spend every minute of every day
with him.

I push the handle down and open the door, stepping
into the room nervously.

I pretty much define awkward right now. I glance up to
see Jude lounging on the bed. The TV is on and he's leant
against the headboard, watching it. I can't for the life of me
tell you what is on the screen because he's almost naked,
except for his boxers. His hands are behind his head, and
every muscle in his torso seems to be popping out in the
morning light. Shit. *Look up!* I scream at myself.

His eyes stray away from the television and land on me.
He grabs the remote and switches the TV off. In the sudden
silence, all I can hear is my own heavy breathing.

He clears his throat. "I'm going to go handle some
things while Caleb gets you breakfast. Oh, and we need to dye
your hair."

"My hair?" The fuck?

He moves off the bed and pulls a t-shirt out of the chest of drawers. "Yeah, your hair. You're dead, remember? Which means the hair is gonna have to be dyed or something. Sorry."

"I thought I was only supposed to be here for three weeks?"

He frowns. "You are. It's just a precaution."

I narrow my eyes at him. "For what? I'm dead, remember? I'm hours from home. No one here knows who I am or gives a shit what colour my hair is."

"Joe knows what you look like." He cocks an eyebrow.

I roll my eyes and move to the bed. I sit in the middle with my legs crossed, watching him. "Great. Well, my old life is ruined. What the hell, I suppose you might as well just destroy my identity."

"Really?" He huffs, crossing his arms over his chest, his biceps straining and stretching the thick ink over his muscles. "Get off the fucking cross." I feel my temper rise to the surface instantly. He has screwed up every aspect of my life.

"Fuck you, Jude! You're a cunt!" I snap.

He laughs humourlessly. "I can't fucking win. I try to kill you, I'm an asshole; I try to save you, I'm a cunt. You want to leave, I let you, and then you come back. What the fuck do you want me to do?"

"Nothing, I want you to do nothing. Just go and take your illegal bets, beat the shit out of some poor unsuspecting bastard, fuck some dirty, AIDSy stripper, hell, drown a kitten..."

He crosses his arms, staring at me with a raised eyebrow. "Drown a fucking kitten? Really?"

"Why do I have to get stuck with you anyway? I want Caleb back. He's nice. He's the only person in this house that isn't a total bloody psycho!"

He taps his foot over the floor as he narrows his gaze on me. "Is this some hormonal female shit? Get that shit under control, would you?" Oh, he did not.

"You!" I scream, crawling onto my knees and moving to the edge of the bed. "Fuck you!" I stab a finger against his bare chest. My boobs are brushing against his stomach, and his eyes instantly drop to my chest. His lips pull up in a smirk, which makes me even more irate. He makes me so bloody angry. I slap his chest, the sound ricocheting around the room.

His eyes narrow, the only warning I get before he grabs my wrists and pushes me back on the bed, pinning my hands above my head. He kneels over me, his face inches from mine. "You done yet?" He growls. I don't answer him. "I would have thought you'd have learned by now not to slap me." He comes even closer to me. "Don't fucking do it again." His voice is a deep rumble that has my skin breaking out in goose bumps, even as it feels like I'm over-heating.

"Or what?" I challenge, before I can even stop myself.

He growls, and one by one the fingers of his free hand move around my throat. He stares at me, his breathing ragged. "Don't test me, Tor."

There's a moment of silence. A moment where I should be scared. A moment where I should apologise, try and get him off me, but I don't. I don't, because some warped part of me wants Jude. A dark, twisted corner of my mind revels in the danger that he represents and rises to the challenge. I'm all too aware of how wrong that is. I have lost everything, and in having nothing to lose, the danger he promises has become an adrenaline shot to my broken and dying soul.

His thumb brushes against my skin as his eyes lock with mine. I can feel his even breath on my lips, his warm fingers tightening around my throat. "Or maybe you want to test me? You like being strangled, Tor?" His voice is husky and raw, sex, laced with danger and possibility.

His lips are so close to mine. My eyes flick to his mouth as a blush creeps over my cheeks. I can remember the way his lips felt on mine last night, his teeth nipping at my throat, his tongue skimming my lips. Our eyes lock, and I watch as that familiar volatile anger gives way to a very male lust. My pulse skitters wildly as he releases my throat and grips my jaw, tracing his thumb over my bottom lip. "You have no idea how many times I've pictured these lips wrapped around my cock," he grates.

I should be repulsed. I should be offended, but I'm not. My breath hitches and my lips part as I try to drag more oxygen into my ailing lungs. A small smile pulls at his lips before he leans forward, his lips brushing mine as he talks. "I want to corrupt all this innocence right here."

And I want him to corrupt me.

I can't take his teasing. I move, pressing my lips against his like the wanton slut that I've apparently become. He releases my chin, his fingers winding into my hair and pulling at the roots hard as his tongue dives into my mouth. My back bows off the bed, trying to get closer to him as my legs spread shamelessly, inviting him between them.

He releases my wrists, moving down my arm and over my body, leaving a trail of fire. His teeth nip at my lip, leaving a sting. I moan against his mouth and he lets out a throaty chuckle as he grabs my knee, hitching it over his hip. He rolls his hips, grinding his hard cock against my pussy, and even the thin pair of lace knickers I'm wearing feel like a fucking chastity belt right now. His lips, his hands, his cock; he uses every weapon in his arsenal to wind me so tight that I'm sure I'm going to snap.

My hands work over his chest, his back, his arms, clawing at the thick muscles. I want more. I need more. He rolls his hips again and my nails dig into his skin, making him hiss.

"You want me?" he rumbles.

I can barely form words. "Yes," I choke out.

"Then fucking beg me for it, Tor," he growls against my ear.

"Please," I moan like a dirty whore.

I can't see his lips, but I can tell from his eyes he's smiling. "Please what, doll?" His voice is a mixture of lust and amusement.

I slap at his chest. "Jude!" His lips cut me off as his tongue dives into my mouth.

His lips have barely touched mine when he tears away from me, rearing up onto his knees. "That's not begging, Tor," he says as he jerks my legs further apart, dragging me down the bed to him. "Beg me!" he demands.

"Fuck you!" I snap. I'm so turned on I can barely function, and he wants me to beg! He's a sick bastard.

"Oh, I intend to," he laughs as he rips my knickers from my body, the material biting into my skin. His eyes move between my legs, and he bites his lip. "Goddamn." I can feel my cheeks heating as my vagina gets the third degree. I'm almost as embarrassed as I am turned on. His hands grip the insides of my thighs, spreading them wide.

"I have pictured fucking this pussy so many times." His expression is pure sex and sin. The devil himself, luring me into hell. At this stage I want to dance around the fucking fire with him.

"Every damn time you run that smart mouth, it makes me want to fuck you raw." He growls as he traces a finger over me before plunging inside. He leans forward, dragging his tongue over my throat. "I'm gonna fuck you until you're so raw, you won't be able to sit down without feeling me," he breathes, thrusting another finger into me.

My hips buck uncontrollably as a ragged groan breaks from my lips. He's brutal and unforgiving, as he is with everything. He pulls his finger out of me, immediately placing it to his lips and slowly sucking it in. He holds my gaze the entire time. Oh, dear God. I throw my head back against the mattress, my chest heaving.

"Fuck me!" I hear myself say. I hear his throaty laugh before he grabs me by my hips, his hold almost bruising. I hear a rustle of material, followed by the ripping of foil, and then he's there, the head of his cock probing at my pussy, begging for entrance. I've never felt this all-encompassing need to have a man inside me, but right now, I just want him, all of him, everything he has to give and more. He lights a fire in me that cannot be extinguished, and in this moment I'm consumed by it.

I press my heels into the bed, pushing up against him. He hisses as he slides inside me. He feels so good, so right.

"Careful. I promised I'd fuck you raw, and I will," he growls, grabbing both my hips and slamming into me. I cry out as he hits the pleasure pain barrier. My body tightens and contracts around him, adjusting to the intrusion. He hovers over me, panting through gritted teeth. "God-fucking-damn, your pussy is something else." He shakes his head.

He stays still for a few seconds before he moves. There's no slow build-up, this is primal and dominant. He rears back on his heels, lifting my hips with one hand and holding me down by my throat with the other. His big body moves over mine with powerful thrusts. He fucks me like his life depends on it, as though he is fucking out all his frustrations.

My head falls back and my eyes flutter closed as waves of pleasure start to ripple through my body. His grip on my neck tightens. "Look at me," he snarls. "Watch me fuck you." My eyes lock with his, and I couldn't look away if I wanted to. He fucks me until I'm writhing underneath him, sweating and moaning his name, and when my body tightens and I'm so bloody close, he stops.

"What the fu—"

He leans over me, lowering his lips to mine. "Beg. Me," he whispers.

I'm so tightly wound, so desperate. He's a bastard. I glare at him and defiantly roll my hips against him. He smirks, and starts to move again. He thrusts in and out of me until again, I'm about to come, and again, he stops.

"I swear to fucking God, Jude!" I shout.

"Beg me." He smiles like the devil that he is.

Fuck it, I'll take one for the team, and when I say team, I mean me and my vagina. I throw as much sex into my voice as I can whilst flashing him a smug smile. "*Please*, Jude. Please fuck me until I come all over you."

That does it. His eyes darken as a guttural growl rips from his throat and he pounds into me. Holy shit, he's like a rabid animal. Everything tightens, and this time he doesn't stop. His fingers tighten around my neck and pleasure explodes across my body. I scream his name as my vision threatens to black out. I feel his fingers dig hard into the flesh of my hip as he lets out a long groan and stiffens between my thighs before falling on top of me.

I can't breathe, and I can barely see as stars dot my vision. Jude rests his forehead between my breasts, still covered in his shirt. Holy shit, he fucks like he does everything else, with total volition and brutal control.

He sits up and pulls out of me, rising to his feet. He says nothing, simply discards the condom and pulls up his boxers before putting on a shirt and a pair of jeans.

"You *are* dying your hair," he says before leaving the room and closing the door behind him.

I sit up and wince. As promised, he did indeed fuck me raw.

What the hell just happened? Since when did the man I hate become the man I want? He's an arsehole, a criminal. I should feel ashamed and yet I don't, I can't. Maybe because every ounce of decency has been stripped from me in this place. Ria never would have fucked Jude, but Ria is gone. The person I was has been taken from me. I'm now the product of what they have made me, what Jude has made me. Ria wouldn't have fucked Jude, because she was scared of him, but Tor would, I would, because I'm a woman without a cause.

Chapter 31
Jude

As soon as I shut the door, I shake my head. *What in the fuck was that?*

All I can manage to do is stand in the hallway. My head is spinning. My breath is ragged. No woman has ever made me feel like that. I couldn't possibly get deep enough in her, touch her enough. That felt right, and it shouldn't. Not one thing about that should come close to feeling right because she's been completely fucked in the head. She doesn't know her ass from her elbow right now. She's been ripped from everything she knows and left with nothing but me. I'm the fucking devil and god at the same time to her because I am the only person who even knows she exists. It's nothingness, or me.

I want to be angry, but I can't. Part of me wants to turn back around and fuck her until she can't fucking see straight. I want to fuck her until she begs me to stop. Fuck, I feel like she just bled into me, and that's not good. The last thing I want is for her to end up believing she belongs here with me.

No woman belongs with me, or in this lifestyle. None. Especially not one like her.

I inhale, gripping the railing tightly as I wind my way down the stairs. I grab a bottle of water from the fridge and go into the den, plopping on the couch next to Caleb.

"Georgia's winning," Caleb mutters.

I glance at the screen and nod. "Yeah."

"John Duglas hasn't paid. Richard said John told you to fuck off."

"Yeah," I mumble, staring blankly at the screen.

"Yeah? He told you to fuck off, and you say 'yeah.'" I glance at him and he lifts a brow, waiting for me to respond. "What the hell's wrong with you? She getting to you that bad?" He laughs, not the slightest idea of how much she's getting to me.

I toss my head back against the cushion and reach for a cigarette. "Not ever met a woman with a temper like hers," I say, pinching the smoke between my lips to light it. That temper makes me want to fuck her into submission every damn time.

"So, she's really just gonna stay here?" He stares blankly at me for a second. "It's nice of you to protect her." He jumps up from the couch and yells at the TV. "Are you fucking insane? That's a flag, dipshit. Dumbass ref!"

I pull in a lungful of smoke. Nice of me? Yeah, I've been a fucking charmer to her, and she's got the psychological and physical scars as a souvenir.

Caleb falls back into the couch. "So, is Ria just gonna stay locked up in your room for however long she decides to stay?

I roll my eyes. I hate that damned name. "Her name's Tor, Caleb. Ria sounds like a fucking bird."

"She likes to be called Ria," he starts to argue, but leans back in the chair and turns his attention back to the TV.

"I left the fucking door wide open, but where else is she really gonna go?"

He's not paying attention to me. He's standing, glaring at the television. "Aw, fuck this. There's no fun in games I'm not betting on." He grabs his keys from the coffee table.

"Where are you going?"

He shrugs. "To the store. Get some food."

I point in the direction of my room. "Take Tor with you."

"Why?" He tosses his hands up.

"Because I said to. I left some hair dye for her, make sure she fucking dyes her hair before she goes out. Let's just say she's not fucking happy about doing it." So unhappy that I had to fuck the temper out of her. Jesus, this is so fucked.

His forehead wrinkles. "What? Why?"

"Don't be a dumbass. We can't take a chance on Joe. It's to cover our own asses." I take a long puff from the cigarette. "Just make sure she does it, and take her with you. She needs to get out."

He narrows his eyes. "Who the fuck are you? She *needs* to get out?" He laughs. "See, she gets to you, doesn't she?" I glare at him, and he holds his hands up. "Hey, I get it. You know I like her. She's crazy, but I like her."

I cover my face with my hands, groaning. This situation I've fallen into is not one I ever intended on being in. Ever.

Chapter 32
Victoria

Caleb holds the door open for me, gesturing for me to get in the car.

"Tell me again why I have to come to the shop with you?"

He flashes me his easy smile. "Apparently you're no longer a prisoner and Jude thinks you need to get out of the house. I knew you'd win him over in the end." He winks at me. I dip my face as I feel my cheeks heat. *Little does he know.*

He slams the door and moves to the driver's side, sliding behind the steering wheel. "I like the hair, by the way."

I pinch a piece of hair between my fingers, staring at the mahogany strands. "Thanks." I hate it. It's just one more part of Ria that is now lost, replaced by Tor, the damaged girl that Jude has turned me into. Yet I willingly bask in his corruption, like some desperate junkie embracing my own destruction.

We drive to the supermarket in silence. I'll admit that although it may be mundane, this small slice of freedom feels liberating.

Caleb doesn't linger, he runs around the shop like it's a bloody hit and run. I have to double check we're not robbing the place.

I glance at the trolley full of beer, pizza, hotdogs, and crisps. *Seriously?* How are these guys still alive? I wrestle the trolley from Caleb and walk off in the opposite direction.

"Ria!" he yells. "What are you doing?"

I glance over my shoulder at him as he huffs after me. "Buying food, obviously, and before you say anything, this is not food."

He flashes me a disgusted look as I head for the vegetable section. "Are you for real? I'm not eating that shit."

"You are not five, Caleb," I sigh.

I move around the shop, ignoring his over dramatic huffing behind me. We pass a small home section, and I spot some picture frames sitting on a shelf. I pick one up and pop it in the trolley.

"Why the hell are we buying picture frames, woman?" he groans. "You're not fucking redecorating!"

"Maybe I'm going to take a picture of you, as a keepsake." I smirk.

He frowns, but says nothing. He's so damn cute sometimes.

"Two hundred dollars!" Caleb shouts, snatching the receipt from me. "This was meant to be a quick trip to the store. Fucking hell."

"Well, if you didn't have five hundred litres of beer, then it wouldn't be two hundred dollars. Now load this shit." I gesture to the shopping cart and laugh at the expression on his face.

He loads the bags and gets into the car next to me. "Never again," he says, shaking his head.

He pulls out of the car park and heads home. I roll my eyes. "You would think I had just tried to wax your nut sack, the way you carry on."

He scowls at me. "You're sick." *Says the guy who helps kill people.*

We're about halfway home, and the buildings are starting to give way to woodland and farmland when I notice Caleb looking agitated. His eyes flick to the rearview mirror and back to the road repeatedly. I turn to look behind us.

"Don't look," he snaps. "They've been following us since we left the store."

I glance in the wing mirror and see a black SUV behind us. I can't make out the passengers. "What are you going to do?" I ask quietly.

"Not lead them back to the house." His face is deadly serious, cold, like his brother's.

"Get the gun outta the glove box," he says, his eyes trained on the rearview mirror.

"I'm not—"

He cuts me off. "I'm not fucking around, Ria. Get it!"

I open the glove box, my hand trembling as I reach for the black pistol. I don't want to touch the damn thing.

"Under the seat, there's a box, get it out," he instructs. I hesitantly reach under the seat and pull out a black box. I open it and several silver bullets fall onto my lap. *Bloody Hell!* I catch Caleb pulling his gun from the waist of his jeans. His finger slowly loops through the trigger. "You need to load that one," he says, his voice too calm.

"I don't know how to load a gun!" I shriek, panic gripping me.

"The button on the side there...push it."

My fingers fumble and I close my eyes as I push the little button. The magazine falls out and I jump.

"Get about ten of the bullets, just push them down in there."

I nervously do as instructed. "Now what?" I ask, staring at the weapon in my lap.

"Slam the magazine in the gun, with your palm."

I attempt to do it, but it won't stay in.

"No, Ria. Fucking hard, like this." He bangs his palm against the end of his gun and I flinch, expecting it to go off. You'd think from all the shit I've endured over the last couple of weeks guns wouldn't still terrify me, but they do.

I manage to snap the magazine in place, my hands shaking so violently, I'm sure I'm going to shoot myself.

"Pull back on the top to put a bullet in the chamber."

I stare at him. "I can't shoot a gun!"

"Well, you're gonna learn because they aren't following us to tell us hello. We're as good as fucked."

He hands me his phone. "Call Jude," he barks, stress marring his features.

I lay the gun in my lap, eyeing it as I fumble with the phone. Caleb pulls off the main road and slams his foot on the accelerator, sending the car bumping down what looks like a farm track. The SUV follows suit, matching our pace. I hear the front bumper smash against a dip as the car gets air.

The phone rings a few times before Jude picks up. "What? I'm busy."

"Jude." I can't hide the panic in my voice. "We're being followed."

"What?" he shouts, the immediate anger in his voice making me tense. The back end of the car slides across the loose gravel, slamming me against the door. "Fuck!" I hiss as pain ricochets up my arm and I drop the phone. The car continues to skid across the road until it bottoms out on the verge, the nose buried in a ditch. Caleb pulls his gun and starts firing through the window at the black truck.

"Ria, move!" he yells. "Get out and get down!" I swing the door open and throw myself on the grass. My eyes fall level with the foot well, where I spot Caleb's phone. I scramble to pick it up as shots ring out around me.

"Jude!" I scream as I press the phone to my ear.

"Where are you?" His voice is low and measured.

"I don't know. We were halfway home, and we passed a farm, and then we took a left onto a gravel track," I ramble. A gunshot pings off the door frame above my head and I scream.

Caleb is hunched down in the seat, but he's going to get himself killed. "Caleb!" I shout at him, but he ignores me.

"Tor," Jude snaps. "You stay down, you hear me?" I can hear a door slamming in the background.

"Okay."

"You got a gun?"

"Yeah."

"Just point and shoot. I'm coming for you." I nod and drop the phone.

"Fuck!" Caleb curses. I glance up and he's gripping his right arm. Blood spreads across the sleeve of his shirt.

"Caleb," I cry out, tears threatening.

"I'm okay, Ria." He hands me the gun and drags himself awkwardly across the centre console. He holds his arm to his chest as he lowers himself to the ground, leaning his back against the car.

"Jude's coming," I tell him.

"Well, by the time he gets here we might be dead. You're gonna have to shoot. Never could shoot worth a shit with my left hand," he laughs.

"What?!" I squeak as bullets continue to rain down on the car. It sounds like really big hail stones and the middle of a firework show.

"Just keep shooting at them. We only have to hold them off until he gets here." I nod and raise the gun Caleb gave me, pointing in the general direction of the shooters. My hand shakes and my breath hitches in my lungs.

Caleb's somehow calm. "Breathe, even breaths. Grip the handle with both hands." I do as he says. "Now squeeze the trigger."

I pull the trigger and the gun explodes in my hand, jarring my elbows. I release a heavy breath.

"Good," Caleb grins. "That's good."

I take steady breaths as the gunfire continues to rain down on us. Caleb hands me another gun and reloads the old one. My nerves are shot and on edge. There's a second of silence and Caleb nudges me, directing my attention to the back of the car. I listen intently, struggling to hear anything over the chaos of gunfire and the hammering of my own heart. Suddenly a guy bursts around the back of the car, gun pointed at me. Everything moves in slow motion. He pulls the trigger at the same time as I do. I hear the whistle of the bullet and the sharp crack as it breaks the air next to my ear. I watch as my bullet hits his chest, and he jerks backwards before hitting the ground. I scramble over to him and take his gun before retreating to my spot behind Caleb once more.

He touches my shoulder and I jump. "You did good, girl." He flashes me a small smile.

I just killed somebody. I should feel something. I feel nothing.

Chapter 33
Jude

Marney swerves, turning onto the dirt trail. Gunfire rings out just as I spot Caleb's car halfway in the ditch. A black SUV sits in the middle of the road with both doors swung wide open, and I don't see my brother or Tor anywhere. My pulse kicks into overdrive, my adrenaline ripping through my veins. I unfasten the seat belt, not allowing the car to come to a full stop before I jump out. All I can hear are the rapid-fire pops from a pistol. I check once more to see if I can locate Caleb and Tor, but I don't have enough time. A bullet whizzes past and dings the hood of my car. I point the gun at the SUV and fire. The guy by the SUV turns, and before he has a chance to pull the trigger, I put a bullet right between his eyes. Gunshots come from behind Caleb's car. A loud boom echoes from the trees as Marney shoots the other man in the SUV. "Fucker," he says, making his way to the bodies, gun still raised.

I jog toward Caleb's car, my blood pulsing through my veins. As soon as I round the trunk, I see Caleb slumped up against the car and Tor fumbling to reload a gun. There's a guy lying on the ground, moaning and clutching his stomach.

My gaze darts to Tor. "Tor!" I shout.

She jumps, jerking the gun in front of her and aiming at me. The pistol shakes in her hands, and I'm afraid she may be so hyped up she'll actually shoot me.

"Hey, put the gun down."

Her eyes dart to the man on the ground, gun still aimed. I inhale, walk over to the guy, and aim at his face. "Fuck you," I mutter, and pull the trigger three times, each times his body jerks.

I glance back at Tor and her face crumples as she points at Caleb. "They shot him."

I look down at him. He's clutching his arm, and his sleeve is soaked in blood. "You okay?"

He glares at me. "Yeah, fucking fantastic." He moves and cringes from the pain. "I couldn't fucking hold the gun after they hit me. It's not bad. Just a pain in the ass."

I look around at the mess surrounding me. The car is fucked with bullet holes. There's two dead guys on the ground, and my little brother's been shot. "Fuck!" I pace through the tall grass. "They're with Joe, aren't they?" I shout at Marney.

He digs through one of the guy's jackets and pulls out an ID. "Simon DeLucas," he says.

I immediately recall Euan sniveling that name out between his ridiculous pleading. "Fuck!"

"I'll take that to mean he's one of Joe's?" Marney looks down at the guy. "Motherfucker," he mumbles, and then puts another bullet in the dead man before walking over to me. "Well, shit. What are we gonna do with this shit right here?" he asks, waving his hand around at the scene.

I pull my phone from my pocket and dial David.

"Hello?"

"I've got a bit of a problem. Two bodies and a car."

"Shit, JP. I'm on patrol. I can get a guy to take care of the cars. Just take the license plate off yours...but you'll have to manage the bodies."

"Yeah, yeah. Okay." I hang up.

I drag my hands through my hair. "We gotta take the bodies back to the house. David can't get them right now."

Marney shrugs and makes his way over to one of the stalky men and grabs his ankles, dragging him through the thick weeds toward the car.

I eye Caleb. He's not going to be any fucking help. "Get in the car, would you?" I tell him before I shoot my gaze to Tor. "And I'm gonna need your help, doll."

Her eyes flick from me to Marney, who's pulling the body across the road and whistling to himself. "No." She shakes her head. "Nuh-uh. I am not dealing with this shit." There's an edge of hysteria to her voice as she starts backing away from me.

I pull a cigarette from my pocket and light it. I wrap my arm around her shoulders as I hand the cigarette to her. "I

272

always have a smoke after I shoot someone. Here, it helps." I shove it in her face and she glares at me. "No? Okay then." I take a long drag and blow the smoke at her, which apparently just pisses her off.

She shoves at my chest. "Seriously? Do you have absolutely no sense of danger, or a moral compass? You're fucking insane!"

"I think you know the answer to that better than anyone." I toss the cigarette to the side of the road. "All right," I say, wiping my palms down the leg of my jeans. I walk to the trunk of the car and help Marney haul the man inside.

We make our way back to the other guy, and I stare at him. This fucker must weigh nearly four hundred pounds. Marney crosses his arms, his eyes trained on the massive man laid out in the grass.

"Little darlin' over there better suck it up."

I chuckle and glance back at her. "Hey little darlin'," I sing out. "Need a hand over here."

She places her hands on her hips and cocks an eyebrow. "You want me to touch a dead fat man?"

"Isn't that what you went to school for?" I can't help but laugh. She looks so damn pissed.

"Oh, yes, Jude. I went to school so I could shoulder press morbidly obese corpses!" Her voice grows more hysterical as she goes on.

"You're being a ball-ache. Just come get his ankles, unless you want to hang out here to see if Joe likes you better as a brunette?"

"You mean his kankles." She narrows her eyes at me. "You want my help?" She raises an eyebrow. "*Beg* me."

Oh, fuck no! I feel the smile fade from my face as I glare at her.

I lean down to grab one of the man's arms. "Unlike you, I don't fucking beg." I smirk. "Now come grab a kankle, would you?"

She stomps over to us like a fucking kid that's not getting their way. Huffing, she bends down to grab one of the man's legs.

"Well," Marney says, grinning like a shit-eating bastard, "looks like you two have been getting along better than you should."

"Oh, dear God," she whines. "He smells so bad, and that's not even the stench of death." She looks utterly disgusted.

We pick the man up, struggling to cart his dead weight across the road.

"Oh, my God. What if someone drives down the street?" Tor lets go of his leg, and it falls to the ground with a thud.

I roll my eyes. "Jesus. No one's driving down the damn road."

"And if they did, we'd just shoot 'em," Marney says with a shrug.

She holds her hands up in front of her and shakes her head. "You are both insane. Fucked up!"

"Fuck, are you just now realizing this?" I groan. "Get his fucking leg and stop your bitching, woman."

We manage to get the man across the road. Sweat is trickling down my temples and Marney's gone into a coughing fit. Tor, she's still holding his leg, her foot tapping over the dirt road.

I climb into the trunk and attempt to lift the man up, but he barely budges. Marney uses his weight to try and hoist the man up, but even that's not enough.

"Tor!"

She huffs and moves, pushing against the body. She's so small that she's in very real danger of being completely crushed by this fat fucker.

"Oh God, I'm going to throw up." She whines as her face presses against his stomach.

"Wait, wait, wait!" I hop down and pull her away from him "Just..." I shake my head. She's no help, and I think part of me got her to do it just to see if she would. "Just go sit in the car with my brother."

"Arsehole," she grumbles before she stomps away.

275

I catch a glimpse of my reflection as I pull open the door to the basement. My shirt is wet, clinging to my body from the gory mess splattered all over it.

"I cannot believe you made me do that!" Tor shouts, following behind me. I cock a brow, turning to walk backward so I can look at her. Blood is smeared all over the front of her shirt.

"Like you've never had someone's guts on you before. Get a grip." I wipe a speck of dried blood from her cheek, before turning to go into my office.

Her nostrils flare. "Do you think this is funny?" she screams. "That was not fucking funny, Jude! I got fucking shot at!" She throws her hands up. "I've got some guy's blood all over me!"

"Well, it was kinda funny watching you feel up a dead guy."

She growls and raises her hand to slap me, but I catch it in the air and squeeze her wrist. I glare at her. Damn, she has a short fuse. "*What* did I tell you about slapping me?" I jerk her body to mine. "You need to rein that damn temper in," I warn, my face inching toward hers. I would rein it in for her if it didn't turn me on so much. I feel her breath on my mouth and I lose it. I growl as I slam my lips over hers in a brutal kiss. *What the fuck am I doing?* She grabs my head, her fingers pulling at my hair. I grip the back of her head, forcing her mouth against mine, making the kiss deeper. A small moan presses through her lips, and I lose all fucking control.

I use one hand to swat the door closed, then I back her toward my desk. She's clawing at my shirt frantically, and I manage to rip my mouth from hers long enough to tear the bloodied shirt over my head. I grab the hem of her shirt and tear it from her body. The long purple scar snaking its way down her stomach makes my pulse lose a beat. I swallow and slam my lips back over hers. Her legs hit the desk and she falls back. I shouldn't do this, but I can't fucking help it. This woman is like heroin: it can fucking kill you, but is so damn good it's worth the risk. Her hands clumsily grip my zipper as she grabs at the waist of my jeans, working them over my hips.

"This is fucking wrong," I groan against her lips as I yank her sweatpants off.

"Everything with you is wrong," she says, her nails scratching down my neck to my shoulders. *Fuck me!*

I work my mouth down the side of her neck, growing drunk on her scent. She pushes my boxers down and grips my cock hard. She strokes me like she fucking owns that shit. I spread her thighs, knocking papers and the phone from my desk in the process. "I'm gonna fuck you until you're just as wrong as I am," I growl.

She thrusts her hips forward and my dick gets the slightest taste of her. I inhale and force her down on the desk, pinning both her hands back over her head. I rub over her breasts as I snake my hands down her body. I can't wait the three seconds it will take to rip her fucking underwear off her.

I push them to the side and shove my cock inside her tight, wet pussy, groaning as she grips me. I toss my head back, digging my fingers into her firm thighs. "Fuck, woman," I hiss as I push into her deeper, just holding my cock there. *Warm. Wet. Motherfucking tight.* If I fucking move right now I may lose my shit.

She wiggles beneath me, her back bowing as she grips the edge of the desk. I drive into her so damn hard her body slides across the desk. Every time I push into her, she moves.

"Fuck," I groan, wrapping my arms around her back and pulling her up.

She's breathing so heavy. "What are you..." she gasps.

I eye the pair of underwear before I grab the sides and tear them from her. I've never been this desperate for a woman. All inhibitions are gone. This is nothing aside from a primitive need.

"I can't fuck you deep enough like this," I say as I drag her from the desk and pick her up. Her legs wrap around my waist as I thrust into her hard and deep. She moans and tosses her head back, her fingernails embedding themselves into my shoulders. She releases a heavy, sex-drunken groan, her eyes fluttering. I kiss down her neck, biting her every few seconds, and with each nip her nails grip me harder.

"Tell me you fucking want it, Tor," I demand as I violently slam into her.

All she does is moan, and I stop, holding myself inside her and pressing into her as hard as I can. She grinds over me, trying to find release. I take the few steps it takes to slam her against the wall, pinning her so she can't move. I'll be damned if I'm not going to get what I fucking want.

I arch a brow and glare at her. "Fucking *tell* me." She stares at me. It's damn torture to hold myself in her, feeling her rhythmically contracting around me and not being able to fucking move. "Fucking say it!" I growl.

She fights against me, her hips bucking over me, and I press her harder into the wall. "Tell me."

She locks her eyes with mine, her hands gripping the back of my head and pulling my face to hers. "I want you to fuck me like you paid for me."

I lay into her, brutally fucking her against the wall. Within seconds she's screaming, clawing at me like I'm taking her fucking life from her. Her pussy squeezes around my dick and I feel every muscle in my body tighten. Sweat beads on my forehead. My fingers grab at whatever part of her body they can find, and I bury my face in her neck, groaning as I come inside her.

Her legs slowly drop to the floor and we stand covered in the blood of a man that tried to kill her, sweaty and breathlessly pressed against one another. I grab her chin and force her to look at me. "The next time you slap me, I will hit you back. Don't fucking test me."

She yanks her chin out of my grip and pushes me away from her. "I may let you choke me, but hit me, and you'd best sleep with one eye open." She scoops up her sweatpants, pulling them on without her underwear.

I glare at her as I pull my jeans up. "Don't fucking slap me, and you won't have anything to worry about."

"Don't be an arsehole, and I won't slap you," she huffs as she pulls on her stained top. Without her bra, her nipples are clearly visible through the thin material. She storms out of the office with a flick of her chocolate-colored hair.

I take a few hard steps into the hall. "Fucking losing your morals, huh? You think maybe showing your tits'll get you fucked by my brother too?" I shout as she walks away. She doesn't say anything, she just flips me the middle finger over her shoulder, her hips swaying defiantly as she disappears around the corner.

I inhale, my fists balling at my sides. I have to force my breaths to even out. That fucking woman gets under my skin like a damn rash. I turn and slam the door behind me so hard that the framing cracks. She does things to me no woman has ever done, and I almost hate her for it.

Chapter 34
Victoria

I've barely spoken to Jude for the last two days. I woke up this morning with him wrapped around me like a vine. My emotions are all over the place. I hate him, but I'm drawn to him. He tried to talk to me, but I'm so fucking angry at him, and I'm angry at myself. Jude could never be accused of being the understanding type, so in true Jude fashion he gave up after all of two sentences and left.

When did this become the norm? When did I stop finding this abhorrent? When did I stop finding him abhorrent?

I'm sitting on the bed watching a game with Caleb. I still have no idea what the hell is going on, no matter how many times Caleb tries to explain the rules to me.

"For the millionth fucking time, woman, it's a penalty if you step out of bounds! That's what the flag is for." He throws his hands up in exasperation.

The door flies open and Jude steps in. "We're going out. Move," he commands before leaving the room.

"So cheery," I mumble to Caleb.

He shrugs. "It's Jude, what do you expect?"

True, very true.

A few minutes later and I'm following Caleb down the stairs. I still don't like walking through this house, or being near his uncles. I can feel their eyes on me, watching me. I don't feel safe unless I'm with Caleb or Jude.

Jude looks up with a glare. "You ready?"

"Yeah, calm down." Caleb grumbles, grabbing a set of keys from the table we're passing by.

I start to ask where we're going, but I decide I'd rather not know because it's not like I have a choice in the matter anyway. We go out to the car and I climb in the front passenger seat.

We've been driving for at least thirty minutes, and Jude does his usual strong and silent thing whilst Caleb and I bicker over the radio station.

"I am not listening to this grungy shit!" I shout at Caleb, elbowing him as he leans between the two front seats.

He laughs and grabs my arm, pinning it to my side. "Let me guess, you want some fluffy English crap?"

"English crap? Because of course, I'm British, therefore I must only listen to my own kind. Idiot."

"Stop flirting with each other!" Jude reaches over and turns the station. He stops on some hard-core metal. "Shut the fuck up. Both of you." He turns the volume up to the point I can feel my eardrums rattling in my head. Jude is drumming his hands over the steering wheel, nodding his head in beat with the music.

"Fucking degenerate thugs, the pair of you!" I shout over the music, crossing my arms over my chest.

He doesn't look at me. He just turns it up even louder. *Ass-hat.* I turn my face to the window, dutifully ignoring him. The world outside is pitch black; there's no moonlight, no street lights. *Where the hell are we?*

Jude takes a sharp right turn, and I slam up against the door from the sudden movement. The car bumps over the uneven road and I peer out the windshield, trying to see where in the hell we are going.

"Is that dirt? Are we on an unpaved road?" Oh, my god, he's taking me out to the woods to bury me. I turn to Caleb. "If you let him kill me, I'm coming back to haunt you, fucker."

He rolls his eyes and smiles.

Jude ignores me, still banging his hands over the steering wheel to the song.

Within minutes we're pulling into a gravel lot. The building in front of us is nothing but painted cinder blocks, a Confederate flag tacked on the dented metal door. The entire lot is littered with motorcycles and a few pick-up trucks. There are several pudgy men in leather vests and bandanas standing to the side of the door, smoking cigarettes.

This is not a place I want to be.

Jude slams the gear into park and turns back to Caleb. "Don't let her out. Don't let anyone come up to the car either."

Reaching under the seat, he pulls out a gun and hands it to Caleb. He reaches back, pulling his own gun from the waist of his jeans and placing a bullet in the chamber. "If I'm not out in fifteen minutes, you leave, got it, Caleb?" He doesn't wait for an answer, he just opens the door, and I watch him walk up to the door and disappear inside.

I spin around to face Caleb. "What does he mean if he's not out in fifteen minutes? What the hell is he doing? Why have you got a gun? Who does he think is going to come near the car?"

Caleb sighs as his eyebrows pull together in a frown. "You know not to ask questions, Ria."

"He's your brother, Caleb, go get him! Stupid arse."

"You want me to go and get him. Seriously? You have met my brother, right?"

I sigh and slump back in the leather seat, crossing my arms over my chest.

The minutes seem to drag by as I wait for something to happen. I don't know what I'm expecting, some kind of shoot-out. I glance nervously at Caleb, who has his finger over the trigger; he's nervous too, fidgety as he stares at the front of the door.

"Come on, Jude," Caleb mumbles. I glance at the clock and my stomach knots when I realize it's already been ten minutes.

Just when I'm about to beg Caleb to go in there, the door swings open and out walks Jude. He comes around the front of the car, and he looks pissed. He slings the door open and slouches into the seat as he starts the car. He puts the car in reverse, the wheels spinning up dust as he backs out onto the dirt road.

"You call Marney and you tell him to have John Duglas killed. Fucker didn't pay and now he's pissed me off," Jude growls, and slams his foot over the accelerator.

He grits his jaw and hunches slightly as he presses the pedal. I glance down, and in the dim light of the dashboard I can see a dark patch spreading over his right thigh. I slam the button for the interior light, and brush my fingers over the darkening patch. They come away sticky and red.

"Pull over!" I shout at him. Caleb leans forward between the two seats, glancing at the growing patch of blood on Jude's thigh.

Jude shoots me a look of absolute defiance, then shifts the gear.

"Fucking pull over you crazy fucking dickhead!" I growl. I swear to god, he has a fucking screw loose.

"Do you want to die? Because if I pull over that just might happen. There's a few guys pretty pissed at me back there, if you hadn't noticed," he says, his eyes darting down to his leg. "You know, stab wound and all."

I look at the speedometer. We are going one-hundred miles per hour down this fucking gravel track. I shake my head, his entire thigh is now covered in blood. "You keep going and you'll pass out and crash this fucking car. Pull over. Caleb, you drive!"

He winces, then groans. "I'm fine."

"Jude," Caleb starts.

"I swear to god, Jude, do not fucking push me right now!" I know I sound hysterical, because I am bloody hysterical.

He takes a hard left turn and the car fishtails; my entire body crashes up against the door, almost knocking the breath out of me. The tires scream as they hit pavement, and he speeds down the road, going well over one-hundred and ten now. The streetlights bounce off the metallic paint of the car hood and I can see the pain etching its way over his face.

"It's just a cut. I'm not bleeding out for fuck's sake, please shut up so I can think," he yells, and I watch his knuckles turn white as he grips the steering wheel.

Stubborn arsehole. Fuck this. I undo my seat belt and lean into the back, snatching Caleb's gun off the back seat where he left it. He moves to stop me, but I point it at him.

"Sit the fuck down, Caleb," I snap.

He cocks an eyebrow, a nervous smile pulling at his lips as he holds his hands up. I turn and point the gun at Jude. I don't put my finger over the trigger, because quite frankly, I'm more likely to shoot myself than him.

"Pull. The fuck. Over."

His jaw twitches and he glares at me from the corner of his eye. "You're gonna shoot me if I don't? You're a fucking lunatic. You put the damned gun down right now, or..." He winces from the pain that must be shooting up his leg.

"I am so not fucking around right now. I don't give a fuck whether you bleed out. I just don't want you taking us out with you. Now pull the car over, you selfish fuck."

With a sudden movement, he grips the barrel of the gun and snatches it from my hands, flipping it around so that it's now aimed at me as he's driving. "Don't fuck with me. I'll pull over in just a minute when I find a place we won't get shot in, okay?"

I glare at him. His face has gone pale and a deep frown has etched onto his features. He's losing blood, and as much as he likes to think he's invincible, he's clearly feeling it.

"You're being unreasonable," I huff.

The car swerves into a petrol station parking lot and he shoves the gear into park. "Caleb, hurry the fuck up and get in," Jude groans, grabbing his leg as he lifts himself out of the driver's seat with a grimace. He opens the back door and lays down across the leather seat. He punches the back of the seat and shouts. Caleb puts the car in gear and pulls away.

I turn around and squeeze myself between the front seats, perching on the edge of the back seat next to Jude. I turn on the interior light for the back and quickly find the tear in his jeans where the blade went in. I rip the material open to reveal the bloody mess that is his leg. He grits his teeth, and his leg twitches.

"Hold still," I tell him.

"Don't fucking touch it and I'll be still," he says, and jerks his leg away.

"Man up, Jude. It's just a scratch. Jesus." I look more closely at the wound, which is still bleeding, but not too much.

His eyes narrow and harden on me as he bites down on his bottom lip. I know he wants to curse at me, but all he does is pull in a heavy breath and groan.

"Caleb, do you have a cloth or anything in here?" I ask.

He shrugs. "Don't think so."

I roll my eyes. Helpful. I yank my jumper over my head and wad it up, pressing it against his leg. He lets out a stream of curse words as I push down on the wound.

Grabbing my ponytail, he yanks my face down toward his. "That's not a fucking scratch, and it fucking hurts!"

"You're being a baby," I say slowly, and he pulls harder on my hair. "Five minutes and we'll be home. I'll stitch you up and find you some painkillers, okay?" I hope it's only five minutes, because he's still losing blood, and due to the fact that he wouldn't pull over earlier, it means that he's now lost a lot.

"What the hell happened, Jude?" Caleb calls from the front.

Jude sucks in a breath. "He didn't have the money. Again." We hit a pothole and the sudden pressure on his leg makes him groan. "I threatened him and he didn't like it. I guess he figured stabbing me would show me he was serious. Well"—his breathing is falling uneven now—"he fucked with the wrong person."

By the time we get back to the house, the backseat is saturated with blood and Jude is drifting in and out of consciousness. Caleb manages to pick him up, but even then I have to help him with Jude's massive weight. *Jesus, what the fuck does he do to weigh this much?*

As soon as we walk through the door, the house is a flurry of activity with serious faces all around. I guess it's not often that Jude gets stabbed.

Once he's in their medical room, I'm shouting at Caleb for various supplies. Much to my surprise, they have a stockpile of medication. I inject him with Morphine before looking at his leg. The wound is deep but clean, a simple clean-and-stitch job. The painkillers knock him out pretty quickly, leaving me to stitch his leg easily.

After I've cleaned his wound up, a couple of the guys take Jude upstairs and put him on his bed. They flash me wary looks but leave the room when Caleb ushers them out.

They still don't trust me, and I don't trust them. Maybe they think I'm going to kill Jude. A couple of weeks ago I might have, but now...now things are different. Twisted. Warped. Wrong, maybe, but I won't kill him.

Caleb squeezes my shoulder once before leaving the room. At least *he* trusts me. Jesus, if I was going to kill him I would have done it by now. Okay, so there was the time I held a razor to his throat in his sleep, but, well, we know how that ended.

I cover him with the duvet before heading to the bathroom.

"Tor."

I spin around. His eyes are half-open, and his head is turned on the pillow.

"Are you okay?" I ask quickly, worried that he's in pain.

He smiles and pats the bed next to him. "Come sleep." His voice is slurred, and he sounds drunk.

"I just need to wee, and then I'll come to bed."

"Wee." He laughs, impersonating a British accent, which he still sucks at. "You sound so girly...and British." This is so not Jude, the drugs must be working a treat.

I shake my head and go to the bathroom, leaving him chuckling to himself.

When I get back his eyes are shut and I think he's asleep, until I get into bed.

"You're back." He smiles and swats at me.

I sit on the bed with my back to the pillows. "I'm back." I have to force the giggle down my throat.

He twists his head to the side and looks up at me, pinching a stray piece of hair that's fallen over my shoulder.

"So pretty, Tor. Pretty and innocent and British." I try hard not to smile, because never in my wildest dreams did I ever think Jude could be cute, but he is so bloody cute when he's drugged up. "You have a sexy voice." He grins at me.

I glance away from him and cover my mouth with my hand, trying not to laugh. "Is that so?"

He closes his eyes and falls back against the pillows. "Mmm. And you have a dirty mouth." He trails a finger along my bottom lip, his eyes intently staring at them. "I like you." His eyes lull shut then pop back open, and he clears his throat. "I like your mouth, I mean. I like it so much I think you should stick my cock in it." He laughs again and his hand drops to the bed beside him like dead weight.

"Wow, what a charmer you are." *Cute and horny apparently.*

His eyes narrow and his lips curl up. "I'm just joking. Kinda..."

Is it wrong that I want to pet him right now? I like him like this, maybe I should just start spiking his whiskey or something.

"Fuck," he groans. "You have fucked me up, doll. I'm so fucking high right now." And then he laughs. Again.

"Well, that's what happens when you go around getting yourself stabbed," I tell him.

Shrugging, he looks up at me. "A, it was a scrape, and two, I'll stab you with something, and you'll like it," he slurs.

Oh, dear God, did I overdose him or something? Shit. I shouldn't laugh at him, because if he remembers any of this in the morning he will be so pissed, but I'm half tempted to film it. Caleb would love this.

"Awe, shit," he mumbles, sighing heavily. "You have fucked me up so much my dick won't even work." His hand rubs over his crotch in desperation. "Why won't it work?"

I sigh and roll my eyes. "Jude, really? You've just been stabbed. Your dick is fine. You don't need to keep checking whether it's still there." I slap his hand away from his crotch. "Stop playing with it."

"Fine." He huffs again and adjusts on the bed. His eyes skim over the room, stopping on the picture of his mother and sister. He studies that picture for a few moments before his eyes languidly come over to me. Another small huff. "You think I'm a horrible fucking person, don't you?"

I press my lips together. What a loaded question. "I think you're a person who does horrible things." I say quietly.

Jude's nostrils flare and he nods, then looks back at that picture.

I can sense his anguish, and there's this part of me that can't help but want to ease it. Call me stupid. "I refuse to believe that you're the monster I once thought you were."

292

"You're smarter than to believe that. You know I am." Suddenly he grabs my hand. "But I swear I never would have brought you here. I'm sorry."

I bite the inside of my cheek as I stare into his dark green eyes. I can't argue with him, because it's true, I never should have been brought here, but I guess the apology means something. This is Jude. He never apologises for anything.

"You didn't want me here anymore than I wanted to come here, Jude." I say, trying to ease his conscience. *Why am I trying to ease his conscience? Why do I even care? Shit.*

"I want you here now though," he whispers. "Fuck, did I just say that out loud?" His eyes are fluttering. He can barely keep them opened. "I don't want you to leave me."

My heart clenches in my chest. God, what is he doing to me? I don't know if I can do this. I like that he wants me here, and that is beyond fucked up. I sit up on the bed and swing my legs off the side, keeping my back to him.

His hand grabs my wrist and his fingers dig into my skin. "I know I've done some bad shit, but I would never really hurt you." He draws in a large breath, possibly yawning, then says, "I would kill anyone who even thought of hurting my girl."

My breath seizes in my lungs. "Jude, I..." Shit, what do I even say to that?

"Come here." He tugs at my wrist, pulling me toward him, and I glance over my shoulder at him.

His eyes have gone all puppy dog. "Please," he says. "That's not a word I say often, you know?"

"Really, I hadn't noticed." Two more seconds of the eyes and I give in, laying back on the pillows next to him. I glance across at him, and he flashes me a cute smile. My heart clenches in my chest. When did he become someone who has the ability to make my heart clench? It was easier when he was just an arsehole, and as time goes on, all these small acts of good amongst the torrent of bad are starting to stand out. Jude has so much bad on his record, there should be nothing that could erase it, but slowly, my mind is starting to forget that. He's the most dangerous man I've ever met, and yet I feel safe with him. I feel protected, and in his own twisted way, I feel cherished. My mind and my heart are at war with each other, and I feel like I'm about to snap from the pressure of it all.

He twists a strand of my hair around his finger. "My sister would've liked you."

I twist my body to face him, and his eyes fix on my face. "Do you miss her a lot?" I whisper. I've watched Jude beat the shit out of people without a second thought, even his own brother, and my mind can't comprehend the possibility that he might care, like really care for somebody.

He remains silent for a moment, staring up at the ceiling. "I almost can't remember them. I'm not sure what I've made up and what's real, you know?"

I nod. "Yeah." I feel the same way about my mum. Sometimes I just can't picture her face anymore.

"I just wanna go to sleep." He closes his eyes and tightens his hold around my waist. "Don't leave me," he says quietly, and I'm not sure if he meant that as an order or a plea.

"I won't," I say to the ceiling. What the hell am I doing?

I've lost track of how long I've been here. Things have become so twisted that I don't know which way is up anymore. I would say it feels like my life is on pause, but of course it's not, because when I press play there's nothing left *to* play. My former life is gone, and the more I come to terms with that, the more accepting I become of this strange life that I'm living.

Then there's Jude. I should hate him, but I don't. I feel safe around him. He took everything from me, and it hurts, but he did it to protect me. In this fucked-up world where enemies lie in wait around every corner, sacrifices must be made. Euan and Joe set me up, tried to use me as a pawn. I guess you could say that I have horrible taste in men, or perhaps fate just took a giant shit on me.

Either way, it is what it is, and for now, I'm stuck in this strange limbo.

I pull the photo from the broken, glassless frame, staring at the image. It breaks my heart to think of what happened to them. Nobody should endure that. Jude shouldn't have had to endure that. To lose your mother and sister is awful, but to lose them because of your father and the enemies he has made...that would destroy a person. Jude is strong in so many ways, but he's also broken.

I slide the picture into the new frame, closing the back. The door clicks open just as I'm putting the picture back on the bedside table.

I look up and lock eyes with Jude. He has this wild intensity about him that always sends my heart into a sprint.

He stops, a frown masking his features as he looks from the picture frame to me. "What are you doing?"

I shrug one shoulder. "I got you a new frame," I say quietly.

"Why?"

"Uh, because you went all Hulk and smashed the last one." I cock an eyebrow at him. "And I know it's important to you, so I got a new one. Well, actually, I think technically *you* got a new one."

He rubs his hand over the back of his neck. "Well, I break a lot of shit, though, so don't go trying to replace anything else I break." He sighs. "Just making yourself at home now, huh?" His eyes slowly lift to mine.

I laugh. "Nothing else to do around here, besides fuck the boss or play with his brother."

He laughs. "You're fucked up in the head, you know that, right?"

"Just know that I wasn't before I came here" I joke.

"Yeah..." His expression falls blank and he crosses the room to pick up the frame. He stares at it, brushing his fingertip over the picture. "That bothers me," he says under his breath.

"Why?" I whisper. My mental state shouldn't bother him. He's a criminal, a killer. No man who can look someone in the eye and pull a trigger should be capable of feeling remorse or empathy, and yet, here he is. I've felt his remorse in every subtle glance, every soft touch. This situation is so far beyond fucked up, it's in its own league. All I know at this point is that things are not black and white. Good or bad, Jude is not the monster I thought he was. Or maybe I just tell myself that to justify my own actions. Let's be honest, they're hardly the actions of a sane girl. Hell, I'm half-starting to wonder myself whether I actually have Stockholm Syndrome. *Jesus.*

"I don't know." His eyes are still fixed on that picture. "Just does." He sighs as he sets the picture on the dresser. "Maybe because of them..." He turns and walks toward me. He stops in front of me, his eyes narrowing as he sweeps a finger over the scar on my throat. "Maybe because you deserve better." He leans in, his gaze dropping to my lips just before he gently kisses me. "But I don't want you to realize it."

Chapter 35
Jude

I wake up, stretch, and my eyes land on her sleeping form. I rub my hand over my chest as I stare at her. She's been her for months. I've actually lost count. Of all the fucked up shit fate has thrown at me, for this, for her...I'm thankful. I press a kiss against her neck and roll out of the bed, my eyes landing on the picture of my mother and sister.

I like to forget that Tor is really only with me because she has nothing else, because I like to think this is what she has chosen--free from all the fucked up shit that actually made her choose it.

She makes me laugh, she pisses me off, she makes me feel guilty. She. Makes. Me. Feel. I care about her, but love, that's an emotion I swore off fifteen years ago, which means I can never give her what she deserves, whether I am all she has or not, I can never offer her things most people take for granted.

I shove my way through the crowded stadium, dragging Tor behind me. Glancing over my shoulder, I catch her smile. This situation has only grown more complicated with each passing day, because I'm beginning to dread the thought of her leaving, but more than that, I fear she won't. She doesn't belong with me. She's too good for this life.

We push past several drunk fraternity brothers and walk to the skybox. The doors swing open and the warmth of the heater hits us. We barely make it a foot inside the room before I hear my name. "JP!" Rodney shouts, shoving several men out of his way.

"Good to see you."

I nod and extend my hand. "Good to see you, partner."

His gaze skims over her body, stopping on her chest. "This your girl?"

I hesitate, my breathing growing shallow. "Yeah." That sounds so fucking strange to me, but she is.

"What's your name, darlin'?" he asks.

She looks nervously at me. I catch her swallow. Maybe she's been locked up with me for so long she's forgotten how to socialize with anyone else.

She clears her throat and smiles warmly. "Tor."

"Well"—his eyes skate over her. "JP's got good taste in women, Tor." Rodney grins and guides us over to the bar. "Help yourself to some drinks. The Saints have done me right this year." He pats my back harder than I'd like. "Thanks to JP here, they've done me *just* right."

He hands both Tor and me a beer, then raises both brows. "One day I'll meet your boss, right? Just have to get in his good graces, I suppose?"

I laugh. "Yeah, he's not much of a people person. Likes anonymity and all."

Rodney nods, placing a beer to his lips and sucking back a few drinks. "Ahh," he says after swallowing. "I can understand why. Sure he has a lot of people that'd like to kill him." He laughs, then squeezes his way through the crowded room to greet someone else who just walked in.

Tor leans into me. "He doesn't know who you are?"

I shrug. "No one really does."

She studies me, sips her beer, then slowly looks over the room before her gaze hones in on me accusingly. "Why are we here again?"

"Business." I shrug and raise the beer to my mouth.

"Business?" She cocks a hip to the side and rolls her eyes. "Please don't kill anyone."

I shove a hand in my pocket and laugh. "I'll try."

I lean against the wall, watching as one of the men in full-on game attire approaches us. "JP?" he asks.

I nod, taking a sip from the beer.

"Phil Crocker," he says. He awkwardly holds his hand out to shake mine, releasing a rolled up wad of cash into my palm.

I take the cash and slyly slip it into my pocket. I flash a grin and arch a brow. "It's all there, right, Phil? I'm not gonna go to the bathroom and count it and find you shorted me, am I?"

"No." His gaze darts around the room like we're doing a fucking drug deal. Jesus Christ.

I nod and take another drink beer. "Good."

Phil walks off and Tor narrows her eyes at me, stepping closer until her chest is brushing my stomach. She slips her hand in my pocket and her eyes widen. "Really? Just like that?"

I smirk, a short laugh rumbling from my lips. "Just like that, doll. Power." I cock a brow. "Fear is power."

The game is in the fourth quarter, and I'm more than ready to leave. Every single person in this room is drunk as piss, yelling and shouting and annoying as fuck. I hate having to do social business shit like this.

Fucking Rodney keeps looking at Tor, and I don't like it. I watch from the bar as Tor smiles politely at various people while she makes her way back to me. I can't help but stare at her. She laughs at something someone says to her, her dark hair falling over her shoulder as she throws her head back. *Damn, she's beautiful.* My eyes skate down her body slowly. That dress is hugging every slim curve, and all I can think about is fucking her.

I'm only half paying attention to the guys next to me as they try to discuss the game with me. Tor stops to squeeze through a group, and Rodney's right behind her. I watch as he places his hand on the small of her back, a little *too* low on her back. I can see the muscles in her shoulders tense as they stop beside me, and his hand moves away from her. I want to punch him right in the face for touching her like that, but this is not the place do that.

The crowd explodes in fits of screams as the clock runs out of time. Rodney shakes me excitedly. "The only thing that could make this better would be if I could take that girl of yours home with me." He grins.

My fingers clench inside my palms, and I attempt to laugh it off.

"Seriously," he says, slightly slurring. He reaches for Tor and I grit my teeth. I watch as he sweeps a stray tendril of hair from her face. It takes every piece of restraint I own to control myself. "How much you want for her?"

Tor bats his hand away, narrowing her eyes at me as though this is somehow my fault.

Rodney grins, his eyes fixing on mine. "Come on, all you ever have around you are whores. Can't share?"

I grab her hand and yank her to me, wrapping an arm around her waist. I glare at Rodney, my pulse throbbing in my temples, my chest heaving from the sudden anger building inside it like a tank. "Fucking apologize to her," I growl, my jaw tightly clenched. It feels like my heart's beating in the back of my damn throat.

He rolls his eyes and lifts the beer back to his mouth. "I was just having fun, JP. Calm the hell down." I can feel the veins in my neck pop. He takes a short sip, licking the froth from his mouth. His gaze veers back to Tor and one corner of his thin lips curve into a smart-ass grin.

Everything inside me ignites. I grab him by the back of his head and smash his face into the bar. I drag him away from the bar and slam him against the wall, repeatedly smashing his skull against it. His hands claw at my arms and he tries to twist free of my hold, but there is no way in hell I am letting him go. "Learn some fucking respect," I shout as I continue to violently bash his head against the wall. The back of his head is bleeding, and the larger the cardinal-red spot grows, the more I want to keep going.

I hear the other men in the room shout. Tor is screaming, yelling at me to stop. It's all muffled background noise to the loud hammering of my own pulse. I want to kill this fucker.

"Let him go!"

"Get off him!"

Strangers are shouting, and I know it's only a matter of time before these guys try to tear me off of him. Something bumps against the back of my knee. Suddenly Tor is hanging off my arm.

She grabs my chin, turning my face toward her. Her eyes lock with mine, wide and blue, and pleading. "Jude." She shakes her head. "Stop."

303

I release Rodney and he slumps down the wall, barely coherent.

"You okay?" she asks, her soft hands still clinging to my face.

I'm breathing heavily, and all I can do is shake my head no at first. After several deep breaths, I shout, "Fuck no! I want to kill him."

"Look at me." I look at her, only her. "Just breathe. Calm. Non-murderous thoughts." She smiles, and the anger starts to dissipate. She's like a bright fucking light, pulling me back from the darkness.

My pulse is slowing, my breathing falling more even, and for a second I find myself thinking she may be the one thing that can save me from myself. Even with all she's been through, she still has this innocence to her that fucking consumes me, and I want to protect that. I refuse to let her become tainted by the filth that surrounds me.

"Nobody's gonna talk to you like that!" I take a calming breath.

There's understanding in her eyes as she nods. "It's fine." She glances over her shoulder at the room of people staring. "Look, let's get out of here."

I turn. All eyes are fixed on us. It's apparent none of these pansy-ass business men know how to handle a 225-pound pissed-off guy. I take a step and my foot hits something. There's a groan from the floor. I look down to see a guy lying on the floor, his knees bent to his chest, his hands tucked between his thighs cupping his junk, and his eyes squeezed shut.

"Yeah, he was about to bottle you over the head," Tor explains, shrugging. I glance up at her, and a pleased grin makes its way onto my lips. *Damn, that shouldn't be hot, but it is.*

As soon as we get outside, I turn and pin her against the wall next to the door. People pass us, most drunkenly singing and celebrating.

"Jude?" She glances up at me with those innocent eyes and it hits me in a place that I'm not sure should ever be touched.

"You shouldn't be getting in the middle of a fight," I breathe across her lips. I hear her inhale deeply as her fingers cling to my shoulders. "If anyone hurt you, I'd fucking kill them. You're my girl." There is so much more to say than just that, but I can't and I won't say it. Whatever this is, it needs to remain unsaid because it is wrong on numerous levels.

"Didn't want him to ruin your pretty face." She smirks. "It's your only redeeming feature." Her voice is low and raspy as her eyes fall to my lips. *Damn, I wish she wouldn't look at me like that.*

"My face isn't my best asset." My lips barely brush against hers. "And you damn well know it." I smirk.

She bites at her bottom lip as her fingers trail from my shoulders to wrap around the back of my neck.

"I am rather fond of your face, though." She pushes onto her tiptoes and closes the space between us, placing a tender kiss to my lips. I crave this. I crave her. Even the devil needs something to break through his darkness at times. And that's what Tor does...she rips through my darkness. I wrap my arms around her small waist, pulling her body close to mine to kiss her deeper. When I release her she's breathless, her cheeks flushed. I fucking love that I do that to her every fucking time.

"Let's go before we both get arrested," she says.

I chuckle as we weave through the masses. "I don't get arrested. Too many cops and politicians owe me, doll. I'm untouchable."

Untouchable, except with her. She touches places inside me that shouldn't be alive. She makes me weak, and the fucked-up thing is that I like it. She takes my control and challenges it, and it drives me insane, but I get off on it. She forces me to fucking feel. Honestly, obsession isn't enough to explain this pull between us, because it's more like an addiction. I know it will kill one of us, but at the moment the high seems fucking worth it.

She glances back at me, smiling like she couldn't be any fucking happier, like she's forgotten why she's even with me. She's stopped thinking of me as the person holding her captive...because I'm really not. She doesn't belong with me, much less in this life, and for that I feel guilty because I'm nowhere near willing to let her go.

Chapter 36
Victoria

I stare at my reflection in the mirror, trying desperately to figure out who the hell this girl is looking back at me. I've told myself for months now that this is just temporary, that I will leave as soon as it's safe, but when will that be. The longer I stay here, the less reason I can see to leave. I don't know what I'm doing anymore. I don't know what I want.

Jude's sordid life of corruption has tangled with mine. I think nothing of the fact that he carries a gun or that he gets stabbed in the leg. I thought nothing of shooting a man, I felt nothing. It's all just par for the course. Slowly this is becoming my normal. What scares me the most, though, is that I'm okay with that. Why am I okay with that?

Jude has managed to impress himself into my world effortlessly. He has caused me pain and watched me break, only to put me back together again, and in a weird way, he's made me stronger. I feel untouchable when I'm with him, because he's untouchable. He protects me and fights for me in ways that no one else ever has, and I feel instinctively protective of him in return.

Every day it becomes harder to remember why this is wrong. I can't deny that I feel for Jude, even while I hate myself for it.

I think I might be falling in love with him, and of all the things I thought he might do to me, loving him was not one of them.

I know that I'm nothing more than a willing bed warmer, a hostage he was forced to harbour. Men like Jude aren't capable of love, and I know that. I question my own sanity on a daily basis. How the hell do you even fall for a guy like Jude?

I always told myself that passion and love don't matter, spoken by a girl who had never felt it. They matter, and losing them will hurt more than any of my physical wounds.

I know I need to leave before I get any deeper, before the scars run so deep that I may never be redeemed, but walking away from him might very well be my destruction.

Chapter 37
Jude

"He'll find you." Marney nods. "He wants you, Jude. That girl's dead as far as he's concerned, and you know it."

Leaning my elbows on my desk, I steeple my fingers over the bridge of my nose.

Marney goes over to the bar and opens the cabinet. I hear him unscrew a bottle. There's a steady pour, then it stops and starts again as he fills another glass. Holding out a drink to me, one side of his thin lips twitch up. "No better time to drink that than now."

I glance back at the bar to find my vintage bottle of Maker's Mark, the label worn down from the years my dad poured from it. I haven't touched it since the day he died.

"You gotta do something, Jude. You ain't got no choice." A raspy cough rumbles up his chest and he sets the drink down.

"I know I don't." I inhale as I run my finger over the glass and wonder if this is how my father felt. Is this what it's like to be at your wit's end? Nothing seems logical anymore.

"What are you gonna do with the girl? Huh?" He shakes his head and holds his lips to the glass, but doesn't drink. "Who would've thought a woman could fuck so much shit up?"

Marney has no idea exactly how fucked up this all is. It's more than fucked, it's a clusterfuck of fucks. I care about her, and I don't care about anyone. Caring about someone the way I care for her causes you to make stupid-ass decisions, it makes your entire life irrational, illogical.

"Jude, you gotta do something." Marney shrugs. "We gotta do something, or we're all fucking dead, and we don't need to be worrying about some girl in the process. Joe's a barracuda."

I take a swig of the aged bourbon, and the scent of it makes me think of my dad. It hasn't finished burning its way down my throat, and I'm already filling my mouth again with the stout liquor. Taking a cigarette from the pack on my desk, I twist it between my fingers. "I don't know what the hell to do," I mumble.

Marney's eyes narrow and he tilts his head to the side like he's just had some realization. "She's really gotten to you."

"No."

I light the cigarette and take a long drag, locking my eyes on Marney's.

He nods and twist the knob to the lamp, the yellow light from the old bulb shadowing his face. "Women fuck everything up. Your father was just like you before he met your mother. It happens to the best of us. It's hard to be a criminal when you're in love, just remember that."

What in the hell is this decrepit old man rambling about? I'm not in love with her. I am *not* in love with her...

"Jude, Joe and your dad weren't always enemies. They fell out over a woman."

I stare at him from across the room, watching him nervously shift his weight on his feet.

"Hell," he sighs, and tips back his drink. "Your mother was Joe's wife."

I feel my jaw loosen and my brow crease. "What in the hell are you talking about?"

"Now, I know this is gonna be hard to swallow, and your mother was a wonderful person, so don't let that change in your mind, but she and your dad weren't ever married."

He must see my jaw clenching because he holds his hands up and waves them like he's surrendering before he clears his throat. "Jude, your mom left Joe when she found out she was pregnant with you. She and your father had an affair."

I shake my head, unwilling to even contemplate what he's saying because I've always viewed my mother as a saint, and this tinges that image.

Marney gulps back another swig and nods. "She just disappeared and Joe had no idea where she went. *None.* And do you know what a fucking feat that was?" A nostalgic glaze coats his face momentarily, and then his smile fades.

"And what, Dad just kept working with him even though he'd knocked up his wife?"

He shrugs. "Yeah, why wouldn't he? Joe had no idea. No reason to make him suspicious."

My stomach churns a little at the thought of it all.

"But he found out, all right. Took the bastard ten years, but he found out, and he made both her and your father pay."

I take the drink and empty the entire glass into my mouth, staring up at the ceiling as I swallow it back.

"Jude, your father loved her, and she loved him. Now, I'm not saying what they did was right, but..." He walks over to me and puts his hand on my shoulder. "I guess what I'm trying to say is, your dad went soft when he met your mother. Joe was a bastard. He beat her, he fucked around on her, and all your dad wanted to do was save her, protect her." He squeezes my shoulder gently. "You want to protect the things you love, the things you think can't be replaced. Just be careful."

I stand, gripping the edge of my desk and letting everything sink in. There is a deeper reason for Joe wanting to kill me than I could have ever known. I epitomize everything he fucking hated. I am a physical reminder, a surviving piece of the two people who betrayed him.

I happen to look into the hallway and see Tor standing just outside the doorway, staring into the room, but I don't think she realizes that I see her. Honestly, I don't give a flying fuck if she does.

"She doesn't belong with me."

Marney nods. "If you see that, then you do love her."

I hear one of the lines ring, but ignore it. I can still see her out the corner of my eye. "Love is a luxury I can't afford, and you know it," I say.

Marney's lips press together before he raises the glass to his lips.

The answering machine finally picks up. "They say you have your mother's eyes," a deep, thick Yankee accent snarls into the line, and I know it must be Joe. "And I swear to God I will take pleasure in cutting those damned things from their socket, you bastard. I know where you are now, and I will kill you."

The line goes dead. I grab the phone and hurl it across the room. Marney rises and shakes his head. "Now what you gonna do?"

Chapter 38
Victoria

Marney moves past me, leaving Jude's office. His eyes lock with mine and narrow as he shakes his head. He doesn't want me here.

My mind reels over what I just heard. Everything is becoming so twisted; it feels like the odds are permanently stacked against us, and I'm just waiting for the other shoe to drop and it all come violently crashing down around us.

What we're living, it's a lie, and it will end, one way or the other. I just need to get out before he breaks me, because loving him *will* break me.

I take a deep breath and knock on the office door.

"Come in," he answers gruffly.

I step through the open doorway and close the door behind me. Jude glances up as I walk in, his dark green eyes locking with mine. Something passes between us, this familiarity that feels as easy as breathing. He has this power over me that I can't fight. He's still the scary guy I met when I got dragged in here months ago, but there's a softer edge to him, a vulnerability that I can now see, and that scares me even more.

"I want to leave," I blurt.

His eyes narrow on me before he pulls a pack of cigarettes from his inside pocket. He places one against his lips and lights it, taking a slow drag. "No," he says, exhaling a cloud of smoke.

I tilt my head forward, trying to escape his intense stare. "Jude..."

"I said no, Tor. No!" he growls. His tone leaves no room for argument, but I can't back down.

"I need to leave, Jude. I can't stay here forever." I sound frantic, even to my own ears.

He stands and stalks around the desk toward me. "Need, or want?" His voice is a low timbre that rumbles over my senses.

"Need," I whisper as he comes to a halt inches away from me. His proximity makes me shiver, and my heart skitters against my rib cage. Every fiber of me wants him, and I hate that I do.

His hand reaches out, stroking over my jaw and down my throat. My breath hitches, and I clamp my thighs together, trying to fight my natural reaction to him. He leans in until his lips are almost touching my neck.

"I know what you need, Tor."

"You don't know me, Jude." My voice hitches.

His lips kick up in a smirk, his thumb grazing under my chin. "Oh, *I* fucking know you." I need to step away from him, his closeness clouds my judgement. I take a shaky step backward and he cocks an eyebrow in response.

"Jude..." I try to warn him.

He laughs as he takes another drag from his cigarette. "This isn't up for discussion," he says, exhaling a long stream of smoke.

"This is my fucking life, Jude, and *this* isn't a life!" I shout at him. I know it's stupid, and I know it'll piss him off, but I just need out.

I hear his teeth grind against each other. "And neither is being six feet under in a grave!"

"The only reason that I'm under threat is because I'm associated with you!" I watch the anger roll over his features. I should back off at this point, but my temper surges, pressing me to make him see, whatever that takes. Staying here will only destroy me in the end. He will destroy me.

He drops the cigarette onto the floor and stamps it out before closing the space between us, placing his chest against mine. His eyes narrow as his breathing becomes ragged. I instinctively back away from him, and he follows me. Step by step, he stalks me, pressing me until my shoulder blades touch the cool wall. He pushes his body against mine, and all the oxygen seems to get sucked out of the room. He overwhelms me simply with his presence.

"You will always be in danger, with me or not. The only way you will leave me is in a fucking body bag!" He slams his palm flat against the wall beside my head. His face is inches from mine, his breath touching my lips. "Do you hear me? I won't let you leave me!"

"So I'm a hostage now?"

His head shakes violently from side to side. "You are not. Fucking. Leaving."

"I can't do this anymore. Please, Jude," I beg.

"What can't you do anymore? Huh, what is so fucking horrible about all this?"

"Everything! This, us, you..." I take a deep breath and force out the words that I know will cut him. Playing on his guilt, I scream, "I *hate* you. You're a monster, and as much as I try to pretend otherwise, you will always be a monster. I can never forgive you for what you've done to me."

He growls, narrowing his eyes at me. "What I've done to you? What the fuck have I done to you?" His eyes lock with mine, demanding, commanding.

"I would rather take my chances out there with Joe than stay and be your own personal whore," I spit.

"You are not a fucking whore!" he shouts. His hand slams around my throat and his fingers clench tight. He's so close, his lips are almost touching mine. "You'd rather be dead than be with me?" His grip tightens slightly, and my fingers claw at his forearm.

The words are simple enough, but I can hear the vulnerability in them. I know Jude, and he's not as emotionless as he likes to pretend. On some level I believe he needs or wants me, but this is not right. I feel like I'm losing my mind, whilst my heart feels like it's shattering in my chest. I close my eyes as several tears slip free, sliding down my cheeks. I can't answer him. I can't say yes. I just can't, but if I say no, then he'll never let me go. I *need* him to let me go.

His fingers remain clamped around my neck, his hold tight, but not enough to suffocate me. I hear him inhale sharply before his forehead touches mine, and his warm breath fans across my face.

"Please, let me go, Jude." I'm begging. "You don't want this, and neither do I."

"You've no idea what I want." His voice is low, soft and controlled, and that terrifies me. I can cope with his temper, I can handle his brutality, but it's in the moments when he's gentle and kind that scare me the most, because it's in those moments that I feel something for him, something tangible, something real, something I shouldn't.

"You know what I want, Tor? Huh?" The look in his eyes nearly kills me. He looks hurt. He has hurt me so many times, and yet his pain breaks me in ways that I never thought possible. His hand moves away from my throat, gripping my jaw. He forces me to look at him. "I want fate to stop fucking me." I feel his rough fingertip skim across my cheek, brushing away a stray tear. Without warning, his lips slam over mine.

He kisses me hard, without mercy. He kisses me like he owns me and he damn well knows it. "You don't want to leave me," he says softly against my lips, the slight stubble on his face scratching against me. "You just feel like it's wrong that you want to stay. Stop fucking with me."

My pulse skitters wildly as his lips brush against mine. God, I can't do this.

I open my eyes and meet his intense gaze. "Jude, I think I'm in love with you," I breathe out before I realise I've said it. I never intended to tell him, but he's not letting me go. I need him to acknowledge how warped this really is, how fucking toxic this path is that we're on.

He releases my chin and takes a small step back, putting some much needed space between us. His eyes become cold and unreadable. This is the man that I saw the first day I walked into this office. This is the man that scares me, and this is the man I need to see so that I can walk out of here without a backward glance.

He paces in front of me, dragging his hands through his hair. The silence seems deafening in light of my confession. Finally he glances up at me. "You're right. You should leave."

I nod as pain ripples across my chest. This is what I wanted, for him to let me go. So why does it hurt so much?

I nod once more, keeping my eyes on the floor. "Okay then," I whisper, my throat tightening. I don't wait for his response. I walk out of the office. As soon as I turn the corner into the hall, I break into a jog and head to Caleb's room. I don't even knock, I just turn the knob and open the door before falling through it and slamming it behind me.

The room is empty, which I'm grateful for. Caleb is of course going to know about this. He'll have to, because I'm staying in here tonight. I stagger back and slide down the wall as tears spill down my face. Shit. I should have kept my mouth shut. Why did I tell him? Because I'm an idiot, that's why. I told him because a niggling gut instinct knew that it would freak him out, knew that it would force him to let me go. I guess the stupid bloody girl in me is feeling stung by the rejection.

I swipe angrily at the tears. I'm angry at myself, really. This isn't his fault, I mean seriously, what kind of person gets kidnapped and then falls in love with the guy holding her? The kind of girl who was tortured and broken. A girl who evolved in order to survive, even if that meant becoming someone she no longer recognises.

I stay in Caleb's room until the light starts to fade. I'm lying on his bed in the fetal position when he eventually comes in.

"I thought you might be in here," he says quietly. "Jude was looking for you. Asked me to come check in here."

But wouldn't come and check himself, of course. "Here I am." My voice sounds raspy and hollow.

He sits on the bed next to me. "What's going on, Ria?" He strokes a strand of hair away from my face, tucking it behind my ear.

"I asked your brother to let me go," I whisper.

His eyes narrow. "Huh, he didn't mention that. How did that go?"

"It went the way it always goes when Jude doesn't get his way. He grabs me by the throat and orders me into submission." I pause. "Only this time it didn't quite end like that." I pick at a loose string on the blanket I have wrapped around me.

His eyes narrow, and I see concern fall over his face. "What do you mean?"

I look up and meet his dark eyes, so full of compassion, so unlike his brother's. "I told him I love him, Caleb." Even to my own ears I sound small and broken. Pathetic.

He inhales heavily before releasing a long breath. "And what did he say?" He's not even surprised. How could he have seen it, and I not?

"He told me that I was right, and I should leave."

"Goddamn it," he mutters as he stands and turns away from me. "You're not going to, though, right? It's not safe."

"Caleb, I am in love with Jude, a man who would kill me without a second thought if I pushed him." I'm not sure that I actually believe that anymore, but I'm the one in love with said killer, so clearly my mind isn't exactly in the best place to call judgement.

"He would never kill you, Ria. Trust me on that."

"I don't trust anything anymore," I murmur.

Caleb stays with me. It's not pretty. I don't think I've ever experienced true heartbreak. My heart isn't broken, it feels like it's bleeding out, shattering inside my chest.

I press my palm to my chest as my body heaves with sobs. Caleb holds me against him, letting my tears soak through his shirt. He doesn't say anything, there's nothing to say. My own stupidity has brought me to this point. I thought that Jude was my absolution in this hell. I'm painfully aware of how ironic that is. We lay here in silence, my broken sobs the only sound in the room.

I cry until I'm all cried out. I will be out of here soon and this entire nightmare will be behind me. My life will never be the same, but at least I'm alive. I will survive. What doesn't kill you makes you stronger, and I, of all people, know that.

My eyes get heavy, and I fall asleep with Caleb's arms around me. He may well be my only friend left in the world, and the thought of leaving him hurts just as much as leaving Jude.

I wake to the sound of low voices. "Just leave her alone," Caleb whispers.

"She's mine, Caleb. Remember that," a low growl that is all Jude threatens.

Strong arms are holding me against a very solid chest. I squint an eye open, and am looking at the side of Jude's neck as he takes easy strides down the hall. "What are you doing?" My voice is hoarse from crying.

He opens a door and then slams it shut behind him. "You're not sleeping with my fucking brother." I know him well enough to hear the barely restrained anger behind his calm words.

He lays me down on the bed, pulling the duvet over me. His scent engulfs me, a subtle combination of cigarettes and his cologne. The smell makes me feel safe, protected.

"I don't want to stay with you," I whisper groggily, sitting up. I watch as he pulls his shirt over his head, the dim light of the lamp playing over his tattoos.

He leans over me, his fingers winding into my hair as he brings his face close to mine. "You are *not* staying with my brother. You overestimate my self-control."

"It's Caleb!" *What the hell is wrong with him*?

"You're mine, Tor. Do you fucking hear me?" he growls.

I frown. "I'm leaving. I'm not yours, I never was."

A small smirk kicks up the corner of his lips. "I may let you go, but you will always be mine." His eyes search mine desperately. I don't know what he's looking for, but he looks haunted. For the first time since I met him, he looks shaken. That vulnerability pulls at something deep within me, something that pines for him, for this strange connection we have, no matter how twisted it might be.

"I can't do this with you." My voice hitches and I try to pull away from him.

His fingers tighten in my hair, holding me in place. "There's no can or can't about it, doll. This just is." His lips brush over mine, tenderly, reverently. My body instantly responds to him, and my battered heart feels whole again the second his lips touch me. His lips move over mine and he holds me as though he'll never let go. It's the sweetest form of torture. I squeeze my eyes shut as tears slip free, sliding down my cheek.

He pushes me back onto the bed, hovering over me. His eyes trace my face, a small frown line creasing his eyebrows. He gently brushes away my tears. "I'm sorry."

I shake my head, because I don't want to hear it. There's too much to apologise for, and yet he has nothing to apologise for. I foolishly did this to myself, but even in the midst of my despair, I still want him. Despite everything, I still need him.

His lips move back over mine, and my hand skims up his defined chest, wrapping around his neck, trying to hold him to me. I wish that nothing outside of this existed, because this right here is simple and easy. This is right.

His hand releases my hair, and cups my face. His eyes lock with mine, and something passes between us, something so pure and beautiful that it should not exist amongst this darkness. What we have is like a poppy blooming from the blood-soaked soil of war. A beautiful tragedy.

His thumb strokes over my bottom lip. "I can't change who I am." He kisses me gently, his lips barely brushing against mine. "I wish I could." I hear everything he doesn't say. He can't change what he is. Our worlds are so different, and in a different time, a different place, maybe he would love me, but this is hell, and in hell there are no happy endings.

His hand strokes over my neck, and he drops his face to the crook of my neck, inhaling deeply. "I wish I could..." he whispers.

Chapter 39
Jude

"I wish I could..." The scent of her makes me weak. I pull in another deep breath, savoring the way she smells, the way she feels beneath me, because this will be the last time I ever have her like this, and that damn near kills me.

"So do I," she chokes.

When did I become this man? When the fuck did I start to care about someone? My chest tightens. This is too much; I suddenly realize I'm not the man I thought I was, at least not with her. I can't change that I'm fucked up, that my life will end in nothing but ruin; I can't be the man she deserves. I can't change my fate, but I can change hers.

I feel her fingers trail down my arms as I gently kiss her neck. My throat tightens, and all I can do is hold my lips against her skin while my fingers tangle in her hair. All I want to do is tell her I'm sorry; really, I want to beg her not to go, but as selfish of a man as I am, I won't do that. I love her and I want to tell her, but I can't, and damn is this hard because I would do anything for her, even if it means losing her.

I tilt her chin back and trail kisses along her collarbone, her neck, her chin. I rest my lips against her and shut my eyes. Closing the gap between our mouths, I feel her lips tremble as they touch mine. I inhale and kiss her hard, deep, as mercilessly as I can. My mouth never leaves hers as I reach for the hem of her shirt. Her fingers claw at my back and her legs wrap around my hips. I tear my lips from hers and pull the shirt over her head, immediately slamming my mouth back down on hers because I can't get enough. I can't kiss her hard enough. I just need her. Right now.

I fumble with the zipper of my jeans, and she pushes the waist down. I grab her, kneading her skin in my palms as I take her underwear and tear them off of her. I glide my hands over her, trying to burn each detail of her body into my mind, because this is all I'll ever have. This fucking moment right here is my last with her. I trace my fingers over her, her legs smooth beneath my palms as I sink my hand between her warm thighs. "Fuck," I growl when my finger slides over her. I tease her entrance, groaning against her neck as I slip a finger in. *She's fucking mine. All mine.*

I roll my bottom lip along her mouth, breathing heavily as I kiss down her neck, down the middle of her breasts, my hands raking over her body. My tongue circles her tight nipple, and I bite down gently before I make my way down the curve of her side. She grabs the back of my head as her fingers twist in my hair and her back bows from the bed. I turn my head and kiss down her arm to her wrist, my hand caressing over her breasts. I trail my tongue over her stomach, her hips, spreading her legs as I lay down between them. I grip her thighs as I release a breath over pussy, and she tugs my hair, her hips raising from the bed.

"Don't move," I groan against her, locking my eyes on hers.

I slowly roll the tip of my tongue over her. The taste of her makes every piece of man in me want to fuck her hard right now, but I want to give her something more than just primitive desire. I groan again, my fingers digging into her hips. I gently kiss over her, nipping her before flicking my tongue along her wet slit. She moans, jerking my head to the side as she wiggles underneath me. All I can do is stare at her. I fucking want her so bad. I want to fuck my goddamn soul into her so she know she belongs to me. I slam my mouth over her pussy, growling as I circle my tongue over her swollen clit, my tongue darting deep inside her. Her hips buck, and I pin them down. She's breathless, her chest rising and falling in deep, desperate swells. I press deeper into her, so deep that my teeth scrape against her as I fuck her with my mouth. She groans as her hands fly to the headboard. Her legs fall weightlessly to the side, her heels digging into the bed as she rolls her hips, grinding her pussy against my mouth. I drag her clit between my teeth and bite down. I hear her nails scratching against the headboard as her hips buck wildly, and she cries out my name like it's a damn prayer.

I sit up, abruptly grabbing her ankles and yanking her down the bed to me. I roll on top of her, covering her lips with mine in a desperate kiss. I can't possibly get close enough to this fucking woman. My hand grips the back of her head and I rip my mouth from hers, our eyes locking. My chest is heaving, my heart slamming against my ribs, and all I can do is stare into those steel blue eyes, losing a piece of myself to her. She wraps her legs around my waist and I push into her, slow and steady as inch by inch of me is covered in her warmth. I pull her up, setting her in my lap as I thrust deep into her. My arms close around her, bringing her chest flush with mine, the beads of her nipples brushing over my slick skin with each deep thrust. Her heels dig into my ass as she moans, her hands finding their way to the back of my head. I fist her hair and bring her face to mine, resting my forehead against hers as I fuck myself into her. Our gazes are locked, our bodies tangled, and my fucking heart is ripping from my chest as tears streak down her cheeks. I grip the back of her head. "I'm sorry, Tor. I'm sorry."

She nods, crying as she pulls in a hard breath. I kiss her, the salty taste of her tears touching my lips. *This is not fucking fair.* I drive into her harder. I'm fucking angry. I'm fucking hurting. I don't want to let her go. I want to make her feel what she does to me, I want to make her physically feel how badly I need her, how in fucking love with her I am.

"I'm sorry," I breathe again. That's all I can say. That's all I will say. Her nails carve into my shoulders, and she buries her face in my neck. I feel her entire body shake, her muscles tense, and her pussy clenches around me. I press into her harder, clinging to her like she's life itself as every last inch of me tightens. I groan, my body raising from the bed as I come and fall back onto the mattress, pulling her down on top of me.

We lay there, her face buried in my neck, my arms holding her to me. We don't say another word to one another. I think we can't at this point, because what is there really to say? I'm losing everything to give her nothing...but really, nothing is better than anything I can give her. She falls asleep in my arms, and I comb my hands through her long hair, every so often feeling tears roll onto my shoulder as she cries in her sleep. This is what I've done to her. She can't even find peace within dreams. And what in the hell has she done to me? There are no fucking words for a woman who can soften a heart as cold and empty as mine. I know there is not another woman that will make me feel this way. Nothing this wrong should feel this right.

Chapter 40
Victoria

I wake up to bright sunlight streaming through the open curtain. I roll over in the bed to find Jude gone. My chest aches with disappointment, but I know it's probably for the best. I just need to go without seeing him. Last night was too much. I saw a side of him that I've never seen, and it only makes me love him more. Every fibre of my being wants to believe that he feels something for me, but he hasn't said it. They say actions speak louder than words, but sometimes you need to hear the words.

I sit up in the bed and lean down, picking up my shirt from the floor. I'm used to feeling sore and used after a night with Jude. I don't this morning.

Fuck, I need to get my head together. He fucks me up. I didn't want to see him last night because it hurts, but Jude, being Jude, doesn't give a shit. He takes what he wants without apology. He wants me, he wants to own me, possess me, and he doesn't want to share me, even if that means leaving me and my bleeding heart in the hands of his brother, my friend. I wish I could hate him, it would make this easier.

There's a soft knock on the door, so soft I almost am not certain I heard it. The door opens slowly and Jude steps in. My heart squeezes, faltering in my chest. I glance up at him slowly. His hair is messy, like he's been dragging his hands through it, and his eyes are distant.

My lungs seize under that scrutinizing stare. I tear my gaze away, unable to look at him.

Each step he takes in my direction makes me feel weak. I hate myself for feeling anything for him, and the shame and resentment are eating me alive.

"You're leaving in an hour." The bed dips when he sits down next to me, but I still can't force my eyes up. "Did you hear me, Tor?"

I nod. That's all I can do.

He lifts my chin, his fingers curling tenderly around it as he brings my eyes up to his. "I want you to do exactly as I say. You have to promise me you will stay safe."

I take a steadying breath before meeting his eyes. Bad idea. "Safe? What's the point in safe when you have nothing?" I whisper. At least here I have nothing, but I have him. Out there I'll be completely alone, a dead girl walking amongst the living. He breathes life into what little existence I have, but for how long? He is what he is, he will never be the guy that you marry, that you have kids with. He chose this life, and in doing so his future will always be precarious. Loving him only puts me in danger and jeopardizes what small chance at a future I have. I could sacrifice my future for love. Love is that which we most cherish, that which countless wars have been fought for and men will willingly die for. I would sacrifice everything for love, for him, but when that love is unrequited...it becomes nothing more than a tragic fantasy, a fleeting dream.

He looks remorseful, and it hurts to see. His eyes drop to the floor as he takes a heavy breath. "You'll do as I say to stay safe. I will have eyes on you, wherever you go." He says sternly. "I promised I would protect you, and I will, even if I can't do it in person."

He's seriously sending people to watch me? I know it's crazy, and I want to say something, but at this stage, I just need out. Once I'm away from here, I can assess my options.

He hands me a bundle of papers bound with a rubber band. "This is who you will be from now on." He undoes the rubber band and sorts through the items. "You're going to London. There's a passport and ID," he says as he hands me the papers.

I glance over the documents in front of me. Documents for Tor Pearson. My eyes slowly move to his, and I search his face for something...anything. Why would he give me his surname?

"Caleb will take you to the airport." He shifts, his leg brushing against mine. "I've arranged for you to have an apartment, or flat, whatever the fuck you call them, and you'll have enough money in an account to take care of you for"—his eyes flick up to mine and I notice him swallow—"for a very long time."

I start to say something but he keeps going, very matter-of-factly, without any emotion. "You must not contact your sister. I'm sorry. You are dead, remember that, because the moment Victoria Deveaux is found to be alive, you *will* be murdered." He swallows heavily. "And the thought of that kills me."

I swallow back my tears, shutting out the little voice in my head that is begging me to take it back, to never leave him. "Thank you." I can't seem to muster the appropriate emotion over this. I just feel...numb, cold.

Jude sweeps my hair away from my neck and I feel him place something around it. I glance down to find a necklace with a hummingbird, much like the one I had when I came here, but it's much more elegant, with emeralds set in the wings. "It was my mother's," he says, adjusting it.

I swallow the lump in my throat as tears blur my vision. It's a small action, one that says a thousand words.

He rises from the bed and I think he's just going to leave me here like this, but he comes in front of me and kneels. Resting his hands on my knees, he glances up at me, holding my gaze. "I *am* sorry."

And with that he leaves me.

Chapter 41
Jude

I stand at the door, my jaw clenched, my hands shoved in my pockets. I hear her and Caleb coming down the hallway and I inhale, closing my eyes momentarily.

When I open them, I see her walking toward me with a duffel bag hung over her shoulder. Everything she now has fits in that small bag. She has nothing, she has no one. She is leaving the only thing she had left—a fucked up life with the man who destroyed her. Her bloodshot eyes make it apparent she's been crying, and that makes me feel even fucking worse. She glances at me, unable to hold my gaze. She doesn't even acknowledge me when she walks past me and steps onto the porch.

Caleb reaches for the door and I grab him. "You watch her get on that plane, do you hear me? You watch it fucking take off."

He nods, but looks utterly pissed at me. "You shouldn't let her leave, Jude."

"She wants to. I don't own her."

"She's not safe."

I shake my head. "She's safer away from me than with me."

He shakes his head again, his face growing red. "You're fucking up."

I look away because I know he's right, but I won't admit it.

He shoots an annoyed look at me as he walks onto the porch, the door banging closed behind him. I watch as he wraps his arm around Tor and leads her down the stairs.

I lean my arm against the door and inhale when I see Tor climb into the car. I press my lips together, my nostrils flaring. *Why the fuck can't I make this work? Why am I letting her leave?* Caleb shakes his head as he opens the driver's side door. The pressure in my chest builds. *Just stop them. Go get her.* My breathing grows ragged, my fingers pulling into my fists. *It would be selfish to stop her. She doesn't fucking belong with me.*

Caleb glares up at me as he backs out of the drive. He's pissed, but there's no way he could understand any of this. I'm not going to lie, watching her leave and knowing she's not coming back fucking hurts. My heart thumps hard in my chest, heat spreads all over me. I just let her leave, hurt and destroyed. Every muscle tightens, and my jaw ticks. The car disappears. "Fuck!" I shout as I slam my palm against the glass door.

I slowly walk down the hallway, lightly pounding my fist along the wall. I know if she had stayed here, she would have grown to hate me. I'd rather let her go now than have her one day realize that I embody everything that she hates. I can't process shit right now, I don't like the unsettled feeling consuming me. I need a distraction. Anything. I head to my office and sit in a daze.

Leaning over my desk, I stare at the wall. My gaze darts around the room and every damn thing reminds me of her. I stand and pace, rubbing my hand over the back of my neck. I realize I will never get her out of my fucking head. I take my arm and rake everything off the desk, my chest heaving. There is not one damn thing I can do to change this, and I can't stand it. I grab the chair and smash it against the wall. *I fucked up.*

I'm wrong for what I've done to her, and I fear I'm wrong for letting her leave me like this, but the thing is, I've never known how to be right. This is all I know, and I know she doesn't belong in the middle of it.

A few hours have passed, and I'm still just as angry as I was when she left, maybe even more so because I realize how fucked up this all is now. Caleb walks into the office and sits on the couch. He looks like he's just been punched in the gut.

He shakes his head and sighs. "I can't believe you let her go."

"She doesn't belong here." I clench my jaw, the unsettling feeling tightening in my chest.

Caleb huffs and tosses his head back on the cushion, rubbing his hands down his face. "Fucked up. It's just fucked up, Jude."

The phone rings, and I ignore it. There's no fucking way I can answer that right now without biting off the head of whoever's on the other end. The machine picks up and my stomach drops the moment I hear Tor's voice. "Jude!" she screams, and then, nothing. Silence. I snatch up the phone.

"Tor!"

A deep sinister laugh rumbles through the receiver. "You fucked up, Jude, and now...now I'm going to fuck her up, just like I fucked up your whore of a mother."

To Be Continued...

Wrath

Wrong Book 2

LP LOVELL   STEVIE J. COLE

Coming Summer 2015

Dear Reader

Thank you so much for reading Wrong. You are the reason we write and without you we wouldn't be able to do what we do, nor would we want to. We write books to immerse you in our world, and pull you out of your own for a few hours.

So thank you for reading. Thank you for taking a chance on Wrong.

We hope that you loved it!

If you would be amazingly kind and leave a review, then we would owe you a leg humping if ever we meet.

Acknowledgements

There are so many people to thank for helping us with Wrong, so here it goes.

Firstly, we have to thank Andi Truckle for being on the cover. We've had a lot of comments about his hotness, and we love the cover. Thank you to Uncovered Models for setting up our photo shoot.

Big thanks to SM Piper. She makes the best covers and trailers, and is infinitely patient with the chaotic disorganization that seems to follow us around.

Thank you to Ashley Mac Editing and Ellen Widom for editing Wrong, and to Kim Ginsberg for your hawk eyed proof reading.

Thanks to our lovely formatter Leigh Stone for making the book look so pretty.

Thank you so much to all the ladies on both of our street teams. You campaign endlessly to put our books in the public eye and it is so, so appreciated.

There are many blogs who have helped us both along the way, and you are all hugely appreciated, believe us. There are a few who are very special though.

Give Me Books and One-Click Addicts. We love you girls and we couldn't do this without you. Thank you for your awesome PR and your mad organizational skills. Thanks to Missy and Devlynn for your fierce loyalty and your willingness to always help. Sarah-Jane, we love you and hope you will soon recover from reading a cliff-hanger...you will forgive us one day.

There are so many blogs and individuals who have helped us, far too many to mention here, but thank you to every single one of you. You know who you are. You guys make being an indie author possible, and we want you to know how much we appreciate everything you do.

We hope we haven't missed anyone out. Just know that anyone who has ever written a review, posted a teaser, or read any of our books...Thank you. Your ongoing support means the world.

LP Lovell

Lauren Lovell is an indie author from England. She suffers from a total lack of brain to mouth filter and is the friend you have to explain before you introduce her to anyone, and apologise for afterwards.

She's a self-confessed shameless pervert, who may be suffering from slight peen envy.

Other books by LP Lovell

She Who Dares series:
Besieged #1
Conquered #2
Surrendered #3
Ruined #4

Facebook: https://www.facebook.com/lplovellauthor
Twitter: @Authorlplovell

Goodreads:
https://www.goodreads.com/author/show/7850247.LP_Lovell

Amazon: http://www.amazon.com/LP-Lovell/e/B00NDZ61PM

Stevie J. Cole

Stevie J. Cole is a secret rock star. Sex, drugs and, oh wait, no, just sex. She's a whore for a British accent and has an unhealthy obsession with Russell Brand. She and LP plan to elope in Vegas and breed the world's most epic child.

Other books by Stevie J. Cole

Pandemic Sorrow Series:
Jag
Rush
Roxy

The Prophecy Series:
Bound by Sin
Bound to the Fallen
Bound by Prophecy

Facebook:

https://www.facebook.com/authorsteviejcole

Twitter: @steviejcole

Goodreads:

https://www.goodreads.com/book/show/22680249-jag

Amazon: http://www.amazon.com/Stevie-J.-Cole/e/B00K9PK3EY

Lightning Source UK Ltd.
Milton Keynes UK
UKOW05f0609050517
300550UK00011B/195/P